"Why hav
blurted

"I like a challenge," Tom said with an easy grin. His eyebrows rose inquiringly. "What would get you interested?"

"Nothing at the moment," she told him, ignoring the thread of awareness that had been spinning between them all night.

"That's hardly encouraging," Tom said wryly, but his eyes were merry.

"It's late," she said. "I should go home."

"Let's relax for a few minutes. It's not even midnight yet." Tom removed two coffee mugs from the cabinet. "Sugar? Cream?"

"Lots of both," she answered. She had no idea why her heart should be racing. Maybe it had something to do with being the focus of attention of a real, live, handsome guy who—unlike the only other man in her life—wasn't a mere five years old!

Dear Reader,

I like small towns. I've lived in one after another—places named Jupiter, Lake Park, Hartsville, Kinston, Grassy Creek. I've resided in big cities, too—Chicago, Charlotte—but I find life more manageable when scaled down to small-town size.

In a small town it's easier to stand out. People know who you are. You can see where you're going, and you know where you've been. Of course, not everyone agrees that this is a good thing. Small-town life has its disadvantages—mainly that everyone knows everyone else's business.

When I wrote *Breakfast with Santa*, I wanted to tell the story of a little boy from a small town who was desperate enough to ask Santa Claus for a real dad. He introduced me to his mother, Beth, who had been searching for love all her life but had never found one that lasted. She deserved a wonderful guy, one who took his responsibilities seriously and wouldn't let her down, and so I created Tom.

Christmas is a season for miracles, but everyone knows that Santa can't bring us love. However, when Santa and the hero are the same person, maybe he can.

So make yourself a cup of hot chocolate, curl up in a comfortable easy chair, pull up that warm afghan against the winter's chill and mosey along with me to Farish, Texas, to find out how.

With love and best wishes,

Pamela Browning

P.S. Please visit me at my Web site, www.pamelabrowning.com.

Breakfast With Santa
Pamela Browning

HARLEQUIN®

TORONTO • NEW YORK • LONDON
AMSTERDAM • PARIS • SYDNEY • HAMBURG
STOCKHOLM • ATHENS • TOKYO • MILAN • MADRID
PRAGUE • WARSAW • BUDAPEST • AUCKLAND

ISBN 0-373-75095-1

BREAKFAST WITH SANTA

Copyright © 2005 by Pamela Browning.

This book is for my parents, Helen and Jack Ketter,
who made me believe in Santa Claus, though
I never did quite believe that you could talk
to him down the kitchen drain.

Books by Pamela Browning

HARLEQUIN AMERICAN ROMANCE

 854—BABY CHRISTMAS
 874—COWBOY WITH A SECRET
 907—PREGNANT AND INCOGNITO
 922—RANCHER'S DOUBLE DILEMMA
 982—COWBOY ENCHANTMENT
 994—BABY ENCHANTMENT
1039—HEART IT THROUGH THE GRAPEVINE
1070—THE MOMMY WISH

Don't miss any of our special offers. Write to us at the
following address for information on our newest releases.

Harlequin Reader Service
U.S.: 3010 Walden Ave., P.O. Box 1325, Buffalo, NY 14269
Canadian: P.O. Box 609, Fort Erie, Ont. L2A 5X3

Chapter One

Bah, humbug!

The Santa suit was too short.

Tom Collyer stared in dismay at his wrists, protruding from the fur-trimmed red plush sleeves. He'd get Leanne for this someday. There was a limit to how much a big brother should do for a sister.

The pancake breakfast was the Bigbee County, Texas, event of the year for little kids, and when Leanne had asked him to participate in the fund-raiser for the Homemakers' Club, he hadn't taken her seriously. He was newly home from his stint in the marine corps, and he hadn't yet adjusted his thinking back to Texas Hill Country standards. But his brother-in-law, Leanne's husband, had come down with an untimely case of the flu, and Tom had been roped into the Santa gig.

He peered out of the closet where he was suiting up at the one hundred kids running around the Farish Township volunteer fire department headquarters, which was where they held these breakfasts every year. One of the kids was hammering another boy's head against the floor and a mother was trying to pry them apart. A little girl with long auburn curls stood wailing in a corner.

Leanne jumped onto a low bench and clapped her hands. "Children, guess what? It's time to tell Santa Claus what you want for Christmas! Have you all been good this year?"

"Yes!" the kids shouted, except for one little boy in a blue velvet suit, who screamed, "No!" A nearby Santa's helper tried to shush him, but he merely screamed, "No!" again.

Tom did a double take. The helper, who resembled the boy so closely that she must be his mother, had long, gleaming wheat-blond hair. It swung over her cheeks when she bent to talk to the child. Tom let his gaze travel downward, and took in high firm breasts under a clinging white sweater, a narrow waist and gently rounded hips. He was craning his neck for a better assessment of those attributes when a loudspeaker began playing "Jingle Bells." That was his cue.

After pulling his pants down to cover his ankles and plumping his pillow-enhanced stomach to better hide his rangy frame, he drew a deep breath and strode from the closet.

"Ho-ho-ho!" he said, making his deep voice even deeper. "Merry Christmas!" As directed, he headed for the elaborate throne on the platform at one end of the room.

"Santa, Santa," cried several kids.

"Okay, boys and girls, remember that you're supposed to sit at the tables and eat your breakfast," Leanne instructed. "Santa's helper elves will come to each table in turn to take you to Santa Claus. Remember to smile! An elf will take your picture when you're sitting on Santa's knee."

Tom brushed away a strand of fluffy white wig hair that was tickling his face. "Ho-ho-ho!" he boomed again in his deep faux–Santa Claus voice as he eased his unaccustomed bulk down on the throne and ceremoniously drew the first kid onto his lap. "What do you want for Christmas, little girl?"

"A brand-new candy-red PT Cruiser with a convertible top and a turbocharged engine," she said demurely.

"A car! Isn't that wonderful! Ho-ho-ho!" he said, sliding the kid off his lap as soon as the male helper elf behind the tripod snapped a picture. Was he supposed to promise delivery of such extravagant requests? Tom had no idea.

For the next fifteen minutes or so, he listened as kids asked for Yu-Gi-Oh! cards, Bratz dolls, even a Learjet. He was wondering what on earth a Crash Bandicoot was when he started counting the minutes; only an hour or so and he'd be out of there. "Ho-ho-ho!" he said again and again. "Merry Christmas!"

Out of the corner of his eye, Tom spotted the kid in the blue velvet suit approaching. He scanned the crowd for the boy's gorgeous mother, who was temporarily distracted by a bottle of spilled syrup at one of the tables.

"Ho-ho-ho!" Tom chortled as a helper elf nudged the kid in the blue suit toward him. And when the kid hurled a heretofore concealed cup of orange juice into his lap, Tom's chortle became "Ho-ho-ho—oh, no!" The kid stood there, frowning. Tom shot him a dirty look and, using the handkerchief that he'd had the presence of mind to stuff into his pocket, swiped hastily at the orange rivulets gathering in his crotch. With great effort, he managed to bite back a four-letter word that drill sergeants liked to say when things weren't going well.

He jammed the handkerchief back in his pocket and hoisted the boy onto his knee. "Careful now," Tom said. "Mustn't get orange juice on that nice blue suit, ho-ho-ho!"

"Do you always laugh like that?" asked the kid, who seemed about five years old. He had a voice like a foghorn and a scowl that would have done justice to Scrooge himself.

"Laugh like what?" Tom asked, realizing too late that he'd used his own voice, not Santa's.

"'Ho-ho-ho.' Nobody laughs like that." The boy was regarding him with wide blue eyes.

"Ho-ho-ho," Tom said, lapsing back into his Santa voice. "You're a funny guy, right?"

"No, I'm not. You aren't, either."

"Ahem," Santa said. "Maybe you should just tell me what you want for Christmas."

The kid glowered at him. "Guess," he said.

Tom was unprepared for this. "An Etch-a-Sketch?" he ventured. Those had been popular when he was a child.

"Nope."

"Yu-Gi-Oh! cards? A Crash Team Billy Goat…uh, I mean Bandicoot?"

"Nope."

Beads of sweat broke out on Tom's forehead. The helpers were unaware of his plight. They were busy lining up the other kids who wanted to talk to Santa.

"Yu-Gi-Oh! cards?"

"You already guessed that one." The boy's voice was full of scorn.

"A bike? Play-Doh?"

The kid jumped off his lap, disconcerting the elf with the camera. "I want a real daddy for Christmas, so there," the boy said, and stared defiantly up at Tom.

"A daddy? I can't bring you a daddy," Tom said, with as much jocularity as he could muster.

"That's what I figured," said the kid as he hopped off the side of the platform near an open door.

"Hey, come back here," Tom shouted, leaping to his feet and grabbing a fistful of blue velvet. But the kid was quick. The next thing Tom knew, he was sprawled on the floor with the boy squashed beneath him. Tom's right hand and wrist had taken the brunt of his fall and pain was shooting up his arm.

"Oomph," said the kid, struggling to get out from under. "Mom—Mom—*Mommy!"*

The helper elf with the beautiful blond hair erupted from the stunned group of kids.

"Mitchell!" she cried, all concern. "Are you all right, sweetheart?"

Tom could have sworn that Mitchell tried to knee him in the groin before crawling out from under the folds of red plush.

"Santa hurt me," he said, his lower lip quivering.

The blonde pursed her lips. Her eyes now had a feisty sheen, at least as seen by Tom, who was by this time grimacing up at her from the floor. Her legs were shapely and smooth. Even in the depths of his pain, Tom noticed.

"Listen, lady," he said when he could talk. "Your son tripped me."

Mitchell, safe in the circle of his mother's arms, growled, "Did not."

"Santa didn't mean to hurt you," said Mitchell's mother.

"Santa never hurts little children," added the photographer elf.

Maybe not, thought Tom. *But Santa certainly has the urge sometimes.*

Leanne was wielding a bullhorn nearby. "Quiet, boys and girls, quiet! Santa will talk to you in a minute. Santa, are you all right?" She frowned anxiously at Tom.

"No," Santa said, clearly and distinctly.

A few children started crying, and two boys slipped out of their chairs and began to chase each other around the room. Another crawled under a table and began to suck his thumb.

Mitchell's mother was staring at Tom's injured hand. "Is— is something really wrong?"

"I've twisted my wrist. It hurts."

Leanne had rushed over and now helped him to stand up. She was the mother of five and knew what she was doing in the first-aid department. Her eyes were full of concern. "Can you move your hand? Can you bend your arm at the elbow?"

"I can bend it at the elbow. Which reminds me, I could use a good stiff drink right about now," he said grimly.

"Very funny," said Leanne.

"Is there a doctor here? Santa is in severe pain," Tom managed to ask.

"He hurt me," said Mitchell.

"Quiet, kid," said Tom. Mitchell's mother gasped and drew her son closer.

Leanne heaved a sigh and shook her long straight brown bangs off her face. "Tom, you're incapacitated. You obviously can't continue as Santa."

"But, Leanne, what are we going to do? All the children…"

The helper's voice tapered off when she saw the murderous expression on Tom's face.

Leanne turned to Tom. "You'd better go to the emergency room. Your wrist is swelling."

"I rode here with you," he reminded her.

"Oh, I forgot," his sister said distractedly.

"Where are your reindeer? Where's Rudolph?" asked Mitchell with interest.

Tom ignored him.

"Beth," said Leanne, sounding as if she was at the end of her rope, "could you drive Santa to the hospital?"

"Me?" Mitchell's mother registered surprise.

"Well, it *is* on your way home," Leanne reminded her. "And Mitchell has already had his chat with Santa."

"Never mind, Leanne," Tom said rapidly. "Mitchell's mom doesn't even know me." Beth was pinning him with a glare that would have stopped a tank.

"Oh, sorry. Beth McCormick, this is my brother, Tom Collyer. Tom, my friend Beth. That takes care of that. Now, Beth, will you *please* take him to the hospital?"

Beth all but rolled her eyes. "Okay, I'll do it," she replied, and Tom knew how she felt. Leanne had a way of extracting favors.

"Don't want to be a bother," Tom said through the pain.

"My car's in the parking lot," Beth said curtly, making it clear that she wasn't happy about this situation. She wheeled and hurried toward the exit, grabbing a coat off a chair back as she went, her son in tow. Mitchell turned around and bestowed an impish grin upon him.

By this time pain was shooting up Tom's arm all the way to his shoulder. Beth put on her own coat first, then stuffed Mitchell into a windbreaker with a hood. Once outside, Beth, her lips drawn into a tight line, silently led Tom to a blue minivan that had seen better days. To the door was attached a magnetic sign; it said Bluebonnet Interiors and was slightly crooked.

Beth strapped the kid into the back seat. Tom folded his tall frame into the front seat beside Beth, noting that the minivan smelled of pungent fresh evergreens, of Christmas.

Tom silently nursed his arm close to his side, wishing he were anywhere but there. Dressed the way he was, his body, toned by strict adherence to military fitness exercises, felt fat. For two cents, he'd shuck the pillow he'd stuffed under the Santa jacket, though he knew he'd better not disillusion Mitchell about Santa Claus. On the other hand, Mitchell probably wouldn't notice. He was playing with a talking storybook, yanking on the string and speaking along with the words.

Beth rammed the minivan into gear. "So you're Leanne's brother?" she said, glancing sideways at him as she wheeled out of the parking lot.

Tom noticed that she had very high cheekbones, exquisitely formed. Like the rest of her. But she had asked him a question. "Her older brother," he said.

"You must be the one who just moved here. The marine." She gunned through the intersection.

"Right. I've bought a house out on Wildeboer Road about half a mile from the elementary school."

"I go to school," said Mitchell. "Day-care school. We take naps there. And make Jell-O. And every stuff."

"And every*thing*," Beth corrected him absently. She hung a left turn in front of the Bigbee County Hospital sign that said Emergency. They stopped under a wide portico.

"I have to go to the bathroom, Mommy," Mitchell announced suddenly as Tom prepared to get out of the car.

"We'll be home in a few minutes, darling," Beth said, eyeing the portly security guard strolling in their direction.

"I really have to go," Mitchell said with an expression of foreboding.

Beth twisted in her seat and focused worried eyes on his face. "If you can wait a few minutes…" she began.

"Right *now,* Mom." Mitchell fidgeted ominously.

Beth drew a deep breath and said in a tone of resignation, "All right, we'll go in." She reached for the door handle.

"Ma'am, you can't park here," said the security guard, glaring suspiciously at Tom, who was by this time standing on the curb in his Santa suit. "This spot is for drop-off and pickup only. No matter who you are."

Beth leaned over so that she could talk to the guard through the passenger window. "My little boy has to use the bathroom," she explained.

Tom's gaze darted from Beth to Mitchell to the security guard. His wrist was throbbing now.

"You'll have to move to the parking lot," the guard said to Beth. "Unless you know how to land on rooftops. We've got a helicopter pad up there. Might work if you were in your sleigh," he told Tom.

Mitchell laughed at this, but then his face went blank and he clutched his blue velvet suit in a strategic placc.

"Mom-*my*," he wailed.

The security guard eyed Mitchell. "Why don't you let your husband take the tyke to the restroom. It's right inside the door."

"He's not my husband," Beth retorted indignantly at the same time that Tom said, "We're not married."

The guard's eyebrows quirked upward. "Oh, I thought you were. As in 'I saw Mommy kissing you-know-who' in the song."

Beth was beginning to appear slightly frantic, and Tom took pity on her. Being Mitchell's mother probably wasn't easy.

"I could take Mitchell inside for you," he offered recklessly.

Beth glanced doubtfully at Mitchell, who was anxiously chewing on his lower lip.

"Oh, dear. All right. If you promise not to yell at him," she said.

"Yell at him? I won't yell at him."

"You were yelling back at the fire station."

"Beth, I'm an ex-drill sergeant. That was what I consider gentle admonition. And if you don't want your kid to go to the bathroom, it's fine with me. Just warn me so I can start building an ark."

She blinked at him.

"Well?" Tom said.

Beth quickly turned to release Mitchell from his seat belt. "Now, Mitchell, you go with Santa to the men's room. I'll be back as soon as I park the car," she said.

Tom caught a glimpse of the inside of her creamy white thighs as she flounced back around and smoothed her coat over her short skirt. He was totally unprepared for the rush of sexual desire that shot through his nether regions.

"Hurry up, ma'am, other cars are in line behind you." The guard was growing more impatient.

Mitchell clambered out of the car and nestled his hand inside Tom's. There was something sweet about the innocence and trust of the boy. Tom was crazy about kids, though he wasn't so sure about this one. Maybe he'd been prejudiced by that awful blue velvet suit. No red-blooded, rough-and-tumble boy would wear an outfit like that without putting up a fight.

"I'll make sure Mitchell gets to the men's room. You go ahead," he told Beth in a gentler tone.

"Yeah, Mom," said Mitchell.

After one long sigh of exasperation, Beth sped away toward the parking lot, leaving Tom in charge.

"I really have to go," Mitchell said imploringly. "Can you take me to the bathroom right now? I can't wait much longer."

"Excuse me," said the security guard, who was standing beside him. "We've got an ambulance bringing in some accident victims in a minute. Could you please clear the area?"

"Sure," Tom said.

"I bet you've been a good little boy this year," the guard said to Mitchell.

"No," Mitchell said, "and pretty soon I'm going to be a lot badder if I don't get to the—"

"Hurry up," Tom said, galvanized into action by the expression on the boy's face.

"That's what I've been *trying* to do," Mitchell said. "But if I have an accident, will you still bring me presents?"

"You're not going to have an accident," Tom assured him. "As sure as I'm Santa Claus." Then he realized what he'd said. "As sure as Rudolph has a red nose," he amended.

"Okay, Santa," Mitchell said in a surprisingly meek voice. "'Cause I certainly could use a real dad."

Inwardly, Tom groaned, but he kept pulling Mitchell along after him. When he'd agreed to play Santa, he'd had no idea that the job would be so difficult. In all sorts of ways.

Chapter Two

As they rushed through the double glass doors into the hospital, Tom looked around frantically for the men's room. A sign indicated that it was located down a hallway to the left.

"This way," he said, pulling Mitchell along and urging him through the door.

Once inside, Tom regarded the kid with doubt. "You, uh, understand how to do this, right?" he asked.

"Sure, I'm not a baby. I'll be six in January," Mitchell said indignantly as he stepped up to the necessary receptacle.

The boy appeared big for a five-year-old, but then, what did Tom know. He moved to one side and studied his aching wrist as Mitchell took care of business. The joint had become so swollen that the bones didn't show, and the skin had turned blue. He probably should have put some ice on it back at the fire station.

"Okay?" Tom asked brightly as Mitchell readjusted his clothes.

"Yeah," Mitchell said in that deep voice of his. "Except for the itching." He tugged at the collar of his suit and made a face.

"Itching?" Tom repeated.

"All around my neck. All over *me*. I hate this suit, but my mom made me wear it."

Tom felt a rush of sympathy. "I don't like my suit much, either," he said.

"Did your mom make you wear it?"

"No, my sister," Tom replied.

"Bummer."

Having established a rapport common to men who did things to appease the women who loved them, Tom ushered Mitchell out of the men's room.

"Ho-ho-ho, we'd better go find your mother," Tom said, though as they emerged into the waiting area, Tom couldn't see Beth. She apparently hadn't come in from the parking lot.

Mitchell pressed close as they approached the admittance area, and there was something comforting about his presence. As Tom slipped his insurance card out of his wallet, he glanced down at the kid, who—life was full of surprises—gazed up at him with a big smile. The trouble was, that smile was on the wrong face. Tom would have preferred it to be on Beth's.

The girl at the desk was efficient in the extreme, so that when the printout with his information spooled out of the computer, she was already on her feet. "Be back in a mo," she said briskly as she disappeared through a nearby door.

"One thing I've always wondered, Santa," Mitchell piped up, tugging at the hem of Tom's red jacket. "How do you manage to get to everybody's house on Christmas Eve?"

Tom, who had forgotten for a span of minutes that he was supposed to be Santa Claus, frowned. "Uh, I have really fast reindeer."

"You mean like the speed of light?"

Tom considered this. "More like a NASCAR racer."

"My daddy goes to car races. He said he'd take me sometime."

"I thought you didn't have a—"

"Sir, you forgot to sign here." The girl was back, and she handed Tom a pen.

While he was scribbling his name with his injured hand and pondering how to become instantly ambidextrous, Mitchell kept talking.

"Last year I left cookies out for Santa Claus and grass for the reindeer. My dad wasn't sure what reindeer ate. We decided on grass because that's what other kinds of deer like, and Starla had a box of real grass on the bar for decoration. She let us use it. Starla's nice most of the time."

Through his pain-filled haze, Tom managed to reply. "You told me you wanted me to bring you a dad."

"Oh, I do. A real dad, I said. My dad's not a real dad because he doesn't live with us. He lives in Oklahoma with Starla. They have a new baby. A girl." Mitchell's deprecating tone expressed exactly how he felt about his sister.

"I guess that's pretty exciting, huh?"

Mitchell scuffed one shiny shoe against the floor. "Nope. I've only seen the baby once. Her name is Ava. Isn't that a dumb name? She's got fat cheeks and lots of brown fuzzy hair. She looks like my friend's new hamster. My friend is named Jeremiah. He's six already and he goes to first grade." Clearly Mitchell held Jeremiah in great esteem and awe because of this fact.

Tom's nephew, Leanne's middle son, was named Jeremiah, and he was in first grade. In a small town like Farish, population eight thousand, there was likely only one Jeremiah that age, but before Tom could comment, the clerk handed him a sheaf of forms. "Here you are, Mr. Claus," she said with a wink. "Right through that door, and you'll be in the first cubicle on the left."

Mitchell pulled at his coat again. "I can go, too, right?"

No sign of Beth yet, and Tom wondered what was keeping her. He eyed Mitchell sternly. "Okay, but no funny business," he warned. "I mean it."

Mitchell's eyes were unfathomable pools of blue. "Okay," he said, surprisingly meek.

At that moment, Beth flew through the door, her hair bouncing around her shoulders and her face alive with concern for Mitchell and maybe even him.

"Everything's fine," Tom told her, mustering a grin. "Mitchell managed very well."

Beth's expression eased, and she smiled back. "Thanks for

what you did. It took me a while to find a parking place—a whole section of the lot was blocked off due to construction."

"I appreciate the ride," Tom said. "I'm sorry it was so much trouble."

"No problem," Beth said breezily. "Let's go, Mitchell."

Mitchell's eyes widened in dismay, and he clutched Tom's hand. "Are we gonna leave Santa here? Without a way to get home?"

"His reindeer will be here soon," Beth said quickly.

"Yeah," Tom said, figuring he could call his friend Divver to pick him up. "With the sleigh and Rudolph."

"Sir," announced a nurse standing in the doorway to the inner sanctum, "the doctor is waiting."

"What if his sleigh doesn't get here?" asked Mitchell. "If we don't help him, he might not bring us presents."

"Hmm." Beth smiled fondly at her son. "If it means so much to you, maybe we could wait for Santa."

"Oh, no," Tom injected quickly, although the idea of riding in the car with Beth again was certainly appealing. "I couldn't impose."

"We'll wait," Beth said, heading for the bank of chairs at the back of the room, where a television set alternately blared out commercials and cartoons.

"But—" Tom began, as the nurse nudged him toward the cubicle. His wrist hurt like hell and the smell of antiseptic stung his nose and he couldn't find the strength or the will to object.

The cubicle was bare and bright, and Tom eyed the young doctor warily. Fortunately, she seemed knowledgeable. "Not broken. Sprained," she said after he came back from X ray. "It's a bad one, too. You'll need to go easy on it for a while."

Tom sighed and winced as she wrapped his wrist in an Ace bandage and applied a sling. In a matter of minutes he was ready to go home.

"With any luck you'll be able to guide your reindeer through rain and hail and dark of night on Christmas Eve," the doctor said.

"You've got Santa Claus mixed up with the postal service,"

Tom said sourly, and the doctor laughed. Everyone seemed to be getting a kick out of his situation but him.

When he emerged into the waiting room, Beth set aside the dog-eared magazine she was reading, and Mitchell jumped up from the coffee table where he had been lying on his stomach and making swimming motions accompanied by dolphin squeals. Several people in the room with varying degrees of injury were glaring at Mitchell with annoyance, and Tom didn't blame them. Beth had no control over the kid. But as she stood and slipped on her coat, he noted the way her figure rounded out her elf costume and immediately forgave her laxness with her son.

Mitchell sang verse after verse of "The Little Drummer Boy," which Tom considered possibly the most annoying Christmas song ever written, at the top of his lungs on the way home. The racket made it almost impossible for Tom, again sitting beside Beth in the front seat, to carry on a conversation with her.

"You'll have to tell me how to get to your house," Beth shouted at him over the din from the back seat.

He gazed out at the lamp posts of Farish, now festooned with red-and-white striped candy canes. During his fifteen-year absence, he'd forgotten that they made such a big deal of Christmas here. "Turn right on Home Avenue, left on Lyndale, head toward the bypass till you get to a four-way stop. Turn right again, and it's the second house on the left. Limestone with dark green shutters," Tom shouted back.

The pa-rum-pum-pum-pums stopped. "Don't we have to drop off Santa at the North Pole?" Mitchell asked.

"I'm visiting here in Farish," Tom stated, earning him a grateful smile from Beth.

"Like me when I go to my father's house in Oklahoma," Mitchell said sagely. "Like I'm going to do this week."

Beth glanced in Tom's direction. "Mitchell is leaving on the sixteenth to spend Christmas with my ex-husband," she said.

She sounded overly mournful. Now if he, Tom, had a chance to get rid of this particular kid for a few days or even a few minutes, he'd be happy. No, make that joyful. Perhaps even down-right ecstatic, though admittedly Mitchell had improved since the breakfast debacle.

"You'll miss Mitchell, I guess," he said, just to keep the conversational ball, if not exactly bouncing, rolling along.

Beth bit her lip—her sensuously curved lower lip—and kept her eyes on the road ahead. "I'll be all by myself for Christmas. I'm going to clean out the closets, cook a turkey, keep busy the best way I can. That's how I'll get through it."

Maybe she was still in love with the ex-husband. Maybe it wasn't only her son she'd be missing.

"You'll be fine," Tom said reassuringly. "The time will go really fast."

"I don't know, since I'm going to close up shop. Well, I don't exactly have a shop. I work out of my home. But I won't be doing much because Christmas week is always slow."

"This Bluebonnet Interiors—it's your own business?"

"Mmm-hmm." She deftly executed a right-hand turn onto Wildeboer Road. Farms started whipping by, horses behind crosshatched white fences.

He wanted to say, *If you're lonely, how about calling me and we'll go out for a beer? Or, I'm new in town, and I might get lonesome over the holidays, too.* But he didn't say either of those things because Mitchell was now kicking the back of Tom's seat where his elbow rested and was sending darting pains up his arm.

"Would you please stop kicking my seat?" he said to Mitchell with remarkable restraint.

"Santa's wrist hurts, darling," Beth said sweetly. She braked in front of his house, a two-story job built in the 1920s.

"Thanks for the ride," he said to her, scrambling out of the car. "And, um, merry Christmas."

"Say hello to Rudolph the Red-Nosed Reindeer for me," said Mitchell. "Say hello to Mrs. Santa Claus."

"There isn't a Mrs. Claus." Tom wanted Beth to realize this.

Not that it made an impression. "I hope your wrist heals quickly," she said, and she smiled slightly. Maybe she was only being polite.

"Thanks."

Beth drove off in a cloud of exhaust, indicating that her mini-van was burning too much oil, and he watched as it disappeared around the corner.

Well, so much for that. He turned to go inside, eager to shuck this stupid Santa outfit and settle down in front of the TV with his ice pack and something potent to drink. Just then, a carload of teenagers ripped across the intersection, and one of them leaned out an open window.

"Hey, Santa, you sleigh me," yelled one of the boys.

Tom bit back a snarl as he stepped through the front door into a sparsely furnished living room that at this moment seemed way too uninhabited.

"Bah humbug," he snarled as he ripped the beard from his face. "Bah humbug, bah humbug, bah humbug!" Even Scrooge couldn't have said the words with more feeling.

Leanne and her harebrained ideas. Next time his sister wanted someone to play Santa Claus, Tom planned to be far away. Even if he had to take an unscheduled trip to the North Pole. Even if he had to walk every step of the way in his bare feet. In a snow-storm, and every stuff.

From the *Farish Tribune:*
Here 'n' There in Farish
by Muffy Ledbetter

It was a hot time in the old fire station on Saturday morning when the Homemakers' Club entertained over a hundred boys and girls at their annual pan-cake breakfast. Leanne Novak, chairperson of the event again this year, says that Breakfast with Santa was a rousing success, despite the fact that the jolly guy had to leave on an urgent trip to the North Pole about halfway through it. Leanne says that the kids who didn't get to talk with Santa taped their requests. The tape will be mailed to the North Pole right away, so don't anyone worry about Santa not knowing what to bring.

Helper elves for the occasion were Gretchen Morris, Tammy Turpin, Nancy DeGroot, Peg Marmo, Helen Duhy, Beth McCormick, Julie Gomez, Sandra Bryant, Jane Funderburk and Tiffany Wiggins-Borg.

Photographer elf Artie Pikestaff says for everyone who attended the breakfast to stop by his shop and pick up your photos with Santa. He'll have them ready before Christmas.

If you have newsworthy tidbits, please call me on my cell phone. You'll find the number at the end of this column.

Till next time, I'll be seeing you here 'n' there in Farish.

Chapter Three

The day after the pancake breakfast, Beth McCormick tackled the chores that needed to be done if her son was going to be ready to go to his father's by Friday.

Mitchell had been invited to play at his friend Ryan's house, which gave her plenty of time to wash and iron his clothes and brush up the nap of his blue velvet suit, which she'd made herself. She liked sewing for her son, though she wished he was more appreciative of her efforts.

Now, where was the duffel that Mitchell needed? Her search led her to the depths of the hall closet, much to her annoyance. "If I could only find a flashlight, this wouldn't be so difficult," Beth huffed as she bent her trim form nearly in half. Several months ago, she'd set a mousetrap in the far regions of the closet, the better to catch whatever was scrabbling around in there. She was unaware of the trap's status at the moment, so she proceeded gingerly.

Suddenly, she remembered the duffel's whereabouts. Leanne had borrowed it when she went to visit her sick mother-in-law a month or so ago.

This meant backing out of the cramped space. As she emerged, Beth spotted the windbreaker that Mitchell had worn to Breakfast with Santa lying on the floor. She started to add the jacket to the laundry in the basket beside the washing machine, but it felt heavy. Wondering what Mitchell was carrying around in his pockets that would weigh them down, she stuck in her hand and pulled out a wallet.

It was a standard man's billfold, fashioned of dark brown leather. Neither she nor Mitchell owned such a thing. She flipped it open, and Tom Collyer's driver's license picture stared up at her. Not that she would have known it was Tom; she had to read his name to learn that. After all, she'd never seen him without the Santa costume.

How had Mitchell—? Well, she supposed, the wallet could have fallen out of Tom's pocket in the car.

She eased Tom's driver's license from its clear plastic case. He was an attractive guy, though his face was more rugged than she would have guessed when it was hidden by Santa's whiskers. She took in the hank of straight dark hair falling over his wide forehead, the eyebrows that angled sharply over craggy cheekbones, the generous mouth that bowed up at the corners and the fine lines fanning out from the deep-set eyes, which were an indeterminate color in the picture. His haircut was precise. Tom didn't resemble his sister, Leanne, who was pleasantly plump and had long straight hair.

Beth grabbed her jacket from its hook by the door before she hurried out of the house. There'd be time to drop the wallet off at Tom's house before she picked up the duffel at Leanne's. Besides, she was eager to know if the rest of him was as interesting as his face.

BETH, SHELTERING BEHIND one of the porch pillars from the cold wind that whipped out of the hills to the north, lifted the heavy brass knocker on Tom Collyer's front door and let it fall. No answer, only the rattle of dry leaves around her feet. She knocked again. Still no answer. She was on the verge of giving up when Tom finally flung the door open.

He was naked to the waist, wiping his damp face with a towel, and his eyes widened in surprise. She must have interrupted his shower. Apologizing came to mind, but she was so mesmerized by the mat of curly dark hair on his chest that she couldn't speak.

"Hello, come in. Shut the door behind you before the wind slams it. It's disaster city around here," he said, wheeling on his heel and taking off before she had even stepped inside. "A geyser erupted in the kitchen a minute before you drove up."

"What?" Beth said, closing the door as instructed and staring after him. His hair was thicker and darker than it had appeared in his photo, and it was wet. So was the top part of his jeans, she noted distractedly. The silver buckle on his belt was embossed with the image of a Texas longhorn. His cowboy boots were scuffed and well-worn, like those of a lot of men around Farish. They were wet, too.

"I really have to—come in, come in—I'd really better get back to Old Faithful," he said, continuing toward the back of the house with a loose-hipped gait that made him seem extremely limber.

Beth noticed a narrow stream of water advancing steadily down the hall toward the rug in the living room.

"Do you have some old rags? Towels? Anything?" she shouted.

"In the linen closet around the corner to your right," he called back, and then he said some words that she couldn't hear but suspected were of the four-letter variety.

Beth found the towels and tossed them down on the plank floor to block the water from reaching the rug, which to her practiced eye appeared to be a good Oriental. She rushed into the kitchen, where she noted immediately that there was no faucet on the kitchen sink. Water was spouting wildly all over the room; it had drenched the walls, the curtains, the wallpaper border below the ceiling. As she watched, Tom, awkward because his right arm was in the sling, threw a bedspread over the place where the faucet should have been. This stopped the geyser.

"Can't you turn the water off?" she asked.

Tom shook his head. "When they built this house back in the Stone Age, they didn't install a cutoff valve. I'd have to turn it off at the meter, and I don't have the right tool to do it. Here, hold this bedspread in place while I get the vise grips. I can crimp the copper tubing under the sink and stop it that way."

When Beth attempted to move into position beside him, she inadvertently jostled his bum wrist. He winced.

"Sorry," Beth said. While Tom ran out to the garage, she held the bedspread, which was soaked but diverted the water into the drain. In a few moments, Tom returned with the vise grips.

His expression was rueful. "I can't do this with only one hand. Could you—?"

Beth had shifted for herself ever since her husband walked out and left her in charge of a house, a yard, a car and a kid. She grabbed the vise grips and, ignoring the water sloshing around her feet, knelt and stuck her head and shoulders into the cabinet beneath the kitchen sink. The vise grips eventually narrowed the soft copper supply pipe until the water flowing from the faucet slowed to a mere rivulet.

In the sudden silence, Tom helped her up. The sling on his arm and the bandage on his wrist were soaked.

"Well, you buy an old house, you have to live with its problems, including faucets that go haywire," he said. "Beth, I'm sorry. You're drenched."

She glanced down at her sodden jacket, her wet leggings, her soggy boots. A substantial stream of water ran between her feet on its way to the foyer.

Beth dashed the water from her eyes and said, "I guess you'd better start building that ark after all."

Tom surprised her by throwing his head back and laughing, a booming laugh that echoed in the house, which she had by this time realized had very little furniture in it. She'd spotted a piano between the dining and living rooms, and beyond that another room, perhaps a den, containing a desk piled with boxes. Stairs led upward from the foyer, presumably to the bedroom area.

With his good left hand, Tom handed her a towel. "I'm glad you can joke about this kind of thing," he said as he picked up his shirt from the kitchen table.

She accepted the towel gratefully and blotted at her face and hair. "Noah kidding," she said.

He stared.

"Is anything wrong?" she said. "Other than the fact that I have all the appeal of a drowned rat?"

He shook his head and smiled. It was a smile that reached all the way to his eyes, which she now perceived were a deep smoky gray and possessed of a devilish twinkle. "The thing is, I don't meet too many women who are so quick on the uptake," he said. "Come to think of it," he added thoughtfully, "I don't meet many women at all." He continued buttoning his shirt, covering up that fascinating thatch of dark hair.

"Well, that will change soon. After all, you're new in Farish," she said, deliberately keeping her tone light. She handed the towel back to him and bent down slightly to peer at her image in the black plastic door of the microwave oven. Her hair was plastered to her head. She tunneled her fingers through the wet mass and tried to fluff it up.

"I'm not exactly new here. This is where I grew up," he said, sounding uncomfortable about it.

She gave her hair a few futile fluffs. "Sorry. I should have remembered. You've been away for a long time, haven't you?"

"Fifteen years," he said. "I was sure I'd never be back."

"Why not?"

He shrugged. "I'm not into small-town life. Everyone knows everything about everybody else."

"That can be a plus," she said. When he didn't reply, she returned her attention to the matter at hand. "Find me a mop and I'll help clean up, since I don't suppose you'd be very good at mopping with that hurt wrist. How's it feeling, by the way?"

"Terrible. I'm in agonizing pain. Maybe you'll stay to help fix dinner?"

"I can't. I have to go over to Leanne's to get a duffel so I can pack for Mitchell to leave on Friday, and then I have to pick him up at his friend's house and—" Beth caught sight of the clock on the range and realized that Ryan's mom would be expecting her at any moment. "And I'd better make a short telephone call." She dug her cell phone out of her purse.

Tom brought a sponge mop and bucket from the back porch while Beth punched in her friend's phone number. "Nancy? Beth. I had to run out for a few minutes, so I'll be a little late picking up Mitchell. No, tell him he can't stay longer. I have to go by Leanne's house and then I'll be right over. Sure, I can drive the day-care carpool Monday. How about trading me for Wednesday? Okay." She hung up and smiled at Tom's ineffectual swiping with the mop. "Here," she said, "you'd better let me wring that out."

He relinquished the mop and watched as she squeezed it into the sink.

"You're not doing such a bad job," she told him as she handed the mop back. He was taller than she had remembered, at least six feet.

"I'm better at this than at playing Santa," he said, the faintest of smiles crossing his lips.

"We appreciated your subbing for Eddie," she told him.

"Leanne has a way of getting people to agree to things they don't want to do. You might say she evoked the Santa clause in our unwritten contract."

"And the Santa clause is what?" She recognized his pun but kept a straight face.

"In return for my dear little sister's invaluable help in getting me settled here, I'm to fill in for Eddie with the kids now that he's traveling more in his job." He started mopping again.

"You?" she said in surprise.

"Is something wrong with that?" He eyed her humorlessly, and she regretted her outburst.

"You don't seem to like kids very much," she said, wishing that they hadn't ventured onto this conversational terrain.

"On the contrary, I like them a lot."

"You do?"

"In fact, I'm going to be working with kids. At the Holcomb Ranch."

Beth's mouth rounded into an O. She'd heard about this guy around town; he was the former marine who was going to teach rodeo skills to high-risk teenagers. She'd never made the connection between the person who was hired to do that and Leanne's brother.

"Leanne never mentioned it," she told him.

"My sister, with her five kids, is more likely to discuss the cost of orthodontia than what her brother plans to do for a living. By the way, my dinner invitation is still on the table," he said.

She realized with amazement that he was flirting with her, and she found it unaccountably sexy. Her interest zinged up a notch, then swooped back down below normal. No way was she going to be influenced by an overemission of pheromones.

She drew a deep breath and focused on a heap of uprooted linoleum scraps in a corner. "Tom, I—"

"All right, so you're going to say no. Yes?"

"Yes."

He cocked his head. "Does that mean you will or you won't?"

"It means I can't. I have a lot to do."

"We got off on the wrong foot the other day. I'm really a nice guy," he said, all charm and sincerity.

"I'm sure," Beth said. She didn't want to be drawn into further conversation with this man who was coming across as so appealing, so she edged around the mop and bucket, trying not to notice the way his wet jeans clung to his thighs. The fluffy white beard he'd worn as Santa hadn't revealed the extreme sensuality of a mouth whose corners were curving upward, a sign that he knew his effect on her.

"I'm running late," she said.

"You haven't yet told me why you're here," he said. He spoke in a low drawl that revealed his native Texas roots.

She felt the color rising in her cheeks. "I almost forgot—I

found your wallet—rather, Mitchell did," Beth said. She dug it out of her jacket pocket and swiped at the water on it with her other hand. "It must have fallen out of your Santa suit in my minivan."

"Thanks, Beth," he said, and she could have sworn that he deliberately let his fingers brush against hers as she handed it to him. She almost let the wallet drop to the floor in her haste to get away.

"Tell Mitch I said hi," he said as she was on her way out the door.

She turned to face him. "His name is Mitchell."

"Sorry."

"Good luck with your plumbing problems," she added lamely. Then she walked quickly down the hall and out the door. Tom followed her, but she didn't trust herself to linger. He was too charming, too sexy and far too interested to be safe.

TOM KNEW HE SHOULD GO BACK into the kitchen and start assessing the damage brought about by the unexpected plumbing failure. Instead, he trailed Beth to the door and watched as she backed out of the driveway.

She had made it clear that she didn't wish to further their acquaintance. But the way she skipped down his front steps, the set of her chin as she hurried toward her car, the altogether delectable derriere, outlined by those tight leggings as she folded herself into the minivan—he couldn't take his eyes off her.

When had she said her son was leaving? Friday? Tom consulted the calendar on the back of the pantry door as he unwrapped the wet bandage from his wrist.

Friday was the sixteenth of December. And Beth was worried about being lonely.

"Well, Ms. McCormick—" a devilish grin spread across his face "—you don't have to worry about that. Not at all."

He waited fifteen minutes, until he was sure that Beth would have left his sister's house before he picked up the phone. "Leanne?" he said when she answered. "Remember that housewarming party you wanted to throw for me? Well, I've changed my mind. Let's have it over the holiday. Like on December sixteenth."

"That's awfully close to Christmas. I'll have a lot of other things to do, and—"

"Leanne, you owe me."

"Oh, I'm not so sure of that. It seems to me we're even."

"I stuffed myself into a Santa suit and entertained a bunch of insufferable little kids on short notice. You promised me the moon, Leanne, and all I'm asking is that we have my housewarming party on December sixteenth." He held his breath.

"May I ask why that particular date?"

He exhaled slowly. "Blond hair. Blue-green eyes."

There was a stunned silence on the other end of the line. "Beth? Are you talking about Beth?"

"I'm talking about finally getting into the Christmas spirit," he said.

"She doesn't go out with anyone."

"It's Christmas. 'Tis the season for miracles. I'll even put up a Christmas tree."

Leanne laughed. "The other miracle is that Mitchell will be out of town."

"Okay, so we can have the party? I don't want anyone to bring gifts. I just want a chance to get together with our friends."

"You told me you didn't intend to get involved in Farish social life."

"I can deal with it," Tom said offhandedly. "Providing there are perks." Like Beth McCormick.

"Okay." Leanne sighed. "I'll do it, but reluctantly. And don't expect Beth to be there."

"I'm sure you can arrange it. That's the whole point."

"Tom—"

"Sorry, I've got things to do."

"What kinds of things?"

"I don't have time to explain. 'Bye, Leanne." And he hung up before she could change her mind.

ON THE DAY that she drove Mitchell through a drizzling rain to the outskirts of Fort Worth, where his father would meet them to drive their son back to Oklahoma, Beth remained stoic. Mitchell sat beside her in the minivan, coloring in his new Christmas coloring book. Beth kept a conversation going to distract herself from the imminent goodbye.

"What did you ask Santa for, Mitchell, when you spoke to him at the pancake breakfast?" She and Mitchell would open presents when he returned from visiting Richie, but maybe there was some last-minute item she'd overlooked.

Mitchell only clamped his lips and went on coloring.

"Mitchell?"

No answer.

"Are you going to keep me in suspense?" They often played the game of coaxing each other to tell something, and usually, her asking this question got a chuckle out of her son, but this time he shook his head and scowled.

"He isn't going to bring it," Mitchell said.

"Bring what, honey?"

"What I asked for."

"Well, he might."

"He seemed like a nice Santa," Mitchell allowed, "but he said he couldn't."

Maybe that was what had set Mitchell off when he'd been having his chat with Tom, aka Santa Claus.

"I'm sure Santa does his best," Beth ventured cautiously.

"I wonder if his arm got better." Mitchell put his crayon back in the box. "So he can bring a big sack of toys to everyone."

"It's probably okay by now."

Mitchell turned the page. "What I wanted couldn't go in a bag. I asked him for a real daddy."

Beth's heart filled with dismay. "You have a daddy," she reminded him gently. "I'm taking you to him right now."

"He isn't a *real* one," Mitchell said with annoyance. "He doesn't live in our house."

"I've told you over and over, Mitchell, why your father doesn't live with us." She'd crafted her explanation carefully, explaining that his parents had decided to live apart because they weren't happy together, that Richie had found a new wife but still loved Mitchell very much, even as much as she, Beth, loved him. Mitchell had accepted this, she'd thought.

"It doesn't matter *why* my daddy doesn't live with us," Mitchell said with extreme patience. "Jeremiah's father is there to throw baseballs with." This was typical kid logic, which probably made perfectly good sense to him.

"There are different kinds of dads, Mitchell. Some travel a lot in their jobs, like Jeremiah's dad. He's not really at their house all the time, you know. Some dads go to an office every day. Some work at home. Some take care of their children while the mommy goes to work. You just happen to have the kind of dad who lives far away. But he's still your daddy, no matter what."

"He has Ava now," Mitchell said darkly. "I bet he's forgotten all about me."

"No, sweetheart, he will never forget you. You'll find out how glad he is to see you in just—um, about an hour now."

"Uh-huh," Mitchell said, sounding unconvinced as he bent over his coloring book again.

Beth decided to drop the topic. She'd said all she had to say about it, and discussing the situation generally made her feel worse. She was determined to keep a stiff upper lip today, no matter what.

She managed all right when she unbuckled Mitchell's seat belt and kissed him goodbye, holding him close for one long hug. She did okay when he ran to her ex-husband's Grand Am, which was parked opposite her minivan in the parking lot of a Denny's Restaurant right off Interstate 35. But when Mitchell clambered awkwardly into Richie's car, she was close to falling apart. She braced herself to speak to her ex, who slid from his seat to help Mitchell out of his bright yellow rain slicker. Tears welled in her eyes when Richie's new wife swiveled and treated Mitchell to a big welcoming smile.

Once Mitchell was situated, Richie, seeming doggedly determined to be civil, walked over to Beth's car and bent to peer at her through the open window. "Are you sure you don't want to come into the restaurant and have coffee with Starla and me? It's a long drive back."

"No, thanks," she said, biting the words off sharply and trying not to let on that she was a basket case.

"Beth, it shouldn't be like this," he said. The waistband of his pants strained across a beginning paunch, and his hairline had receded at least half an inch since this time last year. These observations should have given her satisfaction but only made her sad.

"How should it be, Richie?" Beth asked wearily. "All sweetness and light? When I no longer have a husband? And Mitchell no longer has a live-in daddy?" She'd tried hard to forgive Richie and Starla over the past three years but had failed utterly.

Richie studied the wet asphalt. "We need to get over this," he said finally. "For Mitchell's sake."

Beth swallowed, forcing down the taste of bile. Scenes of Richie's betrayal flashed through her mind: the nights he'd said he was working late, his sneaking into their bed after midnight reeking of Patchouli, a scent Beth never wore. His lies, his denials, his defense of nineteen-year-old Starla of the trim thighs and enormous breasts, who had set her sights on Richie and had never let up until she'd lured him away from his wife and child. Not that Beth blamed Starla, exactly. Richie should have made it clear that he wasn't interested, shown some self-control.

Beth inhaled a bolstering breath. "Mitchell's duffel is in the back seat."

Wordlessly, Richie opened the back door and scooped it up.

She didn't speak until he'd slammed the door. "I'll be here at one o'clock on December twenty-eighth. Call me if you're not going to be on time," she said.

"Okay, Beth. Have a safe trip. And a merry Christmas."

When Beth only stared at him blankly, Richie said lamely, "I mean it, Beth. I really do."

After it became obvious that Beth wasn't going to speak, he straightened and walked away. Mitchell, happy and excited, turned and waved out the window of Richie's car, and Beth waved back. His new red sweatshirt gave him a festive air, and she could hardly bear the thought that he was going so far away.

She wouldn't have anyone to jump squealing onto her bed on Christmas morning, anyone with whom to share breakfast after opening presents or to cuddle with in front of the TV while watching favorite holiday movies. Mitchell had become her whole life since Richie left; Beth often felt that it was the two of them against the world. While Mitchell was gone, she would be miserably alone.

It was against the natural order of things. No one should be alone at Christmas. This was the season to be jolly, wasn't it? A time to be with family, right?

Wrong. Her family now consisted only of Mitchell, and he would be away for twelve whole days.

Chapter Four

Driving home from Fort Worth, Beth couldn't stop thinking about the situation that had produced this sad state of affairs. In fact, she'd been wandering through all the could'ves and should'ves since the divorce.

Back when she was still married, she could've questioned Richie more thoroughly when he'd said he had to work late, but she'd been exhausted from dealing with a toddler all day and hadn't wanted to rock the marital boat. She should've made it clear to Richie that she suspected his infidelity sooner. She could've sought counseling earlier; she should've realized that she was in denial about the disintegration of her marriage; she—

But she hadn't. And if she had, would the course of events have changed? Would she still be married to Richie, who by this time seemed woefully deficient as a husband? And now that she felt that way about him, would she even want to be married to him?

Probably not, she admitted. Certainly not. She'd lost all respect for Richie somewhere along the way, and that didn't bode well for a marriage.

She inserted a cassette of Michael Martin Murphey's "Rollin' Nowhere" in the tape deck, and by the time she rolled into Farish, Beth felt better. The song was about wasting time and having no particular aim in life, which wasn't the case with her. She had her son, her business and her own place to be—Farish, Texas.

Beth always got a positive feeling when she crossed the steel girder bridge spanning the Sabinal River and spotted the sign at the edge of town proclaiming Farish to be "The Small Town with the Big Heart," which Beth's friend Chloe often joked should be amended to add "And Big Ears, Big Eyes and Big Mouths"—a reference to the ever-active gossip mill. Not that Beth found that particular feature of small-town life troublesome; she knew a lot of caring people in Farish.

She still lived in the house that she and Richie had bought when they moved here five years ago, a small white-frame, green-roofed bungalow on the outskirts of town. It was meant to be their starter home. They had figured that they'd be able to move up to a bigger house in the new upscale Hillsdale development outside town after Richie became manager of the local feed and seed store and before their first child started school. However, after the scandal with Starla, Richie was fired and he and his new wife moved away.

The divorce had wrecked their finances, as divorces often did, and moving to Hillsdale was out of the question now. Fortunately, Beth loved her house, which nestled in a grove of pecan trees, and she had decorated it in a shabby-chic cottage style abounding in soft, faded colors. Even though she was able to acquire new furnishings at wholesale prices, she'd avoided suites of expensive furniture, instead shopping carefully for gently used pieces that conveyed an atmosphere of warmth and coziness.

The bungalow, which had no near neighbors, was set back from the two-lane highway that curled down out of a series of hills and continued around a small pond. On the shores of the pond were a county park and playground, where Beth sometimes took Mitchell to play. Today, perhaps due to the cloudy skies and the chill wind sweeping out of the hills, the park was empty. If she hadn't been so upset about saying goodbye to Mitchell, she might have gone for an invigorating walk after pulling her car in the garage, but now she had no intention of doing anything more than putting on the teakettle.

Her kitchen was welcoming and cheerful, with cabinets that she had restored to their original maple finish and blue-and-white checked wallpaper above the beadboard wainscoting. As soon as she walked in the back door and hung her jacket in the closet, her phone rang. It was Leanne.

"You *are* coming to Tom's housewarming tonight, aren't you?" Leanne demanded.

"No," said Beth, cupping the phone between her chin and shoulder while filling the teakettle with water.

"It'll be good for you."

"My nose is red and my eyes are puffy. I miss Mitchell. I wouldn't be good company, Leanne."

"Don't be silly. Why stay home and mope when you can hang out with a bunch of fun people? Chloe is coming, and Julie and Steve, and Divver and Patty, and some of the members of the Breakfast with Santa committee."

"They'll try to cheer me up. I want to wallow in my misery," she said, only half joking. Chloe had been her best friend since they'd both attended the University of Texas, and Leanne, Julie and Steve had been supportive throughout the divorce, but she really wanted to be by herself tonight.

Leanne let out an exasperated sigh. "Tom will be disappointed," she said, employing her best carrot-in-front-of-the-horse technique.

For a moment, Beth couldn't place the man's name. Then she recalled a pair of piercing gray eyes, and the rest of Tom filled itself in. Wide shoulders, ropy muscles, chiseled cheekbones and a shock of dark hair falling across one eyebrow.

She unwrapped a tea bag, her favorite Earl Grey. "How's Tom's wrist?" she asked, being polite. Not that she'd forgotten the rare camaraderie between them on that day at his house when she'd helped him tame a runaway faucet, but she didn't want to seem too interested.

"It's better. Not perfect. So, will you join us?"

"Maybe," Beth said, although she had no intention of going.

She'd told Leanne as much when she received the invitation, but her friend never took no for an answer.

"Good. Be there at eight or so. 'Bye." And Leanne hung up.

Beth brewed the tea and turned on some funereal music before carrying her teacup and saucer to Mitchell's room, where she curled up on the narrow bed with her head on his pillow, inhaling deeply of his sweet little-boy scent. Mitchell had fallen in love with the gentle cartoon ogre Shrek, and she'd decorated her son's room with a matching plaid comforter and curtains that coordinated with Shrek's chartreuse complexion. Mitchell had Shrek coloring books and Shrek T-shirts and a lonely stuffed Donkey that made her tear up when she nudged it aside to make more room on the bed. After a while, lulled by the music and the patter of rain on the roof, she dozed.

When the phone rang some time later, she thought it might be Richie phoning to let her speak to Mitchell before bedtime. She scooped up the receiver and said eagerly, "Hello?"

"Why aren't you here?" asked a familiar male voice, deep and somehow intimate.

Her heart sank to her stomach. It was Tom Collyer.

She levered herself to a sitting position and propped herself against the pillows. "Because—because I'm here," she blurted, saying the first stupid thing that popped into her head. But Tom treated it as if she'd said something witty, and chuckled.

"Everybody's got to be someplace," he agreed. "I was thinking that your someplace should be at this party." She heard lighthearted laughter in the background and glanced outside, where darkness had settled in.

"I've sort of got car trouble," she said. This wasn't entirely untrue, since the minivan had spewed a thick cloud of exhaust all down I-35 today. She'd called from her cell phone on the way home and made an appointment to drop it off at a local garage tomorrow for repair.

"I'll come and get you."

"No," she said hastily. "My car could probably make it." But the minivan was almost out of gas, though she knew better than to say so.

"Good. Can you be here in fifteen minutes?"

She'd trapped herself. "I'm busy."

"Leanne said you'd driven your son to meet his father and were planning a quiet evening. Stop by and let us cheer you up."

"I—" Beth began, but she heard a muffled rustling and Leanne spoke.

"I've got to rush home, Beth, because two of the kids have temperatures, and I don't doubt that they're finally coming down with Eddie's flu. I need someone to stick the canapés in the oven and make sure they emerge as cheese puffs, not incinerated bread crumbs. All you have to do is sit in the kitchen and keep an eye on things. Otherwise, this will go down as the coldest housewarming in history. Will you help? You're the only one I trust with my recipe."

"Do the guests really need jalapeño cheese puffs?" This month she'd already gone over and above what was required of a good friend. Hadn't she fashioned twenty fresh-fir-and-balsam centerpieces for the pancake breakfast and stuffed herself into a silly elf outfit for three hours?

"Yes, or they'll revolt. Steve refuses to go home until he's slaked his cheese-puff craving."

Beth sighed. Although the menu at Farish parties seldom varied from the usual barbecued baby ribs, hot chicken wings and potato chips with onion dip, Leanne's cheese puffs were famous. "Okay," Beth said. "But only until the cheese puffs are all gone."

"Tom says he'll pick you up."

"I'll drive myself."

"Tom says you have car trouble. He'll be there to get you shortly."

"I—" She wished she'd stopped for gas on the way home today.

"Thanks for doing this, Beth. You're a pal."

"And I hope you won't forget it," Beth muttered after she'd hung up the phone. She quickly ran a brush through her hair, pushed a few strands behind her ears, peered at her image in the mirror and applied a new coat of lipstick. Her eyes were still shot through with red, and her nose was swollen. Her blouse and skirt were wrinkled, too, and she didn't have time to change. But she could certainly handle shoveling cheese puffs in and out of the oven for an hour or so.

While she straightened the living room, shoving wallpaper books off the couch and prying the remains of one of Mitchell's half-eaten granola bars off the coffee table, she noticed that her collection of glass and ceramic hearts was dusty, and she went to get a clean cloth.

Beth had been collecting hearts since high school and had received her first ceramic one for her seventeenth birthday. At the time, she'd lived in Houston with her grandmother, a dour old soul who'd never gone out of her way to make Beth's life any easier, and Beth had been working at an ice cream shop to earn money to decorate her tiny, airless and extremely ugly room in Josephine Mitchell's big old house.

The room was a former hallway, assigned to her by Josephine because it wouldn't cost much to heat. It featured faded, torn wallpaper printed with hunt scenes, circa the 1940s, and the wood floor was scuffed and scarred with age. Beth, wanting to make the space hers, had used her first paycheck to buy an area rug in a scrumptious shade of raspberry pink, and when she'd seen the heart-shaped vase in a gift shop, she'd exclaimed over it with her friend Shari. On her birthday three months later, Shari had presented her with the vase over hot fudge sundaes.

Later, she'd bought or received as gifts heart-shaped wall plaques, jewelry boxes, paperweights and perfume bottles. When she and Richie had become engaged, he'd given her a heart-shaped music box. Leanne and Eddie had presented them with a candy dish featuring entwined hearts as an anniversary present shortly after they'd moved to Farish. All of these had been amassed on the shelves between her living and dining rooms, and as she carefully wiped them off, she realized with a jolt that the only ones she'd collected since her divorce were either broken hearts or halves of hearts. Well, that was fitting, she supposed, but now she pushed them to the back of the shelf. The misery that Richie had brought down upon her wasn't something she needed to contemplate right now.

When the doorbell rang, she called, "Come in, it's open."

"Hi," Tom said as he ushered in a rush of cool air. He was wearing his Stetson and a leather jacket, and he stuffed his hands deep into the pockets as he swept his gaze over her. The cold had brought a flush to his cheeks.

Suddenly self-conscious, she dropped the dust rag on the nearby couch and smoothed her hair. "I'll get my coat," she said.

He rocked back on his heels. "No hurry. Only a dozen or so of my closest friends waiting for a cheese puff."

She narrowed her eyes, then decided he was joking. She wasn't in a mood to respond in kind, however, so she went to the closet and pulled her coat off its hanger. Tom sauntered over to the shelf and studied her collection of hearts.

The phone rang as she was sliding her arms into the coat sleeves.

"Excuse me," she said to Tom. "That might be my son." She clicked the phone on. "Hello?"

"Mommy, Mommy, guess what? Ava has a new tooth!"

"That's wonderful, sweetheart," Beth said warmly as she sank onto the hall bench.

Tom continued to survey her collection of hearts, seemingly uninterested in the conversation. He picked one of them up, turned it over in his hands. It was the clear red paperweight from Italy, brought to her by Richie's parents, who had vacationed there a few years ago.

"Yes, it's a big tooth, and she's getting another one. Starla says I can help feed her. Isn't that neat?"

"Mmm-hmm," Beth said, thinking wistfully of Ava sitting in

a high chair and waiting with a gap-toothed grin as Mitchell moved the spoon closer and closer to her mouth. Babies were easy to love, and she had always wanted a houseful of kids.

"Mommy, my room in Dad and Starla's new house is enormous, and guess what—I have bunk beds now! Starla bought me Shrek blankets like at home and every stuff."

"Every*thing*," she corrected automatically.

"Yes, and we just ate spaghetti and meatballs. I love spaghetti and meatballs, Mommy. I could eat it every single night."

"We'll have spaghetti when you get home," Beth said.

"You never make meatballs, only plain old hamburger crumbled in it," Mitchell said.

He'd always loved her spaghetti sauce, which she painstakingly prepared from scratch. "I can do meatballs," she said in her own defense, but she was beginning to feel annoyed. It was always like this when Mitchell was at his father's house; nothing she did seemed as good to him as what Richie and Starla did.

Tom sent her an inquiring glance, which reminded her that they'd been about to leave.

"I miss you, Mitchell," she said. "It's not the same around this house when you're gone."

"Oh, I miss you, too, Mommy," Mitchell said. "I wish you were here."

She had gone to great pains to explain to Mitchell why it was not possible for her to stay with him at his father's, but the fact that he wanted her warmed her heart. "I'll be thinking of you."

"Me, too." There was a pause, then a rustle at the other end of the line.

"Beth?" It was Richie.

"Yes?"

"Mitchell refused to drink his milk at dinner. What's up with that?"

"He—he's on a chocolate milk kick at present, and he only likes it made with Hershey's syrup. In a coffee mug."

"A coffee mug," Richie repeated with a mystified air.

"Yes, um, Mitchell wanted coffee one morning, and I told him it wasn't good for him, and he pitched a fit. I put chocolate in his milk, served it to him in a mug, and that's the only way he'll drink it now."

"I'll tell Starla."

"And he likes bananas sliced very thin on top of his Cap'n Crunch. And don't let him swallow the toothpaste," she added hastily before Richie could hang up. She almost mentioned Mitchell's tantrums, a fairly recent development, but had decided against it. Richie would no doubt get a taste of them soon enough.

There was another pause, and then he said, "Here, I'll let you say goodbye to Mitchell."

Mitchell came back on the line. "Their milk is bad, Mommy. It tastes like a cow smells."

Beth almost laughed. The day-care center had taken the kids on a field trip to a dairy farm recently. "I told your dad that you like chocolate in your milk. You be a good boy, and I'll talk to you again soon, okay?"

"Okay. We're going to a movie tomorrow. Did I tell you that?"

"No," she said, missing him even more now that she'd been reminded of all the clever, funny things that Mitchell would say.

"I've got to go now. Ava's going to bed, and I want to help tuck her in."

"I wish I could tuck you in, too, sweet boy," she said past the lump in her throat.

"So do I. 'Bye, Mom. I love you."

"Love you, too," Beth whispered, and then Mitchell was gone.

Chapter Five

She barely realized that Tom had walked over and was standing in front of her.

"It's tough, huh?" he said, and when she looked up, she saw compassion radiating from his eyes.

She didn't trust herself to speak, only to nod.

He stood watching her for a moment. "Well," he said slowly, "how about explaining this heart collection of yours before we go? I guess hearts mean something special to you, right?"

"I just like them," she said, settling on the simplest explanation. There was more, of course, that prompted her fixation on this symbol of love—her parents abandoning her, never to be seen again, when she was Mitchell's age; the lack of caring and attention in her grandmother's house; the struggle to get along on her own after Josephine denied any responsibility for supporting Beth once she turned eighteen. It was silly, she knew, but adding yet another heart to her collection in difficult times had often reminded her that somewhere in the world, love existed, and that she would find it someday. Collecting hearts was a matter of faith with her, an assurance that things would eventually get better.

Well, they hadn't, not really. But she had Mitchell now, and her love for him was all-encompassing, sustaining her through every difficulty that life threw in her path and making her optimistic about the future.

She wouldn't elaborate on that now. Tom was waiting for her, and she made herself say, "We'd better go."

They walked down the driveway to where he'd parked his blue Dodge pickup, which he explained would be useful for his new job and also for the rodeoing that he intended to do in his spare time.

"I'll be hauling around horse tack and trailers," he told her after he slid behind the wheel, "as well as a bunch of kids."

All she knew about Divver Holcomb's ranch was that the place had belonged to Divver's family for generations. Though most of the Holcomb spread had been sold to the developer of Hillsdale, Divver had recently opened a rodeo school on the homestead portion of the ranch, where he taught bronco and bull riding.

"How did you get interested in teaching skills to at-risk kids?"

He kept his eyes on the road. "After I got back from duty in the Gulf War, I became a drill sergeant at Parris Island, South Carolina, the marine corps training school for recruits. I guess you could say that I met a few guys there who made me think about why kids don't live up to their potential in life. I took college courses on the base and eventually earned my BA in education, did my practice teaching in a middle school with lots of problem teens. I figured out before long that there were parallels between marine recruits who washed out and the problem kids I taught."

Beth was grateful for a subject that required little more of her than listening. She studied Tom's expression in the lights from the dash. "Parallels?"

"The washouts would have been good marines if someone had provided structure and discipline early on. They had the desire to be marines. They were physically fit and highly intelligent. Those middle-school kids had many of the same traits. I concluded that the thing that made recruits succeed and kept middle-school kids out of trouble was someone caring enough to impose restrictions early on."

"Is that the problem with the at-risk kids who'll be coming to the ranch?"

"Could be. After Divver talked to me about the youngsters he wants to help, kids who haven't been turned on by anything or anyone at school or at home, I knew I could make a difference in their lives. If the ATTAIN program gets to them early enough, provides the structure and self-esteem they need, they'll pull themselves together."

"What did you call it—ATTAIN?" she asked, intrigued by the fervor in his voice.

"It's an acronym for Attention To Teens Assessed In Need. The county school board is working with us, and Divver and I have been meeting with experts in education who are helping shape our program. We'll have twelve youngsters from around the state at first, starting after the semester break in January. They'll attend Farish High and room with local families. A van will pick the kids up at the high school and deliver them to the ranch for a half-day of work with Divver and me."

Leanne, when she had mentioned her brother Tom's move back to Farish, hadn't sketched in these details. Basically, all Beth had heard about Tom Collyer before she met him was that he had been upwardly mobile on the rodeo circuit fifteen years ago. Now she felt herself drawn to him in some inexplicable way. Most men she'd met since her divorce were interested mostly in themselves, their cars and sports, in that order. Tom had a passion for helping kids, and the idealism reflected in his eyes made her want to know more about him.

They had slowed in front of his house. Leanne's husband, Eddie, waved genially from a car parked nearby as they got out of the truck. In the house, Leanne, who was rearranging the refrigerator to accommodate another six-pack, straightened as they came in the door.

"Thank goodness! Eddie's ready to leave, and I was beginning to wonder what had happened to you two." Tom, after aiming an encouraging smile in Beth's direction, disappeared through the swinging door into a dining room filled wall-to-wall with people.

Leanne, clearly frazzled, wasted no time in giving her instructions. "I've stored the unbaked cheese puffs on the bottom shelf of the fridge, and you'll need to place them a couple of inches apart on the cookie sheets. Watch to make sure that they brown evenly, and set them out on the counter as each batch is done. Tom will pass them around. Everyone's so busy having fun that no one will notice you."

For the first time, Leanne focused on Beth. "What in the world have you done to your nose? It's a lovely shade of cerise."

"Cried a lot," Beth said truthfully.

"Bad idea. You need other interests, Beth."

"Leanne, didn't I join the Homemakers' Club? Don't I show up for church most of the time?"

"That's not what I meant."

When Beth opened her mouth to protest, Leanne patted her shoulder comfortingly. "I hope you feel better soon, but now I've got to run. Lord, I hope all my kids won't be sick with this flu for Christmas. Thanks, Beth," she said, and she was out the door.

Beth closed her mouth again and studied the current batch of cheese puffs through the glass oven door before parking herself on a stool. On the other side of the kitchen door, she heard her friend Chloe Timberlake talking loudly over music blaring from a stereo, and two other people were arguing about the probable outcome of the Superbowl. When she peeked through the window in the kitchen door, she spied a table full of food and Tom Collyer backed into a corner beside a huge Christmas tree by two equally voluptuous single women, Muffy Ledbetter and Teresa Boggs. Both wore too much makeup, too much jewelry, and both talked too loudly and too fast.

Well, Beth thought as she retreated to her stool in front of the oven, Tom Collyer wouldn't have to worry about meeting women after *this* party. Thanks to Muffy, who had recently started writing a column called "Here 'n' There in Farish" for the local newspaper, word would soon reach all eligible females in Farish that the new guy in town was handsome and personable and in the mood for female companionship.

Beth was heaving a giant sigh when Tom himself marched through the kitchen door bearing a full wineglass.

"I brought you a drink. Or would you care for something stronger?" His smile was disarming, his eyes warm and interested.

She accepted the glass. "This is fine," she said, hesitating briefly before she took a sip. The wine was nice—not too dry, not too sweet.

Tom wrinkled his nose. "Are you sure those things aren't burning?" he asked.

Beth slid off the stool and yanked the oven door open. "Hand me that pot holder, will you?"

He slapped it into her hand, and she removed the cookie sheet from the oven. "Leanne said you'd serve these," she told him as she deftly slid cheese puffs onto a platter.

"Leanne makes a lot of assumptions, but I guess that's no news to you." Tom's eyes sparkled in wry amusement as she thrust the platter at him.

"Hardly, but we don't mind, do we? Much," she added grudgingly as she managed a reluctant smile.

He moved toward the door, then turned back toward her. "Hey, can't I lure you into the living room?"

"I promised Leanne I'd take care of these." She averted her eyes from his hopeful face as she transferred the next batch of cheese puffs into the oven.

"There's no need for you to hide in the kitchen like Cinderella," he said. "Anyway, Leanne told me to cheer you up."

"You'd better get those canapés to your guests before they get cold," she pointed out.

"At least *she* had a handsome prince," Tom replied enigmatically with a jaunty lift of his eyebrows.

Beth stared after him. *Handsome prince,* Beth was thinking. *I had the handsome prince. Also the house in what could pass for suburbs in Farish.* But the glass slipper was the wrong size. And it had shattered to pieces along with all her hopes and dreams for the future, which before her divorce had run along the lines of more kids, an even bigger house and a dog.

Someone plunged through the door from the dining room, her stiletto heels wobbling as she walked. "Da-yumn," said Muffy Ledbetter, grappling with her dress behind her back. Muffy made two syllables out of one even when she was cursing.

"Hi, Muffy," Beth said. "Is something wrong?"

"The zipper on this dress is busted. I expect I'll have to go home, and just when that scrumptious Tom Collyer was asking me about my best bull." Muffy, whose father was a prominent rancher in Bigbee County, was into breeding cattle. But if her low-cut come-hither dress was any indication, she'd like to try out a few breeding techniques herself.

Beth, having been a city girl until she moved to Farish, didn't know much about cattle, but she'd grown proficient at repairs of all kinds since Richie's exit from her life. "Want me to try my luck with that zipper?" she offered.

"Sure 'nuf," Muffy said. She presented her back to Beth, who expertly realigned the two sets of zipper teeth. One tug and it was magically rejoined.

"Gosh, Beth, you're a whiz. Say, why don't you want to come to the party for a while?"

Beth waved at the oven. "Can't. Promised Leanne I'd tend to the cheese puffs."

"Everyone's taking tours of this house. Four bedrooms upstairs, and two baths. It'll be awesome when Tom finishes fixing it up."

"Mmm," Beth said.

"Well, if you're not going to join us, I'll get back to the others. Though why I need competition as drop-dead gorgeous as you, I'm not sure. Tom's probably crazy about blondes." Muffy was a redhead herself, though she freely admitted that her hair color was derived from a bottle.

"Has Beth mentioned that she and I have already met?" Tom inquired as he breezed into the kitchen. He leaned over and plucked the cheese puffs from the oven. "Falling down on the job, Beth? These were ready."

"I was going to take them out," she said with dignity. She picked up her wineglass, took a sip.

Tom seemed unconvinced as he arranged the delicacies on their platter, still favoring his bandaged wrist. "Muffy, how about passing these around?" he suggested.

Muffy looked askance, clearly confused by Tom's air of familiarity with Beth. "Well," she said halfheartedly, "sure I will. Anything to help. Thanks, Beth, for fixing my zipper." She disappeared through the swinging door with a swish.

Tom raised his eyebrows, which gave him a roguish expression. She wished he weren't so attractive. "What was that about a zipper?"

"On her dress. It broke, and I repaired it." In this light his eyes looked silver.

"What's making you nervous? Is it me?"

"I'm not nervous," she said as she spilled her wine down the front of her blouse. Hand still trembling, she went to the sink and blotted water on the stain with a paper towel.

Tom hooked his thumbs through his belt loops and leaned toward Beth as she turned back toward him. "Say, Cinderella, this won't do at all. Want some eyedrops? There's a new bottle in the bathroom medicine cabinet."

She smiled wanly. "I'm coming across as a real nutcase, aren't I?"

He moved away, studied her. "You give the impression of a mother who loves her son very much," he said quietly.

Tears stung her eyelids; she couldn't help it.

"Hey, no crying allowed in my kitchen," Tom said, tipping a finger under Beth's chin and tilting her face upward.

"Seems like you're always having waterworks problems in here," she said, attempting a smile and gesturing toward the now-operational faucet.

"I suspect you need a hug," he said.

She blinked the tears back and leaned away from him, struggling to get down from the stool. He rested his hands on her shoulders.

"Do you mind?" he said gently.

She liked the weight of his hands and their warmth through the fabric of her blouse. "I should put those other jalapeño whatchacallits in the oven," she whispered, inhaling a heady whiff of his aftershave.

"Hang the whatchacallits," he said with feeling.

"My blouse is all wet," she said. But he paid no attention. Instead, he enfolded her in his embrace and pulled her so close that she heard his heart beating slowly and steadily beneath his sweater.

They stood like that for a time, with Beth drawing strength from the warmth of his body and the gentle pressure of his arms around her.

The door opened abruptly. "Beth—" Muffy Ledbetter halted in her tracks and stared at them in consternation. "Well, da-yumn," she said. "What's going on in here?"

Chapter Six

Beth bit her lip, whether in chagrin or stifled laughter over Muffy's perplexed expression she wasn't sure.

Tom handled the situation more coolly. "I was merely giving Beth a hug," he explained, as if this were an activity he practiced regularly. After releasing her, he sauntered to the sink and casually ran water into a glass.

"Oh," Muffy said. "Does everyone get one?" Coyness was built into Muffy like her big bosom and impossibly narrow hips.

"Sure," Tom said easily, his eyes twinkling over the top of his water glass. "We're passing them out as party favors."

Beth made a show of opening and closing the oven door. "In fact," Tom went on, "Beth is helping me. Come on, Beth, let's give everyone their hugs." He grabbed her hand and started out of the kitchen, calling back to the still-perplexed Muffy, "Watch the cheese puffs, Muffy, will you please?"

He propelled Beth into the dining room. "Here's Beth, folks. She's been hiding out in the kitchen."

"Beth! No one told us you were here!" called Gretchen from the back of the room.

"The thing is," Tom said with a grin, "we've decided to make hugs our party favors tonight. Here's one for you, Chloe. Merry Christmas." And he enveloped her in a bearlike embrace. Chloe, never one to lack spirit, turned to hug Divver and his wife, Patty, and then Gretchen hugged Divver and Beth. They were a convivial group, and soon everyone was hugging everyone else, good-humored greetings reverberating throughout the room.

That sort of friendliness might have seemed out of place anywhere else but in Farish, which was the kind of town where you ran into your neighbors at the supermarket and invited them to dinner the same night and where most people had grown up together, as had their parents and grandparents. Beth had to admit that after she stopped being self-conscious over her wet blouse, she liked being hugged. Since her divorce, she had been suffering from sensory deprivation, she realized.

"Beth, where have you been lately?" Chloe asked as she perched on a chair arm across from where Beth stood by the window.

Beth realized she still held a pot holder in one fist, and stuffed it in her pocket. "Driving the day-care carpool. Conferring with clients. How about you?"

"Caring for my grandmother. Toilet training my cat."

"Does it work for cats?"

"I haven't figured that out yet. I suspect it's easier with kids."

Beth smiled at her friend, who was wearing a vintage yellow sweater-dress with shiny over-the-knee boots. Multicolored Christmas-tree lights reflected off her dangling silver earrings, which she'd probably made herself. Chloe had recently streaked her rebellious hair with magenta and done something spiky with her bangs.

"I didn't have any trouble with Mitchell's toilet training, but he wasn't accustomed to kitty litter," Beth told her, and Chloe laughed.

"Beth, I've missed you. It's been a long time since we got together."

Beth thought for a moment. "There's an estate sale near Kettersburg tomorrow. Want to drive over there with me?"

"Grandma's talking about closing the store. There's no point in going to the sale, since we're not buying now."

"Closing the store! She's owned it for years."

"It's become too much of a hassle, even with me to manage it. The state of her health isn't good. I promised to take her Christmas shopping tomorrow. She and I would be delighted if you'd come with us."

Beth shook her head. "I suspect that I'm going to land the account to design the interior of the Kettersburg Country Club, so I need to attend the auction in case they have something I might be able to use."

"The country club, huh? Fantastic."

"Yes, things are going well for me lately businesswise. What are you planning to do if your grandmother closes the store?"

"I want to get back into something arty." Chloe had worked as a jewelry designer for a company in Austin before quitting to help her grandmother.

"But you're so good at selling," Beth said.

"I've managed to sell you a thing or two," she agreed. "Stop in sometime—I may have something you can use for the country club."

"Let's try for lunch one day," suggested Beth. At the moment, Julie was propping open the swinging door to the kitchen, where Muffy was feverishly shoveling cheese puffs.

"You're on," Chloe said. "Anyway, it will be a good time to run something by you."

"Like what?"

"I'm thinking of trying a new venture."

"What is it this time?"

"Oh, it's major, but it has nothing to do with gourmet dog biscuits or feng shui." Those were two of Chloe's past enthusiasms that hadn't proved commercially viable in Farish.

"I'm glad to hear it," Beth said dryly.

Muffy minced out of the kitchen, carefully balancing a tray

in front of her. "Cheese puff?" she asked demurely, just happening to stop in front of Tom. He took one, popped it in his mouth and went on talking with Divver Holcomb, who, unlike the others, who were wearing more traditional holiday garb, had dressed in his usual western shirt and boots.

"Muffy, I'll watch the next batch," Beth told her.

"They're all baked," Muffy said airily.

Beth grabbed a few as Muffy undulated hiplessly by, handing some to Chloe and eating one herself.

"I should go home," Beth said. "It's been a long day. Let out a holler when you're ready to leave. I could use a ride."

"Oh? How'd you get here? Mmm, those were good, though hugging Muffy is kind of a high price to pay for a cheese puff." Chloe delicately wiped her hands on a cocktail napkin.

"Leanne sent Tom to pick me up," Beth said, all reluctance.

Chloe's eyebrows threatened to collide with her multicolored hairline. "She did?"

"Tom and I had met before, at Breakfast with Santa," Beth said. "Of course, Leanne mentioned a month or so ago that she was helping her brother find a house, so I knew he was here."

"Honey," Chloe said, moving closer, "he's preceded by his reputation."

"What does that mean?" Beth asked.

"Tom may have been away from Farish for years, but no one has forgotten him. He was ahead of me in school, so I remember kids talking about his swift departure and the big breakup with his girlfriend. He—"

"Hey, everyone," Tom called from the other side of the room, where he was loading a music roll on the player piano. "Let's have a sing-along."

"Later," whispered Chloe as the group began to gather around Steve, who was pumping the old piano's pedals.

They sang Christmas carols, and Beth joined in with her rich contralto. Still, she hung out at the back of the group of assembled guests while she pondered what Chloe had said. Although

Beth knew many people in her adopted community, she naturally hadn't been privy to things that happened before she arrived five years earlier.

Tom surprised Beth by edging close to her and curving his arm around her shoulders. "You can really sing," he said with some surprise.

Chloe leaned toward Tom. "I've been begging Beth to get involved again in the church choir."

Beth was ready to mention that Mitchell needed her more than the choir did and that practice took her away from him one evening a week, but at that point, the paper piano roll malfunctioned and Steve called Tom to extract it from the mechanism.

When Tom declared the music session over, Gretchen's new husband, whom Beth had met only a few months ago, broke out a pack of cards and entertained them all with tricks. Beth found herself laughing along with everyone else when he produced a jack of hearts from the bottom of Tom's sleeve and an ace of spades from Muffy's low neckline.

As she gazed around this circle of friends, Beth thought reluctantly, *Why, this is fun.* Their faces were familiar and dear, and she realized with a start that she hadn't been to one of their parties since Richie left. In the early days after the divorce, she'd been invited but had always declined, and soon the invitations had tapered off, then stopped.

As it grew later, people began to gravitate toward the door. "I'm riding home with you," Beth reminded Chloe.

"I never got a chance to tell you that I came with Julie and Steve," Chloe said. "If you don't mind stopping by her mom's to pick up the kids, I'm sure it's okay."

Tom heard this exchange as he walked up. "I'm taking you home," he told Beth as he handed Gretchen her coat.

"But —" Beth started, but Tom didn't let her finish.

"No way I'm going to let you out of cleanup duty," he said as he turned toward Divver and his wife.

Exasperated, Beth hurried into the kitchen, thinking she'd get a head start on loading the dishwasher. Muffy, however, had already beaten her to it.

Muffy poured detergent into the dispenser. "Pardon me if I'm too nosy, but I just have to ask. How'd you meet Tom Collyer?"

Beth was accustomed to Muffy's methods of gleaning usable tidbits for the paper. "I drove him to the hospital when he hurt his wrist at Breakfast with Santa," she said offhandedly.

"So, um, is it a casual thing with you two, or what?" Muffy blew a strand of copper-colored hair out of her eyes.

"I'm not interested in him as a date, if that's what you mean," Beth said.

Tom appeared carrying Muffy's coat. "You might be ready for this."

"That's so sweet of you," Muffy replied. Tom held her coat for her, and she slid her arms into the sleeves.

"Well," Muffy said, scanning the kitchen one last time, "you two have everything under control. Guess I'll be on my way. Tom, I hope you'll call me sometime. Daddy would love to talk over our insemination program with you, I'm sure of it."

Tom was clearly amused, but he kept a straight face. "I appreciate your mentioning it, Muffy. I'll be sure to let you know if I develop an interest in, uh, insemination."

Beth stifled a grin, but Muffy didn't seem to find anything amiss in that statement. "Take care, Beth. You and that adorable little boy of yours." She smiled widely and made a sweeping exit, all but catching the hem of her coat in the backswing of the kitchen door.

Tom went to bid goodbye to the last of his guests. "I put the coffee on a few minutes ago," he said, returning as the noise of the last car faded down the street. Beth moved toward the door to the dining room, but he placed himself squarely in front of it, blocking her exit. Flustered, she backed away, but not before Tom's hands captured hers. His were warm; hers, she knew, were cold.

She pulled away. "You take too much for granted," she said briskly as she dumped a stack of plastic cups in the wastebasket.

"Do not," he said.

"Do, too," she shot back.

"If I did, I wouldn't keep trying to wear you down. Anyway, what's wrong with warming ourselves with a cup of coffee before going out in the cold?"

"Nothing. But—"

"But what?"

"Why have you singled me out?" she blurted. "Other women are more interested and available than I am."

"I like a challenge," Tom said with an easy grin. His eyebrows raised inquiringly. "What would get you interested?"

"Nothing, at the moment," she told him, ignoring the thread of awareness that had been spinning between them all night.

"That's hardly encouraging," Tom said wryly, but his eyes were merry.

"It's late," she said. "I should go home."

The machine signaled that the coffee was ready.

"Let's relax for a few minutes. It's not even midnight yet." Tom removed two mugs from the cabinet. "Sugar? Cream?"

"Lots of both," she said. She had no idea why her heart was racing. Maybe it had something to do with being the focus of attention of a real, live, extremely handsome guy who, unlike the only other man in her life, wasn't a mere five years old.

"Let's adjourn to the living room. I need advice," Tom said companionably. When he noticed her dubious expression, he added, "Decorating stuff."

Reluctantly she trailed after him. "This is what I've accomplished so far," he said, his gesture taking in the couch, which hadn't been there the last time she visited, and the two club chairs between the windows.

"You're doing a nice job," she said truthfully. When he indicated the couch, she settled gingerly on the edge of it, and he sat beside her.

"I've put a lot of time and effort into this place, but now I'm stuck. For instance, I want to add a chair rail in the dining room and I haven't the slightest idea how high it should be."

He had positioned himself on the other end of the couch from her, but Beth still felt crowded. She focused on his hands, which were wrapped around the coffee mug. They were big and strong and sinewy, with heavily corded veins. Suddenly, she was unable to keep herself from imagining those hands tunneling through her hair, cupping her face.

"Put your chair rail thirty-six inches from the floor," she said in a strained voice.

"Also, this room could use something at the windows, and I don't have any idea what to get."

"Plantation shutters with wide slats are popular."

"I don't like shutters. I like pulling drapes across the windows and feeling like I'm in a cocoon," he said with a chuckle.

She could easily imagine Tom Collyer bringing someone like Muffy here, switching off the lights, turning up the music and shutting out the rest of the world.

"If you don't mind, I'd better get home," she said.

"Hey, this is business. I'm hiring you to do some work for me."

Business? It didn't feel that way. She tried to steady herself, but there was nothing to hold on to unless she considered Tom himself. He had unfolded himself from the couch and was standing so close that she could discern the flecks in his eyes. Silver, definitely.

"The advice is free," she said, barely able to recognize her own voice over the rush of blood in her ears.

He laughed. "Come on, Beth. Do you have to aim for difficult?"

She searched his expression, noticing the way the lights from the Christmas tree teased golden highlights from his hair. Not only did he have one of the most captivating personalities she'd ever encountered, but she sensed a strength of character in him, as well as a rare empathy.

That was what made her decide to level with him. She forced

herself to stay on point so that her eyes met his with firmness and honesty. "I'm not in the market for a guy," she said. "My life is full with business and child-rearing and keeping up a house that sometimes chooses to fall apart at the worst times." She had regained control, was again able to ignore his effect on her. Though she wouldn't want to push it.

"Okay, Beth," he said. His voice held warmth but also reflected concern. "Don't go and have a hissy fit on me, but I'm going to demolish your arguments one by one. First of all," he said, ticking off the point on his finger, "we were talking business. Besides, you've closed up shop for the holidays—you said so yourself. Second, your mommy duties are moot as long as Mitchell is with his dad. You won't be pouring juice or supervising baths for—um, how long was it?"

"Twelve days," Beth replied in a voice so low she was almost whispering.

"Right, and it would be good for you to have something to take your mind off how much you miss him. As for keeping up your house, I'm available for any repair jobs that you can't handle yourself. Not that I'm so good at it, if you consider my kitchen flood."

When she opened her mouth to speak, he interrupted. "I owe you big-time for helping me that day. It was like the answer to a prayer when you showed up."

"I didn't do much," she demurred.

"You did plenty."

Refusing to meet his eyes, Beth made herself start for the kitchen, found her coat on a hook in the pantry and slid the coat on. As she turned back, Tom was right behind her. He moved in and extended his arms so that his hands rested on the wall on either side of her, effectively trapping her.

"I don't understand what's bugging you, Beth. Maybe your ex-husband did a number on you, but I had nothing to do with it. I wasn't there."

This had gone too far. "Tom," she began.

His hands fell to his sides. "That's all that needs to be said."

His eyes showed compassion and understanding. In a rush of perception, she thought that he could also be a veteran of a love gone wrong. Like seeks like, her grandmother had always said, and Beth recognized the truth in this.

She shook her head as if to clear it. "I'd better work out how I feel about this."

"Would lunch tomorrow help?" he asked, and he smiled down at her.

She should be angry at him for causing her to think about things better ignored, for challenging and pursuing her. For titillating her and making her want to learn more about him. But how could she be angry when he clearly liked her so much? Tom Collyer intrigued her even more so since Chloe had hinted at a mysterious past.

Beth sensed that there was no point in fighting any longer; this was clearly a man who knew what he wanted and would overcome all obstacles to get it. "All right," she said with a sigh. "I'll bring drapery samples so you can study them. That way I can get a feel for the kind of thing you like."

His gaze lingered on her mouth. "You've already got a handle on that," he said.

When he positioned himself to kiss her, she moved quickly to forestall it by deliberately choosing to misunderstand him. "You're definitely not the type for chintz or brocade. Maybe a nice cotton duck or burlap."

He surprised her by laughing, and she used the opportunity to slip away. Now that she'd dodged out of range, he grabbed his coat and shrugged into it.

His hand braced her elbow as they stepped out into a night both clear and cold, myriad stars twinkling high above on a vast field of midnight-blue. She inhaled deeply of the invigorating fresh air, and as an antidote to the undercurrent between her and Tom Collyer, she pictured Mitchell sleeping in his new bed at Richie's. She wondered if her ex allowed him to sleep in the top bunk. She wouldn't have, because Mitchell might fall out or wake up in the middle of the night to go to the bathroom and forget about the long drop to the floor, or—

Tom had said something, and she stared at him blankly. "Sorry," she said, "my mind was elsewhere."

The look he aimed in her direction before walking around to the driver's side of the pickup was wise and knowing. He knew she'd been thinking about Mitchell. As Tom backed onto the street, she faced forward, hoping her embarrassment wasn't evident when the lights of an oncoming car flashed across her face.

"Back to our earlier discussion…I need more furniture," he said. "Leanne suggested that I buy a bedroom set for my guest room in one of those places where you buy the whole room— lamps, rugs, everything. That would be a mistake when it's an old house and could be furnished with antiques that fit the era when it was built. I could use some of your expertise there, too."

"Come with me tomorrow afternoon," she said, the words no sooner out of her mouth than she began to regret them. "I'm going to an estate sale over near Kettersburg. We might find things that would work really well in your house."

"An estate sale? I've never been to one."

"They'll auction off the house's contents. I haven't checked into any of the pieces, but there are sure to be some interesting ones."

"I'd like to go," he said, as if he hadn't expected such good luck, and Beth's misgivings evaporated.

She could keep things businesslike between them; she'd done it before and could do it again. All that was required was not getting too personal, keeping the man at arm's length, and defusing any situations that might get out of hand.

They drove through the quiet streets, which were lit by a bright crescent moon and the Christmas decorations in windows and on lawns. One was a herd of painted wooden reindeer strung with tiny blinking lights. Another was a pudgy Santa perched on someone's chimney. Seeing the Santa figure reminded her how she had first met Tom, and she suppressed a smile at his reluctance to play the part.

"What's funny?" he demanded, glancing down at her.

"I was thinking of the pancake breakfast."

Tom slowed at the entrance to her driveway and made a face as the pickup eased to a stop. "It's not one of my favorite memories—though maybe it could be."

She avoided his gaze. "Thanks for the ride," she said, opening the car door and stepping out.

"I'll walk you to your porch," he said, and she waited while he ambled around to her side of the car. She'd forgotten her gloves, so she kept her hands clenched deep in her pockets. Then, at the door, she had to fumble with cold fingers in her purse for the key.

Tom appropriated the key and inserted it in the lock. The door swung open, and the interior of her house, lit only by a night-light in the foyer, beckoned invitingly. She was sure he was hoping she'd ask him in.

She turned to him. "Noon for lunch?"

"That's good. I'll pick you up."

"Oh, I forgot. I'm supposed to drop off my minivan at Joe's garage tomorrow morning."

"How about if I meet you there?"

She'd wondered who she would get to give her a ride home. "That would be a big help."

He hesitated for a moment, and she was halfway through the open door when he spoke again.

"Leanne said you were fun and that we'd like each other. She was right. Well, about me, anyway. I like you, Beth McCormick. A lot." He raised his hand and casually grazed his knuckles across her cheek. "I'm a patient man, by the way."

She couldn't come up with a fast reply to that, so she only stared at him.

"Good night, Beth. Sleep well."

And then Tom was hurrying away toward her driveway,

climbing in the pickup and waving out the window as he backed out in a plume of exhaust.

She went inside and closed the door with a definitive *click* of the lock. This was all going much too fast.

Maybe she shouldn't have agreed to lunch. But she had. And later, as her eyes drifted closed in preparation for sleep, she was aware for the first time since her divorce of a longing to be desired in the way that a man wants a woman, to be cherished and loved.

Especially loved.

From the *Farish Tribune:*
Here 'n'There in Farish
by Muffy Ledbetter

Leanne Novak and her husband, Eddie, recently threw a housewarming bash for her brother, Tom Collyer, who has recently returned from the marine corps. Some of you recall that Tom was an up-and-coming rodeo star some years back. Lots of people attended the party, including yours truly. We think we'll nominate Tom for the Bachelor of the Year. Oh, almost forgot. Farish doesn't have a Bachelor of the Year. Maybe we'll suggest him for Santa of the Year, instead! (Wink, wink.) We'll bet he has a whole bag of tricks in that sleigh of his.

One tidbit we picked up at the party is that Mrs. Nell Whisenant is thinking of closing her antiques shop on the Kettersburg highway. Nell is recovering nicely from the hip surgery she had in September, aided by her helpful granddaughter Chloe Timberlake. In case you're interested, Chloe says that her magenta hair is a thing of the past. She's into a shade called Desert Dream these days.

Overheard at the luncheonette on Main Street last week: Well, you'll have to wait for the next edition of the Tribune to find it out, 'cause I'm out of space here. Don't forget, if you have news, call me on my cell phone. You can leave a message, and if you don't want to state your name, you don't have to. I'll probably recognize your voice, though.

Till next time, I'll be seeing you here 'n' there in Farish.

Chapter Seven

When Beth and Tom walked into Zachary's restaurant the next day, they both spotted several people they knew. Gretchen was there with Patty, Divver's wife, and Chloe's sister Naomi sat at a table with her sister-in-law and niece. They all studied the two of them with expressions ranging from openly curious, in Naomi's case, to downright flabbergasted, in Gretchen's.

"We're going to give these folks something to talk about," Tom told Beth after they were seated. He was halfway pleased that Beth was momentarily disconcerted, then amused when she ignored what he said and brought drapery samples out of her tote bag.

"I lunch here with clients all the time," she said, maintaining her businesslike demeanor.

Tom had suggested Zachary's because he'd never eaten there. It was located in the recently renovated railroad station, now no longer in use because trains had ceased coming to Farish years ago. He found the place almost too cute for words, with the menu printed on a replica of the old train schedule and a mural of a diesel engine bearing down on them from one wall. Clearly, the flood of retirees moving to nearby Kettersburg, toting hefty pensions and expressing sophisticated tastes, had changed Farish. Then he noticed Gretchen talking behind her hand to Patty, and he grinned at the realization that at least some things around town were still the same.

Beth slid swatches of fabric across the table. "These would all be appropriate."

He tried to focus on the scraps of material, but at the moment he couldn't have cared less. He was much more interested in Beth McCormick. She was wearing a loose multicolored sweater over a pair of snug jeans tucked into a pair of snazzy boots. Her hair was pinned up on one side to show off a small pink ear. Affixed to her earlobes was a pair of simple silver-and-gold earrings that glimmered as she moved her head. The effect was enchanting.

"This would blend well with your Oriental rug," she said, tapping a fingernail on one of the pieces. "On the other hand, so would the stripe. If you're interested in solids, I'd suggest coral." She pulled a swatch of fabric out from under the others.

"Blue," Tom said, staring at her eyes. "I had blue in mind. Or maybe more of a blue-green, to be exact."

"Oh, but the coral would pick up the colors in the rug so much better," she said, busily rearranging the samples. Her pale, strained expression of the night before was gone. She seemed vital, excited, caught up in the pleasure of what she did for a living.

"You are an extremely attractive woman," he blurted, apropos of nothing.

She regarded him with momentary confusion. "We weren't talking about me," she said flatly.

"I am. Why do you hate compliments?" He knew by the way she returned his grin that she understood he was teasing.

"I don't," she said as she tucked the fabric samples away in her bag. "Have you ever met anyone who did?"

"A girl named Meredith Wren used to sock me every time I paid her one. It might have had something to do with the fact that I was eight years old and all my compliments in those days were something on the order of 'You don't sweat much for a fat girl.' She still wasn't speaking to me when she grew up to be the runner-up to Miss Texas."

Beth snickered. "Serves you right," she said.

The waiter took their order, and afterward Tom leaned back in his chair. Beth had relaxed a bit, and he figured he might as well be polite and ask about her son.

"How's Marshall getting along?"

Her expression clouded slightly, and she cocked her head, which made her earrings swing against her cheeks. "His name is Mitchell."

He tried not to wince visibly. Major mistake. Okay, he could deal with it. "Mitchell. Hell of a name for a kid."

"It was my maiden name," Beth said.

Open mouth, insert foot. "Hell of a *nice* name is what I meant." He hoped he didn't sound too insincere; it *was* a nice name, for a banker or a real-estate broker, but not a five-year-old boy.

"I haven't heard from Mitchell since last night," Beth said after a moment or so.

Tom had been prepared for a tinge of self-pity in her words, but he detected none. Last night, she'd been feeling sorry for herself and had made no bones about it.

"Your ex-husband has remarried?" he asked, picking his way through what he suspected was an emotional mine field.

"Yes. Within a week of our divorce." Her forefinger traced one of the luggage tags preserved beneath the thick layer of acrylic on the tabletop.

"Ah. One of those," he said.

She met his eyes ruefully. "Yes," she said.

Their lunch arrived at an opportune time, providing a welcome diversion. He was glad when Beth asked him about his time spent in the marines, which he told her had been an ongoing growth experience.

"Why'd you quit the service?" she asked.

He'd been only five years away from a full pension, but had been at the point where he didn't feel as if he had any more to give to the corps. Also, he'd burned his bridges when he left Farish all those years ago, and he'd wanted to redeem his good name, if it was possible.

He didn't care to get into that right now, so he resorted to a careless lift of the shoulders and said, "It was time to move on. Leanne's here, and I'm godfather to Madelon, Jeremiah and Peter. The job with Divver was the real draw, though." He grinned at her.

She nodded thoughtfully, and he leaned across the table toward her. "Now, how about a thumbnail life history from you."

"I grew up in Houston, worked my way through college, got married. Had a child. Got divorced." She shrugged. "That's about all there is to it."

"What brought you to Farish?"

"My husband's job. Also, my friend Chloe—I met her in an art history class at the University of Texas—was moving back here. This is where she grew up. Chloe introduced me to Leanne, who made it easy for us to meet other young marrieds."

"Leanne's good at social things," he observed.

"Everyone at the party seemed to know you, too."

"Divver and Patty were pals of mine from way back. Others were lowly sophomores at Farish High when I was a senior, and I barely knew some of them, mostly because I was always hanging around the ranch with Divver, training horses, hoping to get into rodeo."

"Leanne told me one time that one of her brothers won lots of rodeo events."

"That would be me. Our younger brother was the high school jock, I was the rebel and Leanne was Leanne, taking charge, bossing people around and getting elected homecoming queen in spite of it."

Beth smiled. "That's our Leanne, all right." She glanced at her watch. "We'd better get moving if we're going to make it to that estate sale before the bidding begins."

He called for the check, and on the way out, they paused to talk briefly with Gretchen, who seemed eager to ask Beth what the two of them were doing together.

"She'll phone Leanne tonight," Tom said with great certainty. "Before morning, my sister will have left several messages on my answering machine, asking me to call her right away."

Once they were in his pickup, he headed toward the Kettersburg highway. "You'll have to tell me where to turn off," he reminded her, speaking over the lively Tejano music blaring from the radio.

"It's at the yellow blinker light south of the state park," she told him. "There's an old roadhouse at the intersection."

"Dolan's?" he asked.

"You've been there?"

"Sometimes my friends and I would sneak over there on school nights to ride the mechanical bull. When I was older, it was our favorite hangout."

"The place closed a year or so ago."

"I won't miss it," Tom said, but he still felt wistful when they passed the tumbledown building.

The house where the estate sale was being held was a stately Greek revival home built in the 1890s. It sat in a rolling meadow overlooking a river lined with cottonwoods and, on the sloping back lawn, featured a lily pond with a waterfall. The sale was held in a large inside room, and they barely had time to register, grab a paddle and find a seat before the auctioneer stepped up to the podium.

Tom felt out of his element in these surroundings. He took off his Stetson, set it in his lap and leaned back with his arms crossed to observe.

One of the first items to be auctioned was a bookcase that Tom liked. He nudged Beth. "That's perfect for my den."

"Want me to bid?" she asked.

He nodded, a little unsure about the proceedings but not about the bookcase. It was made of bird's-eye maple and was the right size to fit behind his desk.

Beth, who obviously enjoyed the bidding process, entered into with gusto, and although others showed interest, she eventually emerged as the high bidder.

"Sold to number 122," sang the auctioneer.

"That's how it works," she whispered. "You could bid on the next item yourself."

"I'd rather let you do it," he said, taking in the bright spots of color in her cheeks.

"Chicken," she accused, and he laughed.

When an elegant old walnut armoire came on the block, she leaned forward and studied it.

"You like that?" he asked.

"It would fit perfectly on the long wall in my living room."

"Go for it," he urged as the bidding began.

Beth didn't bid first, but the person who did backed off when Beth raised the price a hundred dollars. Another bidder entered the fray, but in the end, he shook his head and gave up.

Finally, the auctioneer banged his gavel, and the armoire was hers.

"Ready to go?" Tom asked Beth.

She nodded. "If we buy any more furniture, we'll have to get a bigger truck."

"We could always pick up the stuff later."

"No, I was only kidding. I haven't seen anything else I want."

As they left the auction, Beth handled paying for the items while Tom supervised loading them into the bed of his pickup. Soon they were tooling along the two-lane blacktop toward Farish, exuberant about their finds.

"You really knew what you were doing back there," he said admiringly. "Neither of those other bidders showed signs of backing down."

"You have to read body language," she told him. "I sensed that the first bidder for your bookcase wasn't really interested, and the prospective buyer of my armoire had the earmarks of a dealer who wouldn't pay over a certain amount."

"You must do this a lot."

She shrugged. "I used to, when I was married. Most estate sales and auctions happen on weekends, and I could leave Mitchell with Richie and take off with Chloe for the afternoon. Now it's different. I hate to send Mitchell to day care on the weekends. Don't get me wrong—the day-care situation is wonderful. The women who work there are kind, and they love Mitchell. We're lucky in that respect. It's—it's just that I feel guilty not spending more time with my son, and weekends are best for that."

By this time Beth had lost her self-consciousness, and she continued to talk about her work as they drove back to Farish. "I like being a designer, working with pretty things. Sometimes I feel like a shrink, as well. I often have to psych out my clients, determine what they're really saying when they tell me they want a room to have a 'restful quality.' Do they mean restful as in 'I want to go to sleep'? Or restful as in 'I want to block all intrusions from the outside world so I can get lost in my TV soap operas'? There's a difference, and what's restful to some isn't to others." She laughed. "It's fun."

Sitting beside her, learning more about what she liked about her life, was fun, too. He didn't want the day to end.

As they slowed to the speed limit at the outskirts of Farish, Beth changed the subject. "We could unload the bookcase at your house before we go to mine."

He shook his head. "I'll handle it myself. First, we'll stop by your place and I'll help you put this armoire wherever you want it."

Dusk was falling, and as they circled the roundabout in front of the courthouse, the multicolored lights of the enormous community Christmas tree flickered on. Decorated with ornaments made by hundreds of local schoolchildren, the tree lent an air of festivity to the town.

"It's good luck if the tree lights go on when you're driving by. At least, that's what we used to say when we were kids," Tom said. "You're supposed to make a wish."

"Did you?"

"Sure." He grinned at her.

Beth hesitated. Once, she would have wished something on behalf of Mitchell—that he'd remain healthy, that he'd enjoy his visit with his father—but now the wish she made was for herself.

They continued down Main Street, most of its three-block-long row of shops closed at this time of the evening. In a few minutes, Tom was turning into her driveway carefully so as not to jostle their heavy cargo, and braking to a stop.

Beth kept an old hand truck in the garage, and as she wheeled it to the pickup, Tom unlatched the tail gate. The two of them were able to trundle the armoire easily through the front door and into the living room.

Tom helped her remove the TV from its stand on the long wall, and together they positioned the armoire. When Tom had connected the TV to the cable outlet, Beth studied the effect of the new piece on her decor, then started toward the kitchen. "How about something cold to drink? There's beer in the fridge."

"That's great, 'cause I'm mighty thirsty," he said. He followed her into the kitchen, looking around at the refinished cabinets, the updated light fixture. "I like the way you've pulled this place together," he said approvingly as she handed him a beer.

"I have a lot more I want to do in here, but decorating takes time."

"You can say that again. I've never owned a house before. It's different from renting an apartment, that's for sure."

She smiled at him. "Let's go in the living room," she said.

He followed her and sat down beside her on the couch.

"So," she said. "Your work will pick up after the holidays, I suspect, if you're going to start your first group of incorrigibles after the semester break."

He winced slightly. "We don't call them incorrigibles," he said. "The kids are 'at risk.'"

"Sorry, I was only repeating what I've heard around town." She paused, and when she spoke she was serious, inquisitive. "I'd like to hear more about the program and your involvement. Why you decided to do it, and so on."

He slid back in the couch and stretched out his long legs. "I want to make a difference. That's the main thing."

"You were doing that when you were training marine recruits."

"After a while, it wasn't enough. As I learned more about teaching, I started to contrast training marines to the way I'd trained horses."

She started to laugh but realized he wasn't joking. "Go on," she said.

"I never was one to break a horse's spirit. I preferred gentling a horse, showing him why it was in his best interest to follow a certain course. Obviously, the method wouldn't work with marines, who are, after all, being trained to fight. I began to mull over other ways to train human beings, especially those who needed to develop self-discipline so they could make good choices in their lives. We're going to try some of those methods with the ATTAIN kids." He glanced at her, saw that her expression had softened. "Comments?" He was prepared for her criticism; some people might be insulted to think that the methods that worked on horses could succeed with kids, but she surprised him.

"Only that you're not what I expected," she said in a low tone. "I'm sensing a love and understanding of children."

"True," he said. "Young people have been my life's work." Some of the recruits in his charge had been barely old enough to shave; he'd found working with middle-schoolers more rewarding than he would have guessed when he started out.

"The way you acted at Breakfast with Santa made me suspect you hate children. Or don't like them much, at any rate."

"I'm not good at playing Santa Claus."

He was surprised when she squeezed his arm.

"Also, you were in pain at the time. I'm sorry for misjudging you, Tom."

"You're forgiven," he said.

She dropped her hand. "I'd like it if you stayed for dinner. I cooked a pork loin before Mitchell left, and I could make hot sandwiches."

He wasn't expecting the invitation. He took a moment to adjust to the fact that she had offered it. Maybe she was trying to
make amends for misjudging him, but that didn't matter. At
least she wanted him around.

"Hey," he said, "I'd like that. Are you sure it's not too much
trouble?"

She stood, and he caught a whiff of her hair. Strawberry-
scented shampoo. "No trouble. Actually, I don't want to eat
alone. With Mitchell gone it's too depressing."

"I'm happy to help you out," he said wryly, and she smiled.

"Come on, let's assemble the ingredients for the sauce," she
said, and she led the way into the kitchen.

SHE FIXED SANDWICHES fit for royalty. Together, they assembled
apples, maple syrup and dried fruit, and he oversaw its simmer-
ing on the stove. She poured the concoction over the pork, which
she piled on crusty rolls spread with grainy mustard. She served
these creations with élan—pretty quilted place mats, candlelight,
soft music on the CD player.

"Where did you learn to cook like this?" he asked. He'd eaten
two sandwiches and was considering polishing off a third.

"I took a class in the early days of my marriage," she said,
shrugging.

"Oh?"

"I wanted to be the best wife ever." She got up and started to
clear the table.

He sauntered to the sink with his empty plate. "I'll bet you
were."

"My ex-husband wouldn't agree."

"Let's establish right here and now that the man is an idiot,"
he said, catching her hand.

"He is?" she said.

They were standing so close that he could see the vein throbbing in her temple.

"He is, for leaving you," he said. He removed the dish she

was holding from her other hand and drew her into his arms. A soulful tune was playing on the stereo, something about *love you forever, leave me never,* and Tom thought that if he'd been lucky enough to be married to a woman like Beth, he would have hung on to her for dear life.

She seemed pensive, but she willingly let him dance her in a swooping circle around the kitchen floor, effortlessly following his lead. He held her slightly away and smiled down at her. "Never mind the cooking. Where'd you learn how to dance like this?"

"Does it matter?"

"Not really." He nestled his arm into the hollow of her waist, liking the way her temple barely grazed his cheek. He inhaled the fragrance of her hair, drew it deep into his lungs. If he pulled her an inch closer, their bodies would touch. How would she react when that happened? He felt his palms start to sweat, and he hoped she wouldn't notice. He was as edgy as a teenager on his first date.

When they swirled past the door that led to the hallway, her bedroom came into view. It contained a bed, neatly made. He imagined Beth lying amid the nest of shell-pink sheets, her hair tumbled around her face. Around *his* face.

He wanted to kiss her. To capture her lips with his and indulge himself with a passionate blending of lips and teeth and tongue in a delectable prelude to—

And she would push him away. She'd made it clear that she wasn't ready for a relationship, and perhaps she never would be.

She seemed to melt into his embrace, and he heard her sigh. Surprised, he gazed into her eyes and noticed something he would never have expected. Her eyes were half-lidded, drowsy, gleaming with—what?

"Beth?" he said, unsure of her and of himself.

"Mmm?"

"I meant that about your husband."

"Could we please talk about something else?"

"Like what?" He could have suggested a few things, but he didn't want to push this.

Her lips parted; her head tilted back slightly. Those thick lashes didn't hide the expression in the depths of her eyes. Her mouth was soft and full, lush and inviting. Now—now he could kiss her. Would she mind? He decided to take the chance.

He lowered his head and touched his lips to hers, gently at first, then more urgently. He heard her breath catch in her throat and felt the slight shudder of her body as she swayed against him.

He slid his hands upward and threaded them through her hair, angling her head so that he had better access. She was a responsive woman, Beth McCormick. He longed to free her from the restrictions she had imposed on herself so that she would feel what he felt and want what he wanted.

Tom rocked her to him, fitting his hardness to her curves. He murmured her name, and she pressed even closer. Her head angled, exposing her throat so that he could bestow a string of hot hungry kisses along the sensitive skin below her ear. Electricity hummed beneath the skin where his lips moved.

"Tom? Oh, Tom, I didn't mean for this to happen. "

"Let's stop pretending that there's no attraction, Beth." She might not have been with anyone for a long time, but she certainly remembered how to torment a man. He touched her breasts, cupped their lush curves with his hands, slid his thigh between hers.

"I want—you," she said haltingly, her eyes enormous, her cheeks flushed. "I'm not sure if it's a good idea."

"This isn't one of those casual encounters," he said, making himself speak slowly and carefully. "It's more than that."

Tom saw her wavering, saw doubt in her eyes, and then acceptance and assent. He could have laughed with pure exuberance at the winning of her, but he didn't get the chance because the telephone rang.

Chapter Eight

The next morning Beth lay in bed, watching the play of light and shadow across her ceiling, and contemplated the possibility that wishing on the lights of the town Christmas tree the night before had really worked. After all, Tom Collyer had kissed her, and that had been her wish. Kissing definitely had not been all he had in mind, either. She had been in the mood for more herself.

Last night when the phone rang, Beth had been sure it was Mitchell calling, even though it was almost ten o'clock. She'd broken away from Tom and grabbed the phone, only to recognize Zelma Harrison's strident voice on the other end. She had decided she didn't want the cornices she'd ordered after all, Zelma said, and she hoped Beth wouldn't mind.

It had been a rush order because Zelma had needed the window treatments before Christmas; there was money due on them, and now she wanted her deposit back. Beth had been forced to let Tom cool his heels and presumably other parts of his anatomy for almost twenty minutes while she negotiated with Zelma, and by the time she'd finished, he was cleaning up the kitchen and she was having second thoughts about the wisdom of making love.

Beth had handled the situation gracefully, saying that she'd had a wonderful evening but needed to call Richie to make sure everything was going all right with Mitchell's visit. Even though Tom had kissed her on the cheek before he left, she wouldn't be surprised now if he disappeared for good, though you couldn't actually avoid anyone in Farish. They'd run into each other at the Supersave, exchanging polite but wary smiles. She'd hear about him every now and then from Leanne, who would refrain from telling her if Tom was seeing this woman or that, and Beth would speculate now and then about whether he was involved with someone. She might get a glimmer of what was going on from mentionings in Muffy's "Here 'n' There" column in the *Farish Tribune*. Eventually, she would read a detailed write-up on the newspaper's society page, complete with a picture of Tom's fiancée. Beth had no doubt there would be such a person eventually. Tom was a prize catch.

The house was too empty and quiet, so after going out to pick up the newspaper from the driveway and skimming the headlines, she called Mitchell.

"Hi, Mom," he said when Richie put him on. "We're having pancakes for breakfast."

"That's great," she said, trying for enthusiasm. She wondered if Starla ever made them in the shape of Mickey Mouse's head and, sometimes in the winter, a snowman, as she did.

"Guess what? Ava can crawl! She just started, Starla says. Starla says—"

"Are you drinking your milk?"

"Uh-huh. Starla buys the chocolate kind already mixed at the store. I like it real lots."

Beth refused to comment; she herself never bought chocolate milk in the carton because it was expensive and of dubious nutritional value. "I hope you're saying your prayers at night," she told him.

"Sometimes I forget. Daddy doesn't remind me."

"Oh."

"I have to hang up, Mom. We're going to a company Christmas party this afternoon. Dad says I don't have to dress up. He put my blue suit back in the duffel and said I can wear my old jeans, the ones I really like."

"Those have a hole in the knee." She'd only packed them because Mitchell had insisted they were the most comfortable ones he owned.

"It doesn't matter. I can wear my Shrek T-shirt, too, if I want. I spilled chocolate milk on it yesterday, but Starla says the stain hardly shows."

"Great," Beth muttered. It was a matter of pride to her that her son was always well groomed, but that apparently didn't matter to his father.

"Well, 'bye, Mom. Talk to you soon."

"I love you, Mitchell."

"Me, too."

Beth heard Starla laughing in the background as they hung up. At least Mitchell was having a good time. Still, she would never allow Mitchell to go out wearing those old jeans and a stained shirt, and to a company party, no less.

WINTER, WHEN IT ARRIVED in this part of Texas, galloped in on a wind that cut through the warmest clothes and brought an ache to the bones, especially those injured in long-ago rodeos. Tom ignored the chill's effect on his collarbone—broken in Wichita, 1987—and his right ankle—Tucson, 1989—and drove out to the Holcomb Ranch early in the afternoon to borrow Divver's cordless drill, which he needed for putting up shelves in the closet he had converted to a laundry room.

He and Divver had been best buddies since first grade, when they'd discovered a mutual interest in spitting contests. They'd expanded their circle to include Johnny Snead that same year, mostly because Johnny's mother always included an extra moon pie in his lunch, which Johnny was inclined to trade for almost anything, even liverwurst.

Divver, then and now, was simple, uncomplicated and good-hearted. When the two of them were boys, Divver had been a red-haired kid bearing a striking resemblance to Raggedy Andy. He'd grown into a short, stocky man with a perpetual squint from years of working outside in the sun. He was the founding architect of the ATTAIN program, and Tom admired him more than almost anyone he knew.

Tom found Divver filing papers in his office in the former bunkhouse, where the two of them and Johnny had occasionally spent the night together when they were kids. With a roof over their heads and the fireplace for warmth, the abandoned bunkhouse had rated a notch above camping out. Those had been good times.

Divver rose when Tom's shadow fell across his desk, and he clomped around it to greet him, his footsteps ringing out on the old unfinished wood floor.

"Came to borrow that drill," Tom said, flinging his Stetson onto the antlers of the deer's head hanging above the smoke-blackened mantel. Beneath it, a fat rattlesnake hide sporting a bullet hole was tacked to the wall.

"Yeah, you can take the drill. It's in the equipment shed." Divver angled his chin back over his shoulder.

"Got a minute?"

"Sure, always."

"It's not about work."

"What?" Divver pretended to be surprised.

"It's about a woman."

Divver narrowed his eyes in disbelief. "Who am I, Dr. Phil?"

Tom only shrugged.

"Hell, Tom, aren't you past that kind of thing after what happened with Nikki?"

"It's nothing like that." He preferred to believe that people around here had forgotten about that sad episode in his life.

"What's on your mind, Tom?"

"I want to pick your brain a bit about someone I've had my eye on."

"Muffy? There's nothing I can help you with there, man." From the way he waggled his eyebrows, though, Tom knew Divver thought Muffy Ledbetter was hot.

"Not Muffy. It's Beth McCormick."

Divver began to chuckle. "You devil you. She's a secondary virgin."

"A what?"

"Beth's been married and has a son, but whatever sexuality she had was sealed away after her husband walked out on her."

"Yeah, well, don't be too sure of that." Tom shifted uncomfortably in his chair, wishing that the conversation hadn't swerved in this direction. "What have you heard about the guy who left her?"

"My impression is that Richie McCormick is likable enough, just stupid. Personality a little bland, enjoyed the ladies. Spoiled rotten by his parents, who are nice folks. I met them once in the feed store, and it was clear that they doted on Richie. Kind of reminded me of the way the Sneads were with Johnny."

Tom pictured the Sneads in his mind: two fondly indulgent gray-haired people who'd had to wait until their forties before their only child was born. As far as they were concerned, Johnny could do no wrong. In Tom's view, that was the main reason Johnny, who up until the Nikki Situation had been his best friend other than Divver, had ignored the speed limit and crashed a stolen car into a bridge abutment at the age of twenty-one.

"So this Richie ran off with Starla Mullins?"

Divver nodded, more serious now. "Judging from the scuttlebutt I heard, Richie broke Beth's heart. Lost his job, had to find one somewhere else. Haven't heard much about him since he left. His parents live over in Stickneyville. They visit Beth and her son now and then. Why don't you ask Leanne about Beth, anyway? She's one of her best friends."

"Nah," Tom said. "These women, they grab ahold of a thing, it takes on a life of its own and grows. I don't want my sister to get the idea that I'm more interested in Beth than I really am."

"Or me, either, right?" Divver grinned widely.

"You got it. Now, how about that drill?"

"First let's take a look at the saddle I bought yesterday over to Austin."

Tom followed Divver out of the bunkhouse, aware that he

hadn't fooled the guy but sure that his confidences were safe with this boyhood friend of his. Having a good buddy close by was one of the advantages of living in Farish again.

LACKING EXTRA SPACE in her house, Beth kept shipments and supplies in her garage, and she'd stored Zelma Harrison's cornices there. Late in the afternoon, she decided to refresh her memory about the colors in the medallion print that Zelma had chosen. Someone else might be able to use them.

She marched out to the garage, wrapping her light cardigan around her as she eyed the lowering sky. Weather forecasters were predicting rain tonight, with possible ice if the temperature dropped below freezing.

The cornices, shrouded in brown paper, were propped against Richie's old workbench. When she pulled the paper away, she noted that there was more blue in the print than she'd remembered, and she thought of Tom's living room. The print was sedate and would perhaps complement his Oriental rug.

He had said he'd call. When he still hadn't phoned by three o'clock, she consulted the phone directory for his number. She told herself that she'd be doing Tom a favor; these were custom cornices, and if they fit his living room windows, he could have them at cost. She reasoned that Tom was planning to phone anyway, and she was better off talking with him at her convenience. However, even as she punched in his number, she admitted that the real reason she was contacting Tom Collyer was none of the above.

"Hello?" His voice was muffled and muzzy with sleep.

"Tom, it's Beth." She did her best to infuse her tone with businesslike efficiency, but failed.

A slight pause. What if she had interrupted something important—a date with another woman, perhaps? Her mouth went dry, her palms damp. She clenched and unclenched her fingers and wished he'd say something.

"Beth, what a nice surprise! Sorry, I was waking from a nap

when the phone rang. It takes me a few minutes to get up to speed."

"Oh, we'll hang up if this is an inconvenient time," she began, but he stopped her.

"It's not, and I'm glad to hear from you. I was remembering our junket to the auction a little while ago when I was arranging books in my new bookcase."

"Tom, I have something else that might work for you. Those cornices that Zelma refused could be just the thing for your living room windows. Want to take a quick measurement?"

A rustle, a clearing of the throat. "Sure. Let me get my tape measure. It's across the room."

She imagined him sliding out of bed. Richie had always slept in the nude at naptime and any other time. The image of Tom wearing nothing flashed into her mind and burned itself into the back of her eyelids.

"Got the tape," he declared. "What measurements do you need?"

She went to the sink, drew a glass of water from the tap. "Length and width." He had two windows in his living room, twins with a view of the front yard.

"Forty-eight inches wide, seventy-two inches long," he said. In the background, she heard the *snap* of a metal measure reeling into its case.

"The cornices will fit," she said. "Are you interested?"

"Sure. Could you deliver them now?"

"Now?" she repeated.

"Why not? The weather's getting too bad to go out, but I could cook a couple of steaks for dinner. How about it?"

Beth glanced outside. The wind had picked up and was slapping an occasional raindrop against the window. "I guess I could," she said, suddenly glad for the invitation. She'd back her minivan up to the garage and load the cornices in without even getting them wet.

"Do you need help moving those things?"

"No, I do it all the time. Piece of cake."

"That reminds me, I've still got half of the pound cake Leanne brought over the night of the housewarming. We'll finish it off."

"Sounds great," she said.

"See you soon," he replied.

Beth hurried to find something decent to wear. She hadn't paid much attention to her clothes in the past couple of years and tended to buy all-purpose pantsuits when she required something new. Today they'd be putting up cornices, so she didn't want to get too fancy, but she dug a pair of wool-and-cashmere taupe pants out of the back of her closet and tried them on. They still fit, and she located the matching sweater without much trouble.

When she was dressed, she stared at herself in the mirror. The pants were snugger than she remembered, clearly outlining the shape of her derriere, and the sweater revealed the curves of her breasts more than she recalled. She found a bottle of cologne in a drawer in her bathroom and spritzed some on her throat and wrists. When she saw her reflection, she almost didn't recognize her own polished image. She didn't look like Mitchell's mommy at all.

It had been a long time since she'd dressed with a man in mind, and it felt good.

ZELMA'S CORNICES fit Tom's windows perfectly, and, as Beth had expected, the print brought out the rich shading of color in the Oriental rug.

"We can use plain blue draperies with these, and I have some of that medallion print left. I'll sew matching throw pillows for your couch." She stood with her hands on her hips, studying the effect of the cornices, and it was all Tom could do not to slide his arm around her shoulders.

"You'll make them yourself?" he asked.

"It's not a big deal. Money was in short supply when I was a girl, so I taught myself to sew on my grandmother's old machine."

"She must be proud of you."

She turned toward him, forehead furrowed in a frown. "She passed away a few months before I got married."

"I'm sorry," he said.

"We didn't get along," Beth said, folding the wrapping paper from the cornices.

"I'll put that in the trash can in the garage," he said. He took it from her and disappeared for a few moments.

When he returned to the kitchen, Beth was peering into the toaster oven at the potatoes baking there. "I'm sorry if I talk too much," Tom said as he slid the seasoned steaks under the broiler. "I only asked about your grandmother to be polite."

She smiled ruefully. "I'm not sensitive about the situation. Actually, I'm a better mother to Mitchell because she was mean to me."

Maybe he hadn't heard her right. "You'd better explain that one."

Beth busied herself with taking the sour cream from the refrigerator and spooning it into a bowl. "Because of what I went through with Gran, I'm determined to do the best job I can with Mitchell. No child should have to grow up feeling unloved and unwanted, nor should any child be mistreated as I was."

"Mistreated?"

"Oh, she didn't hit me or anything, and I understand why she wasn't thrilled when my mother and father opted out of parenthood in favor of moving to a commune in California. It's just that there was no warmth in our household, no encouragement, no love. My grandmother couldn't love me. She wasn't capable of it."

"I'm sorry you didn't have a happy childhood. That should be everyone's right," he said. He and Bruce and Leanne had loving, conscientious parents who'd provided them with opportunities that a lot of kids didn't have.

"Unfortunately, some children have a harder time than others. Later, I grew close to Richie's parents, and they provide all the nurturing I need."

"Sometimes in-laws don't stay in touch after a divorce."

"Mine didn't approve of what Richie did. Corinne, his mom,

spent a weekend with Mitchell and me right after we separated, said she loved us both and wanted to remain my friend. His dad, Allen, stops in once or twice a month, gives me advice on keeping up the yard, mows the grass in the summer when he can. They're the only family I have, really."

"Good for you," he said. "So why aren't you with them for the holidays?"

She carried the sour cream to the kitchen table. "They're visiting Richie and Starla so they can be with Mitchell and their new granddaughter on Christmas morning. We're invited to stay overnight at their house in January." She paused. "Anything else I can do to help with this meal?"

"You don't have to do a thing," he said quietly. He was impressed that she was able to relate the story of her unhappy childhood without rancor and that she maintained close ties with her ex-in-laws. Under the circumstances, most such relationships would have broken down.

He silently offered Beth a glass of wine. She accepted it, and he popped the tab off a beer. He leaned back against the counter, appreciating how pretty she was. He'd been lonely since he returned to Farish, despite Divver and Patty's open invitation to visit with them and their teenage daughter anytime. Even hanging out with Leanne and Eddie had palled after a while, though he loved them and their kids. He was always odd man out at such gatherings, didn't have the skill to fit into their family circles when he'd never created one of his own. It was frustrating at such times to feel so out of it, but he knew of no way to reconcile his bachelor status with Divver and Patty's obvious delight in their couplehood or Leanne and Eddie's absorption in their kids.

Thinking about this, he set the beer bottle on the counter and opened the door of the oven a bit farther.

"Now how about you?" Beth asked. "Background information, I mean."

As he flipped the steaks, he grinned. "You already know everything worth knowing."

"Don't be so sure. I haven't figured out how a guy like you manages to stay single until age thirty-four, which is how old Leanne said you are."

"Thirty-five, and maybe I never found the right woman," he said, fielding that one easily. It wasn't as if the question hadn't been asked before, and he'd developed a stock answer.

When the steaks were done, he arranged them on a platter. Beth asked if she could say grace, and he told her to go ahead. The blessing was a simple one, but it reminded him of how important church was in Farish; perhaps he'd start attending himself.

The steaks were tender, the potatoes fluffy. Even the salad, on which they'd collaborated, was perfect. Beth appeared relaxed and at ease, laughing at his jokes, contributing some of her own. She had brought a few decorating magazines, and after dinner, they sat close together on the couch, thumbing through them as Tom told her what appealed to him in some of the rooms and what didn't.

When the rain began to harden into ice, coating the tree branches outside the windows, Tom built a fire in the fireplace, and soon it was crackling away, little sparks flitting up the chimney like so many fireflies.

This inspired him to relate how, on long summer evenings while the adults in the family cooled off with tall glasses of lemonade on the back porch, he and Leanne and Bruce used to catch fireflies. They collected them in mason jars and turned out all the lights in the house, then used the jars as flashlights as they brushed their teeth and got ready for bed. The captive insects were still glowing on their dresser tops as they drifted off to sleep. Later, their father would sneak into their rooms, gather up the jars and release the fireflies into the night so they wouldn't die. There was more, too, that he recounted: fishing off the bridge outside town, upsetting his parents by trying to fly off the barn roof at his grandparents' ranch, lighting forbidden firecrackers with Bruce and Leanne in the far pasture.

"Sounds like an ideal childhood. Except for the firecrackers, of course. Too dangerous," Beth observed, leaning back so that her hair spilled against the cushions.

"We were careful," he said. He longed to slide his hand under that long gleaming mass and pull her close. He didn't, though he wasn't sure why. Maybe it had something to do with wanting to look at her, to marvel at her beauty. Or perhaps it was because he liked listening to her voice, which had a soothing tone that put him in mind of river water slipping over stones.

"I can't imagine growing up any other way," he said honestly. His childhood had centered around his parents' home and their grandparents' ranch, where he and his siblings had learned to ride and rope and run the barrels. They'd each had a horse, and his earliest memories were of being perched on the pommel of his dad's saddle while his mom followed on her own mount. After the grandparents died, their ranch had been sold, its upkeep too expensive.

"I wish Mitchell could have that kind of life," Beth was saying wistfully. "Instead, he goes to day care five days a week. He doesn't have any siblings except for Ava, and she's far away."

"You didn't have brothers or sisters and you turned out okay," he pointed out.

"I was lonely."

"That's because your grandmother was a cold, unloving person."

"True, and it's why I bend over backward to be kind and affectionate toward my son."

She spoke earnestly, and he admired her for the way she cared about Mitchell. Yet he remembered her leniency with the boy on the day of Breakfast with Santa. Not only had she defended him when he was being bratty, but she'd allowed him to disturb other people in the hospital waiting room. Didn't she understand that being a responsible parent meant that sometimes you had to lay down the law? That you couldn't be unfailingly nice to a kid when he was acting up? That you had to exert control for the child's own good?

Apparently not, because she was talking about the importance of understanding small children.

"I keep in mind that Mitchell's still very young. He should feel only love in his life. I mean, the world can be a nasty place. That's why I'm protective of him."

Tom stood up abruptly. He didn't want to say anything to upset Beth, but Mitchell would soon find out that people didn't like kids who didn't behave. It wasn't fair to a child to let him think that the whole world would put up with bad behavior.

"Another glass of wine?" he said, changing the subject. He'd hoped his time with Beth would be about them, not about her son.

Beth handed over her glass. "I shouldn't drink so much of this," she murmured. "It makes me sleepy."

He went to the kitchen to pour refills, relieved he'd avoided a major discussion that would only have created a barrier between them. When he returned he saw that Beth had tossed pillows from the couch in front of the fireplace. "I hope you don't mind," she said. "This seems so cozy and warm."

It did indeed, and he was glad to stretch out beside her. The rain beat against the windowpane, the fire began to die and the wine sang in his veins of things that the two of them might do together. He curved his arm around Beth's shoulders and pulled her to him so that her head rested on his chest.

"I should leave," she said, though she made no move to do so.

"Please don't. Driving could be dangerous until the ice melts. Besides, it's good to relax and just talk. On the other hand, we could...do something else."

"Like what?" she asked playfully.

"Like this," he said, gently kissing her temple. "And this." He bent his head and captured her lips. They tasted of wine, and they were so very soft. He drifted with the kiss, taking his time.

"I really *really* should go," she said when he let her come up for air.

"I really *really* wish you wouldn't."

"Tom, I'm not ready to make love," she said quietly. "I'm still not comfortable with—with—" Her voice faltered.

"Being with a man?"

"I haven't dated since the divorce. I'm out of practice."

"I'll be glad to help you out," he said. "We could practice all night long."

To his relief, she laughed, but she didn't reply, only continued gazing at the fire.

"I want to make love to you, Beth. It doesn't have to be to-night."

"I'm feeling so—so sleepy. When we make love, I'd like to be more wide-awake. Would like to anticipate and plan for it."

If this were anyone else, he'd think she was making excuses. He almost chided her for putting off the inevitable. But, he realized in a moment of clarity, Beth meant what she said. He also intuited the unsaid—that making love, for her, was a major event, not just a quick tumble. This was new in his experience, in a world where people slid in and out of bed with various partners as if the act were no more important than any other bodily function—say, a sneeze. He found Beth quaint. And sexy. And altogether remarkable.

"Tell you what," he said, his voice close to her ear. "You decide when and where it's going to happen. Surprise me."

"Mmm," she said. "I like that idea." She snuggled nearer and slid her fingers trustingly under his hand where it rested on his chest.

He felt his heart beating through the bones and flesh of her hand, thrumming a soothing rhythm that, along with the music of the falling rain, lulled them both to sleep.

Chapter Nine

WHEN BETH WOKE UP in Tom's living room the next morning, she had no idea where she was. Instead of opening her eyes to the familiar sight of her own flowered chintz curtains, she saw a fireplace with its logs reduced to ashes and a Christmas tree in the corner. Her head was pillowed on a couch cushion on top of a beautiful Oriental rug, and she was wearing the same clothes she'd worn last night. A collage of images surfaced from memory—putting up the cornices with Tom, eating dinner, staying until the storm abated—and she sat up abruptly.

"Tom?" She smelled coffee and frying bacon. A watery sun filtered through the glittering tree branches outside the living room windows, melting the ice so that it dripped steadily onto the ground. A blanket that hadn't been there last night was spread across her legs.

He appeared in the doorway, smiling. "Good morning, sleepyhead."

"What time is it?" she asked as she scrambled to her feet.

"Almost eight o'clock. I've already showered and shaved."

"I'd like to wash my face," she said. "I'm embarrassed. I should never have drunk so much wine."

"You can use the bathroom at the head of the stairs. Clean washcloths and towels in the linen closet, and you'll find a package of toothbrushes in the medicine cabinet. Help yourself. There's only one tube of toothpaste, but I don't mind sharing."

She pushed her hair out of her face and smiled. "I'll be right out," she said.

She'd never seen the upstairs of Tom's house, and she peeked into each of the four bedrooms. One was obviously Tom's room. It was enormous and contained a large bed and an oak dresser. The others were large but unfurnished. Wide windows admitted a lot of light, and here, as downstairs, flooring was the original pine planking.

After she washed her face and brushed her teeth, she felt better. She thought about taking a shower, but she hadn't been invited to do that, and undressing in his house seemed too intimate, too forward. She stared at herself in the bathroom mirror, realizing that she looked almost as different as she felt, and she wasn't exactly sure why. Maybe it was that she didn't have any motherly responsibilities at present. On one level, that didn't feel comfortable. On another, the one where she was when she was with Tom, it felt wonderful and special and—well, fun. Sometimes these days she tended to forget that recreation for a twenty-nine-year-old woman wasn't necessarily whooping down water slides or indulging Mitchell in an intense game of Candyland.

Eggs, bacon and grits were on the table when she appeared in the kitchen. "You look scrumptious," he said when she walked in.

He did, too, attired as he was in a plain navy-blue sweatshirt and well-worn jeans, along with the usual boots. "Thanks," she said easily, sliding into the chair she'd occupied last night for dinner. "So does the food."

"Dig in," he directed, and she helped herself. The eggs had been cooked with cheese, the grits was creamy and the bacon crisp.

"This is really good," she said.

"Breakfast is my specialty. Whatever you want—omelettes, waffles, *huevos rancheros*—I can do. I decided on scrambled eggs this morning, instead of waking you to ask what you wanted."

"That's fine with me." She paused. "The weather's cleared," she said, glancing outside. The ice storm had graced the backyard with exquisite artistry; icicles trailed from the shed roof, and every shrub sparkled in the sunshine.

"The front that came through last night has broken up, but you were wise not to be on the roads before the ice began to melt."

"Be that as it may, I'd better go home. I have last-minute shopping to do."

"I promised to help Eddie put together a couple of bikes for my nephews this morning. Otherwise we could go together."

"Doubtful," she said.

"Oh?"

"I'll need to drive to Austin to find what I want," she told him. It was an hour's drive, and she went a couple of times a month.

"Well," he said, "the roads should be safe by now."

He would be amazed if he knew what she planned to buy. But that was a secret she wasn't ready to divulge just yet.

Speaking of secrets, her spending the night at Tom's house wasn't likely to remain one around Farish. When she was backing out of the driveway a half hour later, who should cruise by but Muffy Ledbetter, whose expression registered surprise and astonishment when she recognized Beth's minivan.

Oh, great, Beth thought with dismay. The last thing she needed was for Muffy to mention in her column that she'd seen her leaving Tom Collyer's house.

Beth managed a halfhearted wave, which Muffy returned. Muffy would undoubtedly believe the worst. But so what? Did it really matter?

Amazingly, it didn't.

THE MALL IN AUSTIN was thronged with last-minute shoppers, but they might as well have not been there for all Beth cared. She found herself humming along with Christmas carols in the stores, smiling at people she'd never met and never would. She was on a mission to buy new lingerie.

As she made her way from store to store, she was amused to realize that she was studying the garments the way she imagined Tom might. Did he prefer seductive black lace or red silk? Neutral beige or pristine white? She hadn't shopped for lingerie in a long time, and when she came to a specialty store that showed an elegant nightgown and pegnoir set in the window, she went in.

Inside, however, the inventory was slightly more racy. No, a *lot* more. In fact, she was utterly fascinated. Were there women on this planet who actually wore such things? One item, a shocking pink corset, had no front and no back, only lace straps holding a minibra and thong together. Beth decided that she'd have to be a contortionist to get into it. She lingered over a black slip with only a few bits of lace binding it together at the sides and wondered what good it could possibly do; wasn't a slip supposed to keep people from seeing what you were wearing under a dress? While she was pondering this, a perky salesclerk bounced up to her and asked if she needed help.

"I—um—"Beth couldn't help it. She blushed furiously. The clerk only kept smiling, so Beth tried again. "I'm planning a special night with a man," she managed to say.

"Ah," the clerk said knowingly.

Beth took heart from the thought that the woman probably heard this sort of thing all the time.

"Right this way," the clerk said, leading her to an alcove. "This is our bestseller at Christmas." She held up a red lace teddy. It was a whole lot smaller than any hanky Beth had ever seen.

"I'm not—" Beth started to protest.

"Oh, but, sweetie, you are. With a figure like that, you could wear this. Believe me, when your man sees you in it, he'll be all over you. Besides, it has a Santa cap to match." She held up a red hat edged with white marabou and faked a French accent. *"Très chic, non?"*

"I'll try it," Beth said in order to avoid choking with laughter.

She was summarily guided to a fitting booth and left alone to stare at the red garments in her hand. Then she really did laugh. Chloe would die if she ever knew that Beth had actually tried on this sort of thing.

Once she had the teddy on she had to admit that she *was* sexy. Even so, this particular piece of underwear seemed to have no practical purpose whatever. In the first place, the bra had no cups. The lace underneath, where the cups were supposed to be, provided support enough, so that was okay. There was also no front, only a sweep of lace down the center of her torso that ended in a panty, if you could call it that. In the back, the thong diverged into two strappy wisps that attached to another strappy wisp across her back. It was all too ridiculous to contemplate.

But if she wanted Tom to be "all over her" as the salesclerk said, this was the ticket.

In the end, she bought it, maybe because she couldn't face trying on any more bits of nothing or perhaps because her wearing such a thing was totally out of character. She wanted to surprise Tom, and surprised he would certainly be.

Unfortunately, the teddy was so pricey that she was consumed with guilt for not buying Mitchell more presents, so she stopped on the way home and bought him a Shrek game that he'd begged her for a couple of weeks ago.

When she got the teddy home and spread it out on her bed, she had her doubts again. The usual Beth McCormick wore bras with elastic that had lost its stretch and an old T-shirt for sleeping. That Beth had never owned a teddy. But for an evening of passion with Tom Collyer, she needed to morph into a previous self, the person who had once enjoyed sex. Who had loved and been loved and was thinking about loving again.

Tom phoned as she was rewrapping her purchase in tissue paper.

"Eddie and I got those bikes put together," he said. "It was a hassle. By the way, Leanne said she'd call and invite you to Christmas dinner, but I have another idea."

"I was planning to roast a turkey on Christmas Day," she told him.

"All by yourself?"

"Yes, and I usually make several pans of turkey tetrazzini to freeze for quick meals when I'm working and rushed for time."

"I always cook a Christmas goose. How about if you and I cook Christmas dinner together? Alone. Well, except for the goose."

"Fine, but I've never heard of goose tetrazzini," she teased.

"That might be one of the drawbacks of my plan," he allowed, sounding amused.

She paused, but only for a heartbeat. "Wild-rice casserole would taste good with goose. So would salad and pumpkin pie."

"Great," Tom said. "And how about going to the Hartzell pageant with me on Christmas Eve?"

"I'd like that," she said. The annual pageant was a project of the Hartzell family as their gift to the community, and it depicted the nativity in miniature tableaux set up on two vacant lots downtown.

"The festivities start as soon as it gets dark, so I'll pick you up around five-thirty. Okay?"

"That sounds fine," she said.

After they hung up, she cleaned her closet and discovered, at the very back of one of the shelves, a box of candles. Humming, she went to find every candleholder she owned. Setting the scene for seduction was great fun, she decided as she placed the candleholders here and there around the house. She carried in extra boughs of evergreens that she had stored in the garage after making the decorations for Breakfast with Santa, arranged them on the mantel, strung them along the staircase, banked them on top of the new armoire. Then she nestled the candles among the branches.

She regretted not having bought a fresh tree, but all the good ones would be gone by now. Anyway, she'd never wanted a tree without Mitchell around.

Now she wished she'd considered one. That symbol of Christmas, with its lights and ornaments, might have cheered her up, and it would have been something to share with Tom.

BETH LOVED THE MAGIC of the Christmas pageant—the dramatic lighting of each tableau, the artistry of the three-foot-tall hand-carved figurines that populated the scenes, the hushed reverence of the crowd as the age-old story of the first Christmas unfolded before their eyes. But she hadn't gone in years. She'd stopped attending when Mitchell had started visiting his father for the holidays.

On Christmas Eve, she and Tom, along with the other attendees, walked from one tableau to another on a gravel path along the river. When they came to the scene of the shepherds coming to worship the newborn Jesus, Tom slid his arm around her shoulders.

"I'd forgotten how special this is," he whispered.

She put her arm around his waist, certain that she wouldn't have been here if Tom hadn't invited her. Being at the pageant again made her understand that she'd shortchanged herself in years past; she'd thought it would be impossible to find joy in the Christmas holiday without her son. She never would have guessed that all she had to do to feel part of things was to go through the motions and let the spirit of the season envelop her. With a sense of wonder she let this sink in, and she knew that never again would she sit home and ignore the celebration going on around her.

She had Tom to thank for this new attitude, and she darted a grateful glance up at him. She was surprised to discover that he was looking down at her at the same time, and they exchanged a smile that somehow, in the middle of this crowd, was undeniably intimate.

As soon as they'd seen the whole pageant, they followed other pageant-goers toward the town square. Almost every door bore a wreath, and most of the houses had lights strung amid the shrubbery. At one of the side streets, Chloe appeared with a group of carolers and grabbed Beth's arm.

"Come along," she said. "Choirs from all the churches are

converging on the courthouse to sing on the steps. You, too, Tom."

Beth, more willing than not, found herself singing along at the edge of the group as they walked, Tom on one side of her, participating in his deep baritone, and Chloe singing soprano on the other. The stars twinkled brightly, and the moon cast the bare tree branches in silver. The world seemed like a beautiful place in these moments, their voices spinning a magical web that bound them all together in peace and love.

Soon they arrived at the square, where the courthouse was brightly illuminated for the holiday season. Along with everyone else, they climbed the wide steps and took their places between the tall white pillars. Someone dimmed the electric lights as volunteers handed around candles stuck through circles of gilded cardboard, and then there was the sound of lighters and matches being struck. In a matter of moments, more than a hundred candles were lit, and in the glow of their flickering golden flames shone the faces of Beth's fellow townspeople and friends. There was Gretchen and her husband standing one pillar over, and Divver and Patty Holcomb with their daughter, Amy, occupying the step above them.

A choirmaster from one of the churches led them in singing "O Holy Night," a song that featured a solo by Teresa Boggs. And then, their voices ringing out in the frosty air, they were wishing one another "merry Christmas" and "happy holidays," and invitations were being issued to drop over sometime soon.

As Beth and Tom drifted away from the group, Chloe came running after them. "Would you two like to go with some of us to Gretchen's house to admire their new leg lamp? You remember, like the one in the movie *A Christmas Story.* It's a present from her mom."

Beth and Tom exchanged amused glances. "Well," Beth began.

"Afterward a bunch of us are going to Zachary's to grab a late snack."

Wordless communication passed between Beth and Tom, and she knew that he wasn't in the mood to be with other people any more than she was. "Thanks, but not tonight," she said.

"Okay. Call you soon," Chloe said before hurrying off.

"Well, I don't own a leg lamp, but let's go back to my house," Beth said wryly. She'd stashed away a bottle of wine for the occasion, and then there was that red teddy in her bottom dresser drawer.

"Good idea. I have a surprise for you."

"What?" she asked, smiling up at him.

"I'm not telling." His eyes held a secretive gleam.

She wondered about this all the way home, but Tom gave her no clues.

At her house, he said, "I'll come in the back door. You go in the front."

In response to her quizzical look, he only smiled. "Go ahead. Unlock the kitchen door for me, will you?"

Beth rushed to comply, switching on the lights in the house one by one as she hurried from front to back. By the time she arrived in the kitchen, Tom was waiting for her on the back stoop. When she opened the door, she saw that he was standing beside a small tree planted in a huge pot.

Speechless, she stepped aside while he hauled it in. "I bought a live Christmas tree so you could plant it somewhere on your property later," he said. "Where do you want it?"

She recovered her powers of speech and asked him how he'd managed to get the tree into her backyard without her seeing him.

"Divver and Patty dropped it off on their way into town after you and I had left for the pageant. He buys a live tree for his family every year, so I asked him to find one for you, too."

"It's wonderful," she said, taking in the shape and color of the little Afghan pine. She directed Tom to the living room, where she pushed aside the comfy old armchair in one corner. "We'll set it here. I'll dig the box of tree decorations out." She'd spotted it in the back of the hall closet when she'd been looking for Mitchell's duffel.

After they'd brought out the lights and ornaments, the garlands and the Christmas angel for the top of the tree, Beth inserted a disk of Christmas music into the CD player, and soon Tom had spread the lights on the tree's branches. Beth stood on a chair to drape red and green velvet garlands from branch to branch while Tom offered advice, and then they collaborated to hang gold and silver balls, Tom handling the top of the tree, Beth the bottom. When they had finished, he offered his hand and pulled her to a standing position.

"Tinsel?" he asked.

She shook her head. "I like it better without."

"So do I," he told her, giving her shoulder a companionable squeeze.

She smiled up at him. "Thanks for bringing the tree."

"I couldn't have you celebrating Christmas without one," he said, gazing down at her.

She went into the kitchen and returned with glasses of wine on a gilt tray. While Tom leaned against the mantel, she went around the room lighting candles that bathed their surroundings in a golden glow. Then she switched off all the lamps so they could admire the effect.

"Wait," Tom said, when she would have taken the matches back to the kitchen. He caught her and swung her around to face him. Their eyes met; his were silvery in the candlelight, and his gaze was tender. He stroked the side of her face, a gentle feathering from cheek to jawbone, and she leaned into his hand. Heat radiated from his body, warming her, chasing away the chill. Emotion swept over her, but it wasn't the raw lust she had felt in her younger days when she'd fallen for Richie. It was something entirely different and new, built of respect, and the certainty that the two of them were meant to share something deeper than friendship. She savored the moment, thinking about the preparations she had made to be with him.

"Tom," she said unsteadily, but this time it wasn't a warning. It was an invitation. Her head tilted back, and his hand molded to the curve of her head as his mouth covered hers and her arms pulled him close.

He felt so big and strong, his muscles hard against the palms of her hands, and she gave herself up to the kiss. His lips were insistent, seeking, making her forget who she was. Mitchell's mommy—that had been her identity for a long time now. But Tom made that part of her fade away, leaving a woman who felt like a stranger to herself. Who wanted to be desired as a woman, and loved as a woman, and who wanted to reciprocate in a way that left no doubt that she was one.

He stopped kissing her, captured her face between his palms. "Wait," she murmured, her eyes dancing with excitement. "I have a surprise, too."

He seemed puzzled as she backed away.

"You'll see," she said.

In her room, she undressed quickly, tossed her sweater and slacks in the back of her closet and quickly unwrapped the teddy from the tissue paper. She put it on, got the straps twisted, took it off and started all over. When she studied her reflection in the full-length mirror—*Omigosh.*

Everything showed. She might as well have been naked. Yet she wanted to be sexy and seductive, and—*gulp*—she was. Or at least her body was, but her hair wasn't right, and when she settled the matching Santa Claus cap on her head, it definitely didn't help.

Usually, Beth wore her hair straight and pushed back behind her ears, but that wasn't the right style for the temptress in the mirror. Tonight, when Teresa Boggs had been singing her solo at the courthouse, Beth had noticed that Teresa's hair was tousled, wild and unfettered.

For the first time, Beth considered how she might get the same effect, short of combing her hair with an eggbeater. Tentatively, she poked her fingers through her hair to her scalp, then whisked them around. Liking the result, she did it again. Her reflection convinced her that she was now fit for seduction.

In a moment of misgiving, she reminded herself that she could forget about this ridiculous teddy and Tom would be none the wiser. She could slip into the plain blue silk kimono that she kept in the back of her closet and slink out into the hall. Tom would turn to her, register surprise, and then—but no. She'd gone too far to back out.

She lit a single candle on her dresser, and then, feeling self-conscious, she opened her bedroom door and walked slowly to the arch between the foyer and the living room.

"Merry Christmas," she said, her voice cracking slightly. "I, um, thought you might like a teddy bare."

Tom had been rocking back on his heels as he studied her heart collection. When he heard her voice, he whirled around. His eyes grew enormous as a slow appreciative smile spread across his face.

"I always did like teddy bears," he said. Very carefully, he set his glass down on the coffee table and walked to where she stood. "I've never seen you more beautiful," he said, and then, making this feel like a homecoming more than a seduction, he folded her in his arms.

She lifted her lips to his, and they kissed long and passionately. Tom's lips were warm and firm, and they stirred a response from the depths of her soul. He released her, raised her hand to his lips and kissed it tenderly. There was no need for words between them; all had been said that needed saying. She willed herself to remember these moments forever as he swept her into his arms, carried her into the bedroom and kicked the door closed behind them.

Tenderly and reverently, he laid her on the bed. He peeled away his clothes, and she was fascinated to watch him emerging from pants and shirt and socks and underwear. He was a magnificent specimen of a man, his sun-bronzed skin shimmering in the candlelight. She opened her arms to him and drew him down beside her.

He stared at her in the candlelight. "I'm crazy about you, Beth McCormick," he said unevenly. "Crazy for you and this—this wonderful Christmas present."

Her heart filled with emotion at his words. She had waited a long time to find a man who was kind and caring in a way that Richie had never been, who was steadfast and sure and saw something special in her. Maybe Tom was that man. She was investing something of herself in that hope as she offered herself to him tonight, and she had an idea that Tom understood and appreciated that fact.

They sank against the pillows, and Beth gave in to the sensations evoked by his hard palms against her skin, caressing her breasts, sliding downward across the strip of lace on her belly. He dipped his head down to her throat, his breath fluttering gently there, and feathered a trail of gentle kisses to her breasts. He cupped them reverently in his palms, kissed each one in turn, murmured her name.

She hadn't expected such tenderness. She had expected passion and strength and, perhaps, haste. Usually, in her experience, all of which had taken place long ago, making love with someone for the first time was awkward. It was different with this man, who was instinctively aware of her, of her breathing, of every slight movement of her body. He took his time, as if he understood that the act would be sweeter if they didn't rush. It was good to be totally in sync while making love; she felt that she could give herself over to it entirely and be lost in the experience. Lost, but somehow happily found.

The teddy fell away, and now nothing kept them apart. He made sure they were protected, and it was his eyes that held her then as much as his arms. She could sense the person inside him, the man that she had grown to care about since the day they'd first met. He had made her feel fresh and new again, unsullied by her unhappy childhood and subsequent divorce. It was as if none of that had ever happened. Not thinking about that, not really, she was living totally in the moment as she rose to him and cradled him between her thighs. Held him there, felt his heat and his urgency. It was incredibly erotic when he started to move, slowly, faster, sweeping her along on a rush of heat and intensity and longing.

Across the room, the candle flame flickered and rose, and inside them the heat swirled until it burst behind Beth's closed eyelids into a hundred candles, a thousand. Without warning, Tom exploded inside her, his gasp close to her ear, and she hung on to him as if she never wanted to let him go.

Was that true? That she never wanted to let go? The possibility ricocheted around inside her brain, colliding with her prior determination not to let anyone—any man—into her life.

She found it difficult to come to grips with what was happening to her. She'd entered into this sexual experience expecting it to be an extension of friendship. Yet now, as she slid one leg across Tom's and rested her head on his shoulder as if that was the natural place for it to be, troubling emotions threatened to overwhelm her.

Tom stroked her hair, kissed her temple. "Sweet Beth," he said. "I meant it when I said I was crazy about you."

She melted at the earnestness of his expression. "I—I'm glad," she said, not wanting to go any further than that. She felt so helpless when it came to talking about this.

He sighed and curled his body around hers, falling asleep almost instantly. Beth lay awake pondering. Making room in her life for Tom wouldn't be as easy as making room in her bed. It would be infinitely more complicated.

And, perhaps, more rewarding.

Chapter Ten

"Merry Christmas," Tom said, and Beth opened her eyes to find him standing at the foot of her bed, holding a tray. On his head he wore a red Santa Claus cap, the one with the marabou trim that had come with her new teddy, and on the rest of him he wore—a white terry-cloth towel?

Remembering last night, Beth pushed herself to a sitting position and clutched at the sheet. Her teddy had somehow ended up on top of the lamp shade. His clothes were in a neat pile on a chair, and his boots were lined up beside the door.

"Merry Christmas to you, too," she said, wrinkling her nose at the wonderfully intermingled fragrances of country ham and freshly brewed coffee.

He set the tray beside her on the bed, swooped down, and planted a kiss on her cheek. "I had an idea that you might enjoy a *real* Breakfast with Santa," he said.

She smiled at him, finding the Santa cap and beard stubble combination oddly endearing.

"You should have awakened me," she said. "I'd have cooked breakfast."

"I didn't have the heart to disturb you. Instead, I ducked into your shower, and afterward, I explored the refrigerator."

"The hat looks good," she told him.

"It would probably be more becoming to you. Want to wear it?"

"No, thanks, and would you mind handing me that robe on the back of the bathroom door?"

Tom tossed it to her. "What about breakfast in bed?"

She stood up and wrapped the robe around her. "I want to wash my face, that's all." She kissed him before going into the bathroom and closing the door.

For a moment, she stared at her reflection. Her face was devoid of makeup, her hair a tangled mess. No wonder, when you considered their impassioned lovemaking of the night before.

"Woman, you're going to kill me," Tom had moaned after the third time, or was it the fourth?

Now, as she struggled to tug a brush through her hair, she almost blushed at the way she had seduced him last night. Not that he had minded. In fact, her preparations had fascinated him, and he'd expressed delight that she was such a willing bed partner.

"You always seemed so cool and calm," he'd said in amazement. "How could I have guessed that you're a wild and crazy woman underneath? And on top, and every stuff?"

She'd laughed at that. "I'm not sure I was so uninhibited before you came along. Ever," she'd told him.

When, after a shower and subduing her hair into some semblance of order, she emerged from the bathroom, Tom was propped up on pillows in her bed, the Santa hat tilted rakishly to one side, the tray on a pillow between his side of the bed and hers. She slid under the sheets.

"You're amazing," she said. "I wasn't expecting breakfast in bed."

"What exactly," he said, waggling his eyebrows at her, "did you expect? More of what we did last night?"

She felt her cheeks heat.

"Admit it," he said. "You've figured out that I'm insatiable."

"Now that you mention it," she replied as primly as she could under the circumstances, "the possibility has crossed my mind."

"And what about you? You're no shrinking violet yourself."

"Couldn't we simply eat breakfast? And not dissect last night?"

"I'm only expressing appreciation for the woman you are."

"I'm not that woman, really."

"Last night liberated you," Tom said. "Right?"

Beth stirred her coffee, sipped and found it too hot. She replaced the cup in its saucer and regarded him. The only answer that occurred to her was that she would revert to Mitchell's mom once her son came home.

"We don't have to talk about it now," Tom said. "Let's enjoy Christmas, okay?"

She took heart from the warm light in his eyes. "Good idea."

"You'd better eat your eggs before they get cold."

The eggs were delicious, and so was everything else. Because he had cooked, Beth insisted on cleaning up, and after that, Tom said he would go to his house to get the goose, which was thawing in his refrigerator.

"I'll be back later," he said, kissing her at the door.

She stood in her warm fleece bathrobe, collar upturned against the chill, and waved as he drove away.

Afterward she hummed as she made the bed, straightened the house, vacuumed the living room. She was hoping Mitchell would call.

When the phone rang, however, it was Chloe.

"You're invited to eat Christmas dinner with my family," she told Beth hurriedly. "I've been meaning to mention it."

"Thanks, Chlo, but I have other plans." Beth knew Chloe would automatically think that she was spending the afternoon with Leanne and her brood, as she had last year.

"You sound mighty cheerful."

This would have been the time to mention to Chloe that she'd spent last night with Tom Collyer, but Beth was reluctant.

"It's Christmas," she said airily, "the season to be jolly, and all that."

"Fa-la-la-la-la," Chloe agreed. "I need to put the finishing touches on the salad I'm making for our family dinner. Merry Christmas, Beth, and we'll get together soon."

After they hung up, Beth wandered into the living room. The Christmas tree that Tom had brought dominated the living room, even with her new armoire against one wall. Maybe she could start a tradition of planting an Afghan pine every year. Mitchell would like that, and perhaps Tom would, as well.

She was caught up short by this thought. She had no cause to believe that Tom would be part of her life next Christmas, and she probably wouldn't have the heart to buy and decorate a tree just for herself.

As she lit the fire in the fireplace, the phone rang again. She hurried to answer it.

"Merry Christmas, Mom!" cried Mitchell.

She carried the phone to the armchair, poked at the newly lit fire to make sure it was burning and sat down. "Hi, honey. Merry Christmas to you, too." The familiar lump was rising in her throat again, and for a moment, the lights on the Christmas tree blurred.

"Mom, you'll never guess what I got for Christmas!"

She blinked to clear the mist from her eyes. "No, I can't. You'll have to tell me."

"Should I keep you in suspense?"

She smiled. "Please tell."

"Santa brought me an electric scooter of my very own!" Mitchell said with glee. "It was under the tree this morning when I got up!"

"An—an electric scooter?" she repeated. She was stunned. Surely Richie didn't believe that Mitchell was old enough to ride one.

"Yeah. It's bright red. I love it, Mommy. Later, Daddy's going to show me how to make it go."

"Oh, dear. Maybe you'd better let me talk to your dad." An electric scooter? For Mitchell, who was only five and still had to be cautioned not to run into the street when they were at the park? She'd give Richie a piece of her mind. She'd—

"Okay, Mommy, I'll get him." She heard footsteps running, then Mitchell calling, "Dad? Da-*ad!* Mom wants to talk to you."

She waited impatiently, drumming her fingers on the table beside the chair.

"Beth?"

"Yes," she said tightly. "Are you out of your mind, Richie?"

A pause. "Merry Christmas to you, too, Beth," he said with more than a hint of irony.

"Never mind that. How on earth could you think that our son is ready to ride an electric scooter? He hasn't even tried the kind you push with one foot yet. He's barely ready for a bike with training wheels."

"All the kids around here have them."

"Five-year-olds?"

"I didn't ask them for their birth certificates. Starla agreed that it would be a good gift, and Mitchell loves it."

"Richie, don't you worry that he might have an accident? Hurt himself?"

"Sure, that's always a possibility, but a boy is a boy. Mitchell's not some namby-pamby wuss. He'll fall down and get scraped up like all kids do, and there's not much we can do about it. He'll be six in January and is big for his age. I don't understand the problem."

Beth shook her head to clear it. "Buying him a scooter wasn't smart, Richie."

Richie let out an exasperated sigh. "It's Christmas morning, Beth. Couldn't we call a truce?"

"I—I'm upset," she admitted.

When Richie spoke again, he sounded calmer. "I bought him a helmet. I'll make sure he understands safety rules. He can ride up and down the driveway and nowhere else. You're making too much of this, Beth."

She was silent, unwilling to back off. Mitchell wasn't ready for an electric scooter. She knew it.

"Do you want to speak to my folks?" Richie asked. "They're right here."

"Of course," she said. She loved his parents, and in a different scenario, the one she'd married into in the first place, she would have been with them every year at this time.

Corinne came on the line first, and she described the awe on Mitchell's face when he first spotted the presents under the tree, related some of his clever remarks as he opened various gifts and ended by telling Beth how much she missed her.

"We'll see you in a few weeks," Beth promised her.

Then Allen took over, his voice gruff but energetic, asking her how she was bearing up during the holiday season and finally wishing her a merry Christmas.

"Thanks, Allen," Beth told him warmly.

Her ex-father-in-law handed the phone to Mitchell, but her son was in too much of a hurry to talk for long. "I'm helping Grandpa put together a swing for Ava," he said with an air of self-importance. "I'm supposed to hand him the bolts."

"Okay, you'd better get back to work," she told him, and then they hung up.

Beth sat for a pensive moment, picturing the scene at Richie's house. She imagined the commotion and excitement, with tantalizing smells wafting from the kitchen and the two children playing with their new toys. But somehow, she couldn't visualize it as well as she had on other Christmases. Maybe that was because she was looking forward to something else now. She had a life that Richie and Starla, Corinne and Allen, and most of all Mitchell, knew nothing about.

It struck her that no one at Richie's house had indicated any interest in her plans for the day. Not even Mitchell. And if they had, she wouldn't have wanted to tell them about Tom.

For now, he was a secret that she hugged to herself.

Tom arrived about an hour later, red cheeked and hearty, carrying the defrosted goose in a brown paper bag. He'd also brought a bottle of chardonnay.

Beth tossed together the stuffing while Tom scouted up the proper pans and racks from her kitchen shelves, and after they'd consigned the bird to the oven, Beth dusted off her grand-mother's heirloom bone china and set the table. From the garage, she brought scraps of spruce and fir left over from the decora-tions she'd made for the pancake breakfast and arranged them down the middle of the lace tablecloth, placing some of the can-dles from last night among them. The evergreens' fragrance scented the house and mingled with the aroma of the roasting goose.

When she stood back to admire the effect of the candles on the table, Tom came up behind her and wrapped his arms around her. "Is that all we have to do? For a while, at least?"

She leaned her head against his chest and closed her eyes. "There might be something else we could be doing," she said, beginning to feel the stirrings of desire. Dimly, she wondered how she could have felt no sexual energy for years, and now that she was around Tom have it to spare.

He ran his hands up under her sweater and caressed her breasts. She turned to him, overwhelmed by her feelings. He pushed her sweater up, traced her nipples with his thumbs, unhooked her bra.

It felt right to be kissing him longingly and lingeringly, to slide her hands through the front buttons of his shirt. Her seek-ing lips never left his as her fingers fumbled with his belt and he unfastened her jeans.

She shivered, not with cold, because it was warm in her house, but with anticipation. Tom felt her trembling and re-leased her lips, his words stirring the hair beside her ear.

"Do we have to make love standing up, or is there somewhere else we can go?"

She didn't want to take the time to lead him to her bed-room, to which he knew the way already. Urgency over-whelmed her.

"Here," she whispered, "right here."

She pulled him down beside her on the big couch, pushed some of the faded pillows into a rest for their heads, shimmied out of her jeans. Soon he was kissing her abdomen, moving higher, trailing kisses toward her breasts.

He was as hungry for her as she was for him, and they reveled in their reexploration of each other's bodies in broad daylight, with the sunlight casting shadows through the shutters at the window. Afterward, Tom cradled her close, his fingers lazily stroking her back. They dozed for a while, woke up, kissed some more, and then Beth slipped on Tom's shirt to go to the kitchen to check on the goose. Tom, dressed only in his jeans and with the top button undone, followed her and watched as she started the rice cooking. Then they kissed again.

"First course, kisses. Second course, salad. Third course, kisses," Beth teased him before she went to get dressed.

After dinner, when he backed her against the refrigerator and kissed her again, she asked him why he kept doing it, even as she ran her hands up the musculature of his back and tangled her fingers in his mussed hair.

He countered with humor in his eyes. "There's nothing else I'd rather be doing," he said, but he sobered quickly. "You're absolutely radiant, Beth, and this is the happiest Christmas I can remember."

"Me, too," she told him, wondering how this could be so. Before, the Christmases when she was married had been the benchmark against which she compared all subsequent ones. She was willing to admit that she and Richie had had problems from the beginning, but Mitchell had made up for those. Mitchell had been the centerpoint of their relationship from the day he was born, so was it any surprise that their son was what had made Christmas so wonderful?

Now this godsend of a man had come along and brightened Christmas for her, made it meaningful again. Instead of feeling lonely, she was truly blessed. How could she ever thank him?

"I can think of a way," he said, and she laughed and let him lead her to the bedroom.

"I wish this day could go on forever," she murmured wistfully, later when they cuddled in her bed together, the comforter keeping away the chill.

"I do, too," he said. "You're one hell of a Christmas present, Beth McCormick."

"Better than a leg lamp?" she asked mischievously.

"If we're going to start talking about body parts, I have some favorites of yours that I'd like to nominate for lamphood," he said.

After Tom had dozed off, Beth willed herself to stay awake so that she could cherish this remarkable day until its very end. But she fell asleep well before midnight in Tom Collyer's arms.

TOM AWOKE IN BETH'S BED on the day after Christmas with a cramp in his arm and an unsettling feeling that time was running out.

As he lay beside her with the dawn light piercing the slit in the curtains, Beth slept beside him. Her chest rose and fell with her breathing, and her hair tumbled over his arm. She might have been an angel straight from the top of the Christmas tree, and he felt bewilderment that he was soon to lose her to another man.

To Mitchell.

Once her son returned, Mitchell's claims on Beth would be more important and far-reaching than Tom's could ever be. Gloomily, he tugged his arm out from under Beth, massaged his numb shoulder and watched while she smiled and turned away, snuggling close to him under the covers.

The thing was, he didn't want to give Beth up. He wanted to be around her as much as their busy lives allowed. He wanted to have long conversations with her on the telephone, to invite her to his house for drinks and dinner, to take in a movie in Austin on the spur of the moment if they felt like it. How much of that would be possible once Mitchell was back in the picture? Probably very little.

"Tom?"

Beth was awake now, and his hand curved easily around her breast. "Mmm?" he said, picturing last night in his mind: the wind howling outside the window as they'd made love, the softness of her skin against his, later, the sweetness of sleep.

"You said you'd show me Divver's ranch today," she murmured. "Want to get an early start?"

"Might as well. I told him I'd feed the horses while he and his family were out of town."

She kissed him before she slid out of bed. "Give me a couple of minutes in the shower."

He stared up at the ceiling as he listened to her opening and closing cabinet doors, turning on the water, yanking the shower curtain across the rod.

This was Monday, and Mitchell was due back on Wednesday. He felt a pang of sadness for what they were about to lose: privacy, and pleasure wherever and whenever they wanted it.

Well, he'd have to adjust, that was all. No matter what he had to put up with, Beth was worth it.

THE TWO-STORY CLAPBOARD HOUSE where Divver, Patty and Amy lived was over a hundred years old. Divver's great-grandfather had homesteaded in a small cabin up Big Horse Creek and built a larger home for his family when he became more prosperous. At one time, the Holcombs had run a large herd of cattle, but Divver and his sisters had sold much of the ranchland to the developer of Hillsdale. Divver preferred horses to cattle anyway, and he'd achieved some success with his breeding program and rodeo school.

Tom related the history of the house to Beth later that morning as they got out of his pickup and started walking toward the bunkhouse.

"How long have you and Divver Holcomb been buddies?" she asked.

"Most of our lives. He and Johnny—" He stopped talking in midsentence, uneasy and reluctant to discuss the past.

"I don't think I know a Johnny," Beth prompted. "Does he live around here, too?"

"No," Tom said curtly. Fortunately, they were walking past the old cookhouse, which was now a utility storage area, and he was able to point out where he and Divver had constructed a lean-to at the age of twelve, and done a fairly good job of it, too.

They kept walking, the subject of Johnny Snead effectively quashed. He couldn't expect Beth to be aware of the taboos; she hadn't lived here then.

Divver's big yellow dog galloped up and sniffed hopefully at Tom's hand for treats. Glad for the diversion, he dug a dog biscuit out of the supply in his pocket and fed it to her.

"Her name's Dallas," he told Beth as she stooped to pet the dog. "Divver and his daughter brought her home when they found her sick and wandering in the city, so that's how she got her name."

"She looks part Lab," Beth said.

He nodded. "Probably. She's a good mutt."

Dallas, primed for more treats, followed them toward the former bunkhouse. "This is where we have our offices and a couple of classrooms," he told Beth, opening the door so she could precede him inside.

She took in the head of the deer and the snake skin hanging over the old fireplace, as well as Divver's old desk, a family heirloom. After Tom told her about all the nights he and Divver had spent here in front of this fireplace on bedrolls when they were kids, she went to peek into the other rooms, which opened off the bigger one.

"This is a classroom," she said, noting the chalkboards, and he nodded. He knew she was wondering about the big oval table in the middle of the room.

"We didn't spring for desks. Kids who haven't been a success in school often don't respond to a classroom setting, so we and our educational-experts team decided on oval tables, where everyone is equal and can feel comfortable contributing to a discussion. The training we're going to do here at the ranch is interactive. Some of these kids have never spoken up in a classroom, but they'll get a chance to do that here."

"Isn't most of what you do going to be practical, hands-on experience? You know, roping and riding?"

"We'll also talk a lot about safety issues and proper conduct, and a classroom is best for that. Come on over here and I'll show you the kitchen."

After the tour, they stepped out into the warm sunshine. Today, he felt young and carefree in a way he hadn't in years and certainly not in the past few months when he'd been working so hard to get the ATTAIN program up and running. He slid an arm around her waist. "How about going for a trail ride? Old Red's the calmest mount in the stable. Even a novice could handle him."

She arched an amused glance out of the corners of her eyes. "All right."

While Tom saddled Old Red and his own horse, Ironsides, Beth went from stall to stall visiting with the other horses. When it was time to mount Old Red, she surprised Tom by swinging her leg smoothly across the horse's back and tucking her feet into the stirrups, heels down as recommended.

"Hey," he said, grinning up at her. "You're pretty savvy in the horse department."

"Did I mention I used to be good at riding? In return for the privilege of exercising horses, I mucked out stalls at a stable near where we lived. It got me out of the house on Saturdays, and my grandmother liked that."

He mounted Ironsides, and they began to ride across the wide fields toward Big Horse Creek. Tom pointed out a trail where whitetail deer often walked down to the water to drink, and as they passed a thicket, a flock of wild turkeys rose into the air and flapped away. Soon they heard the creek burbling as it coursed over rocks and lapped at its steep banks, and they picked their way along the path beside it.

This was beautiful country, with rolling hills and abundant wildlife, and Tom liked sharing it with Beth, who showed no fear in urging Old Red across the creek and who grinned back over her shoulder at him when he suggested that next time she deserved a more lively horse. "You could ride Daisy. She's a spirited mare. Old Red's good for beginners, like some of the kids in the ATTAIN program."

"It's great that you're going to teach those kids to ride."

"It's part of our program. We'll spend time with them—trail rides, camping, learning appreciation for nature. Many of these kids don't have much chance to interact with men. That's why at-risk teens sometimes turn to gangs for male companionship. Divver and I intend to be good role models for our students."

Beth nodded. "One of the most difficult things about my being a single mother is that there's no male role model for Mitchell."

"What about his father?" He had wondered more than once about Mitchell's desperate request for Santa to bring him a daddy, especially since he already had one.

"Mitchell isn't with Richie often," Beth said.

"Because your ex-husband doesn't want him around?"

"Richie loves Mitchell, I don't doubt that. But Richie has a new family. He's committed to Mitchell for Christmas and a few weeks in the summer, and that's it. He hasn't suggested seeing him more frequently, and I—I admit that I would rather Mitchell be with me. Richie doesn't have the best judgment in the world."

Ironsides had been picking up speed, trying to break into a trot. Tom reined him in because he sensed that Beth wanted to talk. Plus he was curious; he wanted to sound out Beth's true feelings for her former husband.

"Tell me about it," he said, and that was all it took for Beth to pour out the story of Richie's buying Mitchell an electric scooter.

"I agree with Richie on one thing," Tom said. "It's no good wrapping a little boy in cotton batting. You can't keep him from getting hurt some." Fresh in his mind was how he had pegged her as an overprotective mother on that first day at the pancake breakfast.

"I won't deliberately put my son in harm's way. No mother would."

"Boys will be boys, Beth."

They rode along the narrow creekside path, and when Beth spoke it was with utter sincerity. "Tom, if it weren't for Mitchell, I'd be all alone in the world. I—I couldn't face that. He's everything to me. Do you understand?"

He studied her as she kept her eyes focused ahead on the path. "Yes, probably," he said.

She glanced at him and smiled wistfully. "I hope so."

He slapped the reins against Ironsides' neck. "Hey, let's challenge Old Red to keep up. Follow me," he said, taking the lead as Ironsides gratefully transitioned into a trot.

Even though he disagreed with Beth's approach to discipline, he had to admire her intention to be a good mother. He understood now, more than before, why she preferred to err on the side of being too permissive rather than too strict. He personally couldn't imagine what it would be like to be alone except for a little boy. After all, he had Leanne, Eddie and their brood to care about him and also his brother, Bruce, though he lived far away.

It was too bad that Beth didn't have more family. She was a lovely woman, sweet and sincere, hardworking and intelligent. Lately, because of his work with kids, he'd given a lot of consideration to parenting skills and had decided that too many parents didn't take their jobs seriously. Some never showed up for parent-teacher conferences; others didn't realize the value of a family's eating dinner together every night; and a lot of people put themselves first, never mind that their kids deserved priority. Beth wasn't one of those. She was the kind of parent who would always be there for her child, who made him the center of her life. Tom respected that.

In a short time, Beth McCormick had become more important to him than anyone else. He was surprised at how close they'd grown, yet he was comfortable with it, with her. He knew without a doubt that he wanted to find out where this relationship was going. He wanted to make it work.

Chapter Eleven

On Wednesday after she'd picked up Mitchell at the restaurant near Fort Worth, Beth was still unloading his Christmas bounty from the back of her minivan when Tom arrived at her house.

"Hey," he said as he stepped out of the truck.

No matter how often Beth saw him, every time seemed like the first. Her heart would speed up and her mouth would go dry and she'd find herself thinking about the pleasurable intimacies they conducted in private.

"Hi," she said, raising a hand to shade her eyes from the sun slanting across the hills in the distance. Then they just stood there, grinning at each other like fools and unaware of anything else.

Except that now Mitchell was home, and Beth was distracted when her son yanked at the edge of her jacket and asked, "Who's that?"

It hadn't seemed important to discuss beforehand how she would present Tom to Mitchell, but now, as Tom walked toward her in that loose-jointed way of his, she wished they had. She'd accepted this wonderful man's presence in her life—and in the back of her mind, though she knew there could be a problem, she had assumed that Mitchell would, too. Yet Mitchell's forehead was knotted in a frown, and the boy's posture was anything but welcoming. She had to remind herself that even though Mitchell had actually met Tom before, Tom had been dressed as

Santa at the time. The disguise had been so complete that she was certain Mitchell wouldn't recognize him now.

"That's a friend of mine," she answered.

"Oh," Mitchell said.

Tom wore his broad Stetson and was dressed for working at the ranch in jeans, a Western shirt and a worn suede vest. She wanted to rush to embrace him, but, mindful of the two curious eyes watching, she moved forward at a sedate pace and held out her hand. When Tom's hand was securely in hers, when she'd managed to telegraph silently to him that she wanted to take this slow and easy, she turned back toward Mitchell.

He was still frowning, but not so much with displeasure as with concentration. Her son was a handsome boy, and she never ceased to marvel at the expressions that flitted across his features. Especially now, when she and he had been apart for so long. When she had missed him so very much.

"Mitchell," she said carefully, "this is Tom."

"Hello," Mitchell replied uncertainly.

Beth smiled at Mitchell. "Let's finish taking your toys in."

"Can we open the presents Santa left here for me?" he asked.

"You might want a snack first," Beth suggested. "Then the presents, okay?"

"Okay." Her son grabbed a plastic bag full of action figures and headed toward the house.

"I hope you don't mind that I dropped by," Tom said to Beth in a low tone. "I missed you."

She'd only been gone since right after breakfast, but Tom had spent last night with her, and she'd wanted to stay in bed with him a little longer this morning. "I missed you, too," she said as Tom pulled her around the side of the minivan where they were out of Mitchell's line of sight and kissed her thoroughly.

"Um," she said, aroused in spite of herself, "we'd better go inside."

He nuzzled the side of her neck. "Lord, but you smell good."

She pulled away and hauled a plastic crate out of the back of the minivan. "Check out Mitchell's scooter," she said on her way past Tom.

He studied the scooter, which was collapsed flat. "It's something a kid would like," he commented in as noncommittal a tone as he could manage, though he agreed with Beth that Mitchell was a little young to be entrusted with such a toy. "Want me to put it in the garage?"

"Sure. Then come inside and have a cupcake with us." She grinned over her shoulder at him.

When she went to check on Mitchell, she found him dumping his new action figures under the Christmas tree, where they joined the gifts that she had carefully chosen and wrapped.

"You didn't tell me you got a tree," he said in an awestruck voice.

"Well, maybe I forgot," Beth said.

"Can we turn on the lights?"

"Sure." She flipped the switch on the wall that made the tree lights spring to life.

After gazing at the tree entranced, Mitchell glanced over at her. "Mommy, is that man going to stay here?"

"He's going to have a snack with us. I made your favorite green cupcakes last night."

"Oh, boy! I love green cupcakes! Starla said to ask you if you'll give her the recipe for them."

The cupcakes were pistachio, and Beth had no intention of sharing the recipe with a rival for her son's affections. "We'll see," she said tersely as she heard the front door swing open.

"Where is everyone?" Tom called, stomping his boots on the doormat.

"In here." She started for the door.

"Does *he* have to stay and eat cupcakes with us?" Mitchell demanded.

Beth cringed. She knew Tom had heard. "I invited him," she said. Mitchell scowled.

"Join us in the kitchen when you're ready," she told him, keeping her tone light. She left Mitchell staring after her as she and Tom headed in that direction. She supposed that she should have warned Tom to stay away until Mitchell had acclimatized himself to being with her again; he was always difficult after he returned from his visits to Richie's house.

"Help yourself," she told Tom, gesturing at the tray of cupcakes before opening the refrigerator and taking a glass from the shelf so she could pour Mitchell a glass of Cherry 7-Up.

"Do I get some of that?" Tom asked.

"If you like. Or coffee, if you'd rather."

"I'd prefer coffee. Don't bother—I'll make it myself." Tom, of course, was at home in her kitchen by this time.

Mitchell came running with a clatter. He stopped abruptly at the kitchen door and took in the spectacle of Tom measuring coffee into the coffeemaker. His mouth dropped open for a moment before he clamped it shut.

"Mom, is he supposed to be doing that?"

Beth's eyes met Tom's. He regarded Mitchell without saying anything, then took the pot and filled it at the sink before emptying water into the coffeemaker's reservoir, leaving her to handle the question.

"Yes, it's okay, Mitchell. Would you like your 7-Up in your Shrek mug or a glass with ice?"

"In my mug. You told me never to mess with the coffee machine." Mitchell went and climbed on his customary chair. He swung his feet so that one of them would strike the table leg.

Flustered, Beth avoided Tom's eyes. "That's right," she said. "It's dangerous to play with the coffeemaker. Tom is an adult, and he's making coffee for us."

Mitchell didn't say anything, just accepted the mug of soda from Beth and stared at Tom. He continued to kick the table leg.

She brought the cupcakes to the table, as well as mugs for her and Tom. Tom waited until she made a slight motion with her head before he sat at the table with her and Mitchell.

"I guess you got some really nice toys for Christmas," Tom said to Mitchell by way of starting a conversation.

"I sure did. Here, Mom, can you peel the paper off this for me?"

Beth took the cupcake from him and did as he asked, but she was concerned that Mitchell wasn't being polite to Tom. "What toys did Santa bring you?" she asked helpfully.

"I told you. A scooter." Mitchell bit into the cupcake, sending a flurry of green crumbs down the front of his shirt.

"Seems like we unloaded a lot of other things, too," Tom prompted.

Mitchell chewed and swallowed. "Yeah. Starla said I must have been a good boy to get so many toys. Can I really open my presents here after we eat?"

"Sure," Beth said. Then, unable to hold back her irritation, she said, "Mitchell, honey, could you please stop kicking the table leg?" She was feeling the beginning of a headache.

The coffeemaker beeped, and Tom got up. He brought the coffee to the table and silently poured mugfuls for him and Beth before sitting down again.

"Mommy, how come you got a tree? You said we weren't going to have one."

"Tom brought it," Beth told him, thinking that this would surely win points for Tom.

"We had a bigger tree at my dad's house. It had lights that blink and lots more ornaments."

Beth told herself that Mitchell was only five years old, didn't understand that such comments were hurtful, and she busied herself dusting the crumbs off Mitchell's front with a paper napkin.

When he finished his cupcake, a gooey bit of frosting was smeared over his upper lip. He swiped at it with the napkin she handed him. "I'm going to open my presents now," he said, sliding down from his chair and starting toward the living room.

"Wait until I get there, please, and 'Thanks, Mom, for the cupcakes,'" she reminded him.

"Yeah. Thanks." He aimed a grin at her and ran out of the room.

Tom blew on his coffee. He didn't say anything, and Beth felt that she needed to apologize for Mitchell.

"He's tired," she said. "And cranky. Richie let him stay up to watch Jay Leno last night."

"That's okay. Maybe I should have called before I came over."

"No, you're always welcome," she said, at a loss to compensate for Mitchell's rudeness.

"I'd better go," Tom said.

"Wouldn't you like to stay while Mitchell opens his presents from Santa and me?"

"No, I just wanted to make sure you were back safely."

"As you discovered, we are," she said, her tone a bit too bright. She stood when he did.

He squeezed her hand as she walked him to the door. In the living room, Mitchell was hopping impatiently from one foot to the other while he waited for Beth.

"How about if I call you later?" Tom said in a low voice.

"Good idea. Then you can tell me about the meeting you and Divver had with the high school principal."

"It went well. He's solidly behind the ATTAIN program and says he can find sponsors if our kids want to put on a rodeo next year. Not that a rodeo will ever take the place of high school football, but sponsoring one will be a way for these boys and girls to show off what they've learned."

"We'll talk more tonight," Beth promised.

At the door, they ducked behind the wall that blocked them from Mitchell's view and Tom kissed her. She rested her head against his strong shoulder for a moment before he slipped out the door.

"Mommy? Is that man going home?"

She went into the living room, thought how good it was to have her son back here in her own house. "Yes, sweetheart. But we'll be seeing him again soon."

"Oh," Mitchell said before grabbing a present from under the tree and beginning to rip the paper off.

"And, honey, his name is Tom."

Mitchell didn't reply.

Beth sat down next to him on the floor and watched as he opened his first present.

"Oh, boy, Mom, this is great. I can't wait to play with it," he said when he saw the game she'd bought him on the day she went shopping for her teddy. He favored her with a cherubic smile before hauling another present into his lap. "So far, this has been the best Christmas ever. I must be the luckiest kid in the world!"

Well, he certainly was the cutest kid in the world. As Mitchell continued to express pleasure and delight over the presents she had chosen for him, she recalled why she loved being a parent. And not just any parent, but Mitchell's mom.

TOM WAS PLEASED that Beth had invited him to her house for dinner the night after Mitchell arrived home. When he walked in, Mitchell greeted him with restrained friendliness and immediately exhibited more interest in playing with his new toys than in being sociable. After eating the delicious chicken stew that Beth had made, Tom and Beth cleaned up the kitchen together and the two of them went into the living room to talk.

Tom was full of news about his work at the ranch; a corporate sponsor had contributed a large amount of money for new tack, and Tom planned to buy it when he went to Amarillo next week.

"Divver's leaving the outfitting of the tack room to me, since he's got his hands full tearing down the old wooden corrals and putting up new metal ones. They'll need to be finished before the semester starts and the kids arrive."

"Do you have to go all the way to Amarillo to buy horse tack?" Beth asked. She was sitting at one end of the couch, he was at the other. They'd agreed that there would be no touching around Mitchell until the boy had time to get accustomed to Tom.

"A fellow I used to compete against in rodeos said he'll give us a good deal. In fact—"he gazed at her steadily, the better to assess her reaction "—there's an exhibition rodeo there that week. He asked me if I wanted to rope some calves."

Beth blinked, and he realized that he'd alarmed her.

"I figured that your rodeo days were over."

"The days when I rode bulls are far behind me, but calf roping—now, that still has appeal," he said.

He'd told Beth enough about his rodeo days that she understood what was involved—the sleepless nights riding from one place to another, injuries that could sideline a guy for months, the harsh punishment on the body. He didn't care to experience all that again, but he'd been practicing roping since he'd gotten back to town in the fall, and he'd be teaching it to the kids in the ATTAIN program.

"You ride bulls and broncos and all that?" Mitchell piped up from the other side of the room, where he was playing cars and trucks beside the armoire.

"I did, but it was a long time ago," Tom told him.

"I wish I could ride bulls," Mitchell said with a spark of admiration. "Horses, too."

"Mitchell…" Beth began, and Tom knew that she was going to squelch that idea.

He winked. "You could learn to ride a horse, Mitchell," he said. "I'd teach you."

"He's too little," Beth protested.

Tom cleared his throat. "I was riding a pony when I was his age."

"Could I learn to ride? Like a real cowboy? Really?" Mitchell's eyes sparkled with excitement.

"Sure. Anytime your mom says it's okay."

"You don't mind, do you, Mom?" Mitchell scrambled to his feet and went to stand beside her.

"It's a useful skill," she said, hedging.

"You like to ride," Tom reminded her gently, remembering her confidence in the saddle.

"I didn't learn till I was much older," she protested.

"Jeremiah rides a pony. He told me so." Mitchell was clearly envious.

"That's right," Tom said. "I taught him to ride a pony at the ranch. His name's Captain, and he belongs to Amy, Divver's daughter. Amy wouldn't mind if you rode him. She's into bigger horses now."

"That is totally cool," Mitchell said with delight. "Isn't it, Mom?"

"Um, yes," Beth said, sounding resigned. "It's time for you to brush your teeth, son."

"What about riding the pony?"

"Maybe," Beth told him.

"I don't have to go to bed right away, do I?"

"No, after you brush your teeth, you can come out and say good-night to Tom, and I'll read you a bedtime story."

"Okay," Mitchell said. He had abandoned his trucks and cars, leaving them in a jumbled mess, and he galloped away, neighing like a horse.

Tom turned to Beth. "Mitchell would enjoy riding Captain." He didn't add that he hoped teaching Mitchell to ride would help him build rapport with her son so they could get to know each other better. This seemed not only necessary but right, if he was going to pursue a long-term relationship with Beth.

"I still believe he's too young."

"Isn't his birthday soon?"

"January fourteenth. " She paused, looked away, then apparently decided to level with him. "I've told you how I worry that he'll get hurt."

Tom couldn't help it; he broke their no-touching rule. He patted her hand where it rested on her knee, wishing he could run his fingers up the inside of her thigh.

"We talked about this, Beth," he said patiently. "You don't want to make him into a—" He stopped when he saw her forbidding expression.

"A sissy?" she provided.

"I was going to say that you don't want to turn him into a child who is afraid of his own shadow," he amended.

"Mitchell is a spunky kid," Beth objected. "He's not scared

of the dark or monsters in his closet or any of the things that frighten some children his age."

Tom hadn't meant to provoke Beth, and he wasn't in a mood to argue. "That's good," he said, backing off and thrashing around in his brain for another subject.

Mitchell galloped back from the bathroom, pulled in his imaginary reins and whinnied.

"Teeth all brushed?" Beth asked.

"Uh-huh." He pawed at the ground with a foot that was supposed to be a hoof. Tom had to grin. He'd been a horse himself for one whole summer when he was seven.

"Well, pick up your toys," Beth said. "What story would you like me to read to you?"

Mitchell whinnied again, then wheeled and galloped toward his room, where they could hear him rummaging around.

Beth leaned back in the couch and smiled at Tom. "I didn't tell you about my day," she said. "You won't believe what happened. Zelma Harrison called and asked me to make up a new set of cornices, this time in dark green moire. She says she got a new bedspread for Christmas, and she's going to redecorate her bedroom. Keep in mind that those cornices in your house were meant for her, and she didn't take them, which could have cost me money. I haven't decided whether I should charge her a larger deposit this time, demand the full price up front or turn her down flat."

Tom was ready to voice his opinion, but Mitchell had returned and was now clattering around the room at full speed, making all the appropriate horse noises. Tom glanced at Beth, sure that she would again suggest to Mitchell that he pick up his toys, but instead, she merely waited expectantly to hear what Tom had to say.

He cleared his throat. Mitchell neighed, took a leap over the pile of trucks and cars and slapped imaginary reins. "Giddyap," he shouted, working himself into a frenzy.

They had a momentary respite when Mitchell whirled and

headed for the hall, and Tom hoped that the kid would continue into his bedroom, but here he was again, tossing his imaginary mane.

"Whoa, fella," Tom said, attempting to inject some levity into his voice, but Mitchell ignored him.

Nonplussed, he realized that Beth was still waiting for him to reply to her question about the cornices.

"I'd insist that she pay me for them before I ordered anything," he managed to say over the whinnying and neighing and galloping.

Beth put out a hand as Mitchell raced past. "Honey, aren't you ready to go to bed? I'll be in to read your story in a minute."

Mitchell neighed a *no* and proceeded to trot up and down the hallway to Tom's left.

Beth turned to Tom again. "Zelma even had the nerve to ask if I'd give her a discount on the fabric. I told her I wasn't in a position to do that, since it had to be special-ordered."

Tom didn't catch all of that sentence because the noise reverberating off the wood floors and ceiling of the hall, which was furnished only with a long pine bench, was deafening.

Finally, he'd had enough. This lack of control on Beth's part was more than he could take, and it was all he could do not to holler at the boy to knock it off. It was unclear to him how Beth could talk with all the racket in the background, and he couldn't understand how she could have asked Mitchell to pick up his toys earlier but sit idly by while he blatantly ignored her request. If Tom were the parent of this kid, he'd lead him to the pile of toys, wait while he gathered them up and escort him to his room. Then he'd read the story, turn out the light and leave.

Since that didn't seem about to happen, he stood and reached for his hat, which he'd left on the easy chair.

"I've got to go," he said gruffly. "Got an early-morning appointment."

Beth stood, too, her forehead creased in consternation. Mitchell, of course, was still being a horse. A very raucous horse.

Over the din, Beth said, "After Mitchell goes to bed, we could…" She nodded toward her bedroom.

For a moment, Tom wavered. To sleep with Beth's fragrant hair tickling his face, one of her breasts cradled in his hand, was so wonderful. He liked waking up and cooking breakfast for her, surprising her with waffles one day, eggs the next. But he didn't care for what was going on with Mitchell right now, and his instinct was to cut and run.

"Sorry," he said gruffly, wishing he could tell her exactly why he was leaving. That, however, wasn't an option. Someone else needed her attention, and that someone would clearly go to great lengths to get it.

Beth bit her lip, flashing the pink tip of her tongue for a moment, and that almost undid him. Then it was as if shades flapped down in front of her eyes, hiding the person he knew and loved.

The thought set him back a good bit. He had, without thinking, admitted to himself that he had begun to love this woman.

"Well, if you must go, you must," Beth said, but he knew she was troubled about his abrupt leave-taking.

Tom paused at the door to caress her forearm for a minute.

"I'll call you," he said, and she squeezed his arm, too. He didn't like to leave Beth like this, since she appeared so bewildered and so resigned. He read disappointment in her expression. And more.

"Good night, Beth," he said, and then he was out the door, breathing in a huge draft of the crisp night air. Behind him, he heard Mitchell whinny again. The sound only made him feel depressed, a contrast to the customary happy feelings he had when he was with Beth.

He zipped his vest as he walked to the pickup. He was about to spend a long night in his solitary bed, and a definite chill hung in the air.

From the *Farish Tribune:*
Here 'n' There in Farish
by Muffy Ledbetter

Guess who's back from Oklahoma! Little Master Mitchell McCormick was seen helping unload presents from his mom's, Beth McCormick's, minivan the other day. Somebody else was helping, too, but I'll let you guess who that might have been. (Hint: Red suit at Breakfast with Santa.) Mitchell went to visit his dad, Richie, and stepmom, the former Starla Mullins, in their new house in Timmonsville, Oklahoma.

In case you haven't heard, Richie and Starla had a baby last summer. Proud grandparents are Corinne and Allen McCormick of Stickneyville and Billie Jo Mullins of Seattle, WA, formerly of Farish. Ava Starleen is almost six months old and sooooo cute! Starla is one of my very best friends, and she reports that Ava just loves her big brother, Mitchell.

Have y'all seen the new decoration in Gretchen and Wayne Morris's living room window? If not, Ryder by and take a look. (Hint:"You'll shoot your eye out!") Those of you who have enjoyed the movie *A Christmas Story* will get it right away. If you haven't seen this ultimate feel-good film, run right out and get the video now.

I'm happy to report that the Hartzell Christmas Pageant did really well this year. Bernie Hartzell is considering putting on an Easter pageant, as well. Good for you, Bernie.

Did you go to the community carol sing on the courthouse steps? It was awesome, especially Teresa Boggs singing her solo.

Please call in news to my cell phone number, which you'll find at the end of this column.

Till next time, I'll be seeing you here 'n' there in Farish.

Chapter Twelve

The morning after Mitchell pretended to be a horse, Beth settled him in front of the television set with one of the new videos he'd received for Christmas and started picking up the cars and trucks he'd left on the floor the night before. She knew she should probably repeat her request for Mitchell to put them away, but he was happily scooping Froot Loops into his mouth with his fingers, and she didn't want to disturb him. Last night's display of horsemanship had almost been too much even for her.

She was willing to admit to herself that sometimes she was at a loss about how to react to Mitchell's shenanigans. Last night, she hadn't wanted to suppress his creativity. But as his behavior progressed, she had been torn between wanting to clamp down on him, which might provoke one of his tantrums, and letting him continue. She was sure Tom had gone home because of Mitchell's bad behavior.

After Tom had left, she'd finally and in desperation gone along with Mitchell's horseplay, hurrying to the kitchen and getting a sugar cube, then using it to lure Mitchell to bed and allowing him to eat it while she read *My Little Pony*. She should have insisted that he brush his teeth again after eating the sugar, but she was so worn out by that time that all she did was tuck him in and kiss him good-night. He'd replied with a whinny, and she'd switched off the light.

Then she'd fallen exhausted into her own bed and gone to sleep. Alone.

Fortunately, when Mitchell woke up this morning he was a boy again. A cheerful, charming boy, who willingly ate all his breakfast, didn't kick the table leg and quieted down when she asked him if he wanted to watch TV for a while.

Mitchell came in from the living room. "Mom, where's my cowboy hat?"

Remembering how much she'd missed him when he was with Richie, she felt her heart overflow with love. She stooped to his level and caught him up in a fierce hug.

"Mommy," he protested, wriggling away.

"I love you, my darling son," she said. "It wasn't the same around here while you were gone."

Mitchell grinned winsomely up at her. "I missed you, too. Now can you help me find my cowboy hat? I'm going to need it when Tom teaches me to ride the pony."

"I put it on my closet shelf for safekeeping," Beth said, taking his hand. "Let's get it together." It was a felt hat, a miniature Stetson that Mitchell's grandfather had given him. She'd stored it on a high shelf because she worried that he would step on it and ruin it.

"Okay," Mitchell said, and off they went.

At least he was looking forward to doing something with Tom. He wasn't totally against Tom's presence in their lives. That was a hopeful sign.

"How about if I drop by this afternoon and make sure Mitchell understands the finer points of scooter safety?" Tom asked when he called later.

Beth leaned back against the kitchen wall, closing her eyes against the waves of longing that washed over her when she heard Tom's deep voice rumbling over the phone wire. "That would be wonderful. He's been asking when he can ride it, and I've been putting him off."

"I'll be over around three."

"Do you want to stay for dinner?"

A hesitation. "I told Leanne and Eddie that I'd eat with them and the kids. She's making my favorite—meat loaf."

"Oh, well, that's fine. Maybe another time."

"Sure. See you soon."

"'Bye."

"Who was that on the phone, Mom?" Mitchell, wearing his cowboy hat and boots, clomped in from outside, where he'd been romping in the dry leaves under the grape arbor, working off some of his excess energy.

"It was Tom, and he'll be over soon to let you show him how well you ride your new scooter."

Mitchell brightened at this. "Oh, boy," he said. "That'll be fun."

"How about if you and I pick up all those Lego in the kitchen?" Beth asked brightly.

"I don't want to."

"We'll do it together."

"I want to play with my new Yu-Gi-Oh! cards," Mitchell said stubbornly. He started to walk away.

"Not so fast. First, we pick up the Lego, then you can play with the Yu-Gi-Oh! cards."

"Oh, Mom," he said, verging on a whine. But he let her propel him to the kitchen, and they soon had piled the Lego in their box. True, she picked up more Lego than Mitchell did, but at least he was cooperating. Experience had taught Beth that this was unusual when Mitchell had just returned from Richie's.

WHEN TOM'S TRUCK PULLED into the driveway later, Mitchell ran out the door with an excited whoop. Beth, who had been working in the kitchen, followed as far as the doorway, wiping her damp hands on a towel.

"Hiya," Tom said to Mitchell as he slid to a stop.

"Hiya," Mitchell replied, scuffing the ground with his feet. He seemed suddenly shy.

Beth knew she lit up at the sight of Tom. She felt her face flush and wondered if Mitchell would notice. He wasn't particularly aware of her, though. He only had eyes for Tom, who favored him with an easy grin.

"How about if we get that new scooter out of the garage," Tom said.

"Okay. Tom." Mitchell added Tom's name as if it was an afterthought.

"I'll finish my chores in the kitchen and be there in a minute," Beth called to Tom, who managed a surreptitious wink. Beth smiled back. Somehow it wasn't so bad that they couldn't kiss upon meeting when he was letting her know that they were on the same wavelength and that he missed kissing her, too.

In the kitchen, she finished putting away the clean dishes. Through the narrow window, she spotted Tom and Mitchell heading into the garage. Mitchell seemed to have lost his sudden shyness and was chattering to Tom nonstop. Tom nodded gravely, as though he agreed with whatever Mitchell was saying. Thinking that this was a positive sign, Beth pulled on a sweater against the cool winter day and hurried outside.

When she reached them, Tom was unfolding the scooter, and Mitchell located the helmet and was dangling it at his side.

"I rode my new scooter in Dad's driveway," Mitchell was saying self-importantly. "I didn't wreck it or anything. My baby sister can't ride a scooter. She's too little."

"That's right," Tom said with a glance up at Beth, who knew she was frowning but couldn't help it. Mitchell was too young for the scooter, but she was certainly agreeable to Tom's teaching him safety and making sure Mitchell understood how to operate it.

Tom expounded for a couple of minutes on the importance of always wearing a helmet and never operating the scooter unless an adult was present to supervise.

"Daddy says I can ride in the school parking lot near his house on weekends and holidays when no one is there," Mitchell said.

"That's at his house, not here," Beth interjected.

"Right, Mom. Hey, want me to show you how to drive it?" He'd put the helmet on, and Tom fastened the strap for him.

Overcoming her many objections to this toy—if that was indeed what a motorized scooter was—wasn't easy, but she was reminded that Tom was here to oversee Mitchell's riding of the thing and to impart safety hints. She bit her lip, unable to dispel a niggling spot of worry.

Mitchell showed Tom the starter switch, and they turned the motor on. Beth was surprised at how quiet an electric scooter was; the fact that it didn't roar made it less threatening. Tom made sure that Mitchell could work the variable speed control, which he proved able to do, and then Mitchell was piloting the scooter down the driveway, concentrating mightily on his task.

Beth ignored the queasy feeling in the pit of her stomach as Mitchell sailed past the row of junipers and the pecan tree near the walkway, then past Tom's truck, whose tires seemed humongous all of a sudden.

"See, Mom? It's not dangerous at all!" Mitchell yelled. He circled at the end of the driveway and headed back, his eyes bright as he coasted to a stop in front of them.

"He's figured out how to ride it, wouldn't you say?" Tom grinned down at her, and all she could do was nod in reply.

"Can I go to the end of the driveway again?"

"I guess so," Beth said grudgingly.

"He's very coordinated," Tom observed when Mitchell was on his third circuit. He cut his gaze toward Beth. "Have you thought any more about pony-riding lessons?"

"I suppose it will be all right," she said. "If you keep in mind that he's only five."

"Almost six," Tom reminded her with a grin.

"Ponies. Scooters," Beth said faintly. "Like I really need all this."

"Here's what you need," Tom said playfully, tickling her ribs while Mitchell's back was turned. "And this." He planted a hearty kiss on her lips.

She straightened her sweater as Mitchell turned around. "Men," she said scornfully. "They think that's the answer to everything."

"What?"

"Sex."

"That wasn't sex. It was affection."

Beth tried to hide her smile but was totally unable. "Tom, you're pushing it."

"Does that mean we can't spend New Year's Eve together?"

"What do you have in mind?" she asked. New Year's Eve was tomorrow night.

"You. Me. We can go out if you like."

"Where would we go?" she asked. The church sometimes sponsored a get-together for singles, but if such a gathering had been announced in recent bulletins, she'd missed it.

"How about Divver's party? He and Patty are having a few friends over," Tom said.

Mitchell, still thrilled with his new scooter, headed down the driveway again.

"I like the idea of putting Mitchell to bed early and spending the evening alone," Beth told him. She'd felt deprived of Tom's presence lately, and she missed being with him.

"I'd like that, too," Tom said, and she only had to glance at him to be convinced of his sincerity.

In that moment, she knew that she had been worrying needlessly. Everything was the same between the two of them.

She threaded her fingers between his. "We'll talk about it more tomorrow. I could take Mitchell to the park to run and play in the afternoon, which will tire him out so he'll go to sleep early without a fuss. How about a late dinner, and I'll cook something you really like?"

Tom squeezed her hand. "Sounds good."

She smiled at him, pleased and comforted that they were still thinking along the same lines. "Mitchell," she called. "Time to put the scooter away."

"Aw, Mom, no."

"I mean it," she said, but Mitchell only ignored her and summoned up a defiant expression that Beth didn't want Tom to notice. Of course he *would* notice. She had the feeling that nothing escaped Tom where either she or Mitchell were concerned.

"Mitchell," she said sweetly and patiently, "come on now."

Beside her, Tom had gone tense.

"Mitchell?"

"Not yet, Mom."

He kept riding the scooter, disappearing behind Tom's truck.

"All right, only a little while more," Beth called.

"I'm due at Leanne's shortly," Tom said. "Guess I'd better get going."

She turned her attention back to him, detected a certain restlessness in his expression, as if he couldn't wait to be gone. She'd never discerned this in him before. He usually was anything but distant, and she'd always felt his reluctance to leave her. She managed a smile and said, "Right."

He bent and kissed her forehead. "More later about tomorrow night," he said.

"Mitchell," she called with slightly less patience than before. "You have to get out of the driveway so Tom can back out. Let's put the scooter away, son."

"That's right, cowboy," Tom interjected.

Mitchell hopped off the scooter in front of them. "You're going?" he asked Tom.

"Yeah, 'fraid so."

"When will you come back?" he asked.

"It won't be long," Tom said. "See you, Beth." He kept his expression neutral.

"Call me," she said, resting her hand on Mitchell's shoulder. They stood like that as Tom backed the pickup out onto the road and aimed a brief salute in their direction before driving away.

Despite her son's enthusiasm for Tom and Tom's reciprocal interest, she couldn't help but realize that she had fallen short of some mark. She knew it probably had something to do with Mitchell's behavior again.

She supposed she could still try to explain about the lack of boundaries at Richie's house, though she couldn't expect Tom to understand. He wouldn't care about Mitchell's other life; he'd only be concerned that Mitchell wasn't minding now that he was home.

Another option was not to make excuses for her son but to put pressure on Mitchell instead of cajoling him along for the next week or so. Unfortunately, she was afraid to come down too hard on the boy. What if Mitchell, now or at some later date, decided that he'd rather go live with his father? Certainly, Richie could afford to give him more expensive toys—witness the scooter. And Mitchell no doubt found living with Richie and Starla easier, since they allowed him to stay up late, wear the clothes he liked, and who knew what else. She, Beth, couldn't compete with that. These were things that Tom, who had never been a parent, couldn't fathom. He wasn't aware of the underlying layers of this situation.

Well, perhaps Mitchell wasn't a misbehaving child, merely one who took his own sweet time about following her orders. Which, when she allowed herself to admit it for only a moment, might well be considered misbehaving after all.

AS TOM HAD HOPED, New Year's Eve turned out to be a time of reconnection for them as a couple. Beth, true to her word, made sure that Mitchell went to bed right after Tom arrived. Mitchell begged Tom to read him his story, and, unwilling to assume any of Beth's duties unless she said it was all right, Tom waited for her to give the okay. She did, and Mitchell chose a book about a big dog that carried a baby away on adventures in a park. Tom liked the book, and he enjoyed reading it to Mitchell, who listened with rapt attention.

"Someday I'm going to get a dog. I'm going to name him Blackie," Mitchell said solemnly.

"Good for you," Tom said. Every boy should have a dog. He'd owned a series of them, starting when he was about Mitchell's age.

After Mitchell fell asleep, Beth served a dinner fit for a king: beef bourguignonne and yeast rolls that melted in his mouth. Tom had brought champagne, and they finished off the bottle in bed after they'd made love. Curled up together, they watched the big ball drop over Times Square in New York, a place that was far away from Farish, Texas. Not that Tom wanted to be there on this night. He liked being exactly where he was.

They fell asleep as they had before, in each other's arms. But the following morning, instead of surprising Beth with yet another elaborate breakfast, Tom crept out into the early-morning fog, socks on feet and boots in hand so as not to wake Mitchell.

It didn't matter. On New Year's Eve, traditionally a time of hope and looking toward the future, he and Beth had managed to recapture the wondrously happy and connected feelings that had sprung up between them, and he dared to believe that everything was back on track. True, he missed the carefree element of their relationship before Mitchell had returned to the scene, but he was beginning to regard Beth's son in a new way.

THE DAY AFTER NEW YEAR'S, Beth's phone rang around ten in the morning. Mitchell was playing at Jeremiah's house, and she was cozily ensconced on the easy chair in the living room, going over her accounts on her laptop computer. She hoped it was Tom calling, since with Mitchell out of the house, they might be able to get together. But it wasn't Tom; it was Chloe.

"Beth, so glad to catch you at home. Can I drop by for lunch?" Her friend sounded harried and upset.

"Of course. We can have tuna sandwiches. Mitchell is at Leanne's, playing with Jeremiah. What's up?"

"We need to discuss my life plan. I'm in crisis. Grandma is definitely closing the shop."

Chloe had helped Beth clarify matters in her mind when she'd split from Richie, and she wanted to be helpful to her friend now. "I'm sorry, Chloe."

"I'm not. Remember the old saying 'When God closes a door, he opens a window'?"

"You've found a window?"

"Hmm, not sure. But business is slow today, so I'll hang the Closed sign on the front door and come over. Maybe I'll stop by the bakery and pick up some cookies."

"I made pistachio cupcakes the other day for Mitchell, and we still have some in the freezer."

"I feel a specific need for chocolate," Chloe said. "Brownies?"

"Sure," Beth replied.

As she hurried off to open a can of tuna, she reminded herself to ask her friend about Tom Collyer's mysterious past.

"I'VE MADE A NEW YEAR'S resolution to get out of town," Chloe said dejectedly once she and Beth were seated.

"This sounds major," Beth said.

"Well, I've decided that though Farish isn't exactly nowhere, it's certainly within sight of it. Hey, do you think that slogan would look good on a T-shirt?"

"No, but if you go printing up shirts saying that, your departure from Farish might be speeded up. The folks over at the chamber of commerce would run you out of town on a rail."

"The hometown boosterism is another thing that bugs me."

"You were born here," Beth reminded her. "Plus you always discouraged me from leaving Farish when I was at loose ends after the divorce."

"You had a great support team here, Beth. It would have been crazy for you to go live among a bunch of strangers."

"I happened to agree with you, and I've never regretted staying." After Richie left with Starla, the people of Farish had closed ranks around Beth, making it clear that she was one of their own. They had loaned her money to start her business, patronized Bluebonnet Interiors and helped her find quality child care. She couldn't have managed without her friends and neighbors.

"Farish doesn't work for me. I'm bored to pieces lately. The best guys all seem to be married, and the ones who aren't, I don't want to date. After Grandma moves to the new residence-care facility in Kettersburg, I'd like to follow my dreams."

"Which are?" Beth prompted.

Chloe's eyes danced as she finished off her sandwich. "Remember when I went to visit my cousin Gwynne in Florida and came back with all that sea glass that I'd gathered from the beach?"

"What does that have to do with anything?"

She slid a tissue-wrapped package from her purse. "This is for you."

"Hey, we agreed not to give each other presents this year," Beth reminded her, but she was touched.

"You'll like this, I promise. It's a thank-you for being such a good friend over the years."

"Oh, Chlo," Beth said as she unwrapped the box. It was small, and rattled when she shook it.

When she lifted the top, she pulled aside the top piece of cotton to reveal a pair of earrings, two pieces of blue-green glass enclosed in silver cages and attached to hooks to fit through her pierced earlobes.

"You made these?" Beth said, blown away by the delicate craftmanship of the jewelry. She held one earring up, and it swayed gently in the air blowing out of the heating duct overhead. For a split second, it was as if she could actually view the ocean in the pale sand-scoured surface.

Chloe nodded, obviously proud of her handiwork. "That glass is the exact shade of your eyes. The earrings had to be yours."

Beth removed the pearl studs from her ears and put the new earrings on. Her friend handed her a mirrored compact from her purse.

"These are stunning, Chlo. I mean it."

Chloe moved forward in her chair. "Listen to this. Gwynne has gone back to school. Her old house on the beach is vacant, and she's worried about kids partying in the place, vagrants camping out, that sort of thing. She asked me if I'd like to stay there. I'd deal with repairs, make the house appear lived-in and—here's the best part—I'd work on my jewelry. A gift shop in town could sell the pieces I make—at least, that's what they say—and I could market some over the Internet. If I could place some of my more original designs at a couple of Palm Beach boutiques—"

"Chlo, wait a minute! You're going too fast for me. First off, what makes you think you'll be good at home repairs?"

Chloe had the good grace to look sheepish. "I can change a light bulb, and that's about it. But you learned, didn't you? After Richie left? So could I."

Beth couldn't help chuckling as she helped herself to a brownie. Chloe was regarded around Farish as a lovable klutz. "Okay, you're going to become a handyman. I can dig it, I guess. Who do you know in Palm Beach?"

"Only one person, Gwynne's godmother. I've met Patrice once. She owns a store on Worth Avenue. It's *the* place to shop in Palm Beach, and if I showed her my designs…" Chloe let her sentence trail off speculatively.

"She'd fall in love with them," Beth supplied.

"Maybe. Another viable alternative is for me to stay here in Farish and sell Mary Kay cosmetics like my sister. It's been good for Naomi—she's on her second pink Cadillac. But that's not me, Beth. I'd have to stop streaking my hair the color of the month and act like a normal person."

Their eyes locked, and the woman intoned in unison, "No way!" Then they laughed.

"Beth, what do you think?"

"Go for it," Beth said seriously. "Life is short, and you've accepted a big responsibility with your grandmother these past couple of years. This may be your chance to do exactly what you want to do, so why not?"

"Why not?" Chloe repeated softly. She glanced at her watch. "Hey, I'd better get going."

"Not so fast," Beth said, resting a hand on her arm. "I've been waiting since before Christmas to hear the scuttlebutt about Tom Collyer."

Chloe hesitated before settling back in her chair. "Oh, that. I can't believe someone else hasn't told you."

"I'm pretty much out of the gossip loop," Beth reminded her.

"It's one of those things that no one talks about," Chloe said in a hushed tone.

"What things?" Beth asked skeptically.

"People pretend Tom didn't do anything, but everyone knows he did."

"For heaven's sake, Chlo, get to the point," Beth said with more than a hint of impatience.

"Tom had a girlfriend, Nikki Fentress. Tall, brunette, long legs and absolutely gorgeous. They dated during his last year of high school and afterward, and everyone expected them to marry. Then Nikki got pregnant, and Tom skipped town. Left her in the lurch."

"He—what?"

"Tom disappeared in the middle of the night and enlisted in the marines. Nikki had the baby right here in the Bigbee County Hospital and raised the child herself until she married and moved away some years back. The baby would be about fourteen now. An adorable little girl named Angelica."

Beth's head was spinning. "I've never heard a word about this."

Chloe went on. "He denied any responsibility for the baby and never saw the kid—I've got that on good authority. Nikki was bitter about it. I can't say that I blame her, can you?"

Beth wondered why Tom had never mentioned anything about it. "I suppose I don't blame Nikki. It would be a terrible thing to be pregnant and alone. And being a single mom isn't easy." Suddenly, the room seemed airless, and she forced her mind to grapple with this new information.

"You can certainly attest to the struggles of single mothers,

Beth. Though you handle it very well, I might add." Chloe stood up. "Now, I really should run. Hey, are you okay?"

"I'm fine." Of course, Chloe didn't realize that Beth had made Tom Collyer part of her life. Had fallen in love with him, maybe. And this most definitely wasn't the time to tell Chloe that.

Chloe sailed toward the front door. She turned. "Maybe you and Mitchell can eat dinner with us before too long. Grandma would like to visit with you before she moves away."

"Give her my love," Beth said automatically.

"Sure will, and thanks for being my sounding board, Beth. You're a great friend." She hugged Beth before hurrying down the path toward her grandmother's sensible old Volvo, which she was driving these days.

Beth closed the door and leaned against it. Memories flashed through her mind, stringing themselves together in logical strands. Tom had always been vague about his past. Except for brief remarks about his childhood friends Divver and Johnny, as well as a few comments about his family of origin, he'd kept mum. Now she knew why. He probably believed that she'd heard the gossip and liked him anyway.

Tom had become increasingly important to her over the few weeks of their acquaintance. But his newly revealed past was a blotch on his character, and not because he'd gotten his girlfriend pregnant. No, that happened to a lot of people. She herself had been pregnant when she and Richie married. Fortunately, they had been in love, and Richie had wanted to marry her as much as she'd wanted to marry him. But if he had walked away from her at that time, she would have been in a difficult situation. She'd have been alone in the world and penniless, not the best circumstances under which to bear a child.

Beth could imagine nothing worse than being left pregnant by the man she loved—no decent guy would do a thing like that. Although Beth had never met Nikki Fentress, she identified with her as she would with any woman in such hard circumstances.

Tom was clearly not the man Beth had thought he was, and

the last thing in the world she needed was someone she couldn't trust, who wouldn't be there for her when things got rough. She'd already said goodbye to one man like that, and she wasn't about to let another one become part of her life. And Mitchell's.

But perhaps she already had.

Chapter Thirteen

Tom called Beth from his office at the ranch a couple of days after New Year's Eve to ask her if she and Mitchell wanted to drive into Austin with him to pick up teaching materials. He would be leaving on his trip to Amarillo at the end of the week, and he was already dreading how much he would miss Beth while he was gone.

Mitchell answered the phone. "Hi, Tom!" he said, all enthusiasm. "When will you see us again?"

"I've been kind of busy at work."

"Have you decided when you're going to teach me to ride Captain?"

"We could start on your birthday. Would you like that?"

Mitchell let out a delighted squeal. "Would I!"

"Okay, then, that'll be the plan."

"I can't wait. I guess you want to talk to my mom?"

"Sure. Put her on." He avoided using Mitchell's name as much as possible; it was pretentious and ill-suited to this particular boy. In his opinion, a kid deserved a rough-and-ready name, one that pegged him as tough. He was grateful for his own no-nonsense name, Tom. Never Thomas, and not Tommy. Just plain old Tom, thank you very much.

Beth picked up the phone, and he was glad to hear her voice. "How are you doing?" he asked, picturing her in her small house, up to her elbows in fabric samples.

"Fine, though I'm kind of busy at the moment."

Something in Beth's tone and manner didn't feel right, but he was at a loss to figure out what it was. "How about if I phone you later?" He expected her to suggest a good time for him to call back, the way she usually did.

"Sure, if you want."

"I'll be through here before dinner," he said. "I'll touch base when I get home."

"Okay," Beth said, and then she was gone.

He stood staring at the phone in his hand. He felt emotionally flattened because he'd looked forward to offering her the trip to Austin as a treat, and she hadn't even given him a chance to mention it.

FOR SOME REASON, Beth wasn't answering her cell phone, and Tom tried her home phone three times that afternoon before she answered.

"I want to see you," Tom insisted when she finally picked up. He was home now, and he leaned back in his chair to admire the blue print fabric on the cornices that Beth had supplied. He remembered her delivering them to his house, then their spending the night in front of the fireplace, waiting for the ice storm to pass. That had been the beginning of everything, the start of what he had begun to cherish as an important part of his life.

"We just walked in from Leanne's," Beth told him. A door slammed on her end of the line, and she sounded harried.

"What's going on at my sister's? Anything interesting?"

"Margery's science project was the big thing. Mitchell, Jeremiah and Ryan played video games. Britney, the hamster, was having a workout in her plastic ball."

"Anything else going on?"

Beth sighed. "I'm pretty tired today. I'm planning to heat up some leftovers and get Mitchell to bed early."

He lowered his voice conspiratorially. "Does that mean that you and I can also get to bed early? Together?"

A long silence. "No, Tom. I want to crash tonight, grab some sleep."

He couldn't believe that she was putting him off again so soon. Before Mitchell had arrived home from his father's, Beth would have been as eager as he was now. No, that wasn't fair. Maybe all those late nights making love had caught up with her. Maybe she was exhausted. After all, she was busy running a business as well as being a mother.

"It's not easy being a superwoman," he said, hoping to get a chuckle out of her, but his effort fell flat.

"I never said I was," she said stiffly.

"Hey," he said. "Are you all right?"

A long silence followed. "I've got a lot on my mind," she finally said. "I've won the contract to design the interior of the Kettersburg Country Club. That means that Mitchell will be spending even more hours at day care."

"He seems to like it okay."

"He does. It's just the guilt thing."

Tom would bet that Beth spent more time with her son than most single parents; she shouldn't feel guilty.

"Congratulations on the contract," he told her.

"Thanks. I hope you'll understand why I'm feeling pushed for time at the moment. In fact, when you called, I was preparing for my first big meeting with the country club people."

For a moment he considered not asking her to go to Austin with him. If she was so busy, chances were she couldn't. But he wanted to sit beside her in his pickup and be the object of flirtatious glances. Wanted to share a laugh, a confidence. With Mitchell, too, of course.

He cleared his throat. "I'm going to run errands in Austin tomorrow," he said. "I was hoping that you and Mitchell would go with me."

If the last silence was long, this one was even longer.

"I can't, Tom," she said, her voice low. "I'm supposed to be in Kettersburg first thing for the meeting."

"I didn't realize it was tomorrow," he said. For a moment he considered reminding her that he would be leaving for Amarillo soon, but he decided against it. He might come across as pressuring her to duck out on her country club clients, and he didn't want that.

"We'll do it some other time," he said. Then he had an idea and blurted it out without considering whether it was a good one. "How about letting Mitchell go with me to Austin?"

"Just the two of you?" She sounded surprised.

"Sure, why not?"

"I guess it would be okay. I was planning to leave him with Leanne because his day care won't start up again until the public school does, and he could play with Jeremiah."

"I'd enjoy his company."

"What time will you leave?"

"I'll stop by your house around eight o'clock to pick him up. How's that?"

"Perfect." She sounded slightly more like herself now, more cheerful.

"Tell Mitchell I'm looking forward to it."

After they hung up, Tom pinched the bridge of his nose between his thumb and forefinger. Even though Beth had softened up toward the end of their conversation, his built-in problem detector told him that something was definitely wrong here.

Not only that, he was beginning to have trepidations. What if he wasn't capable of entertaining an exuberant five-year-old for a whole day?

WHEN TOM PICKED UP Mitchell the next morning, the boy was fidgeting impatiently on the porch, a big smile on his face. He ran out to the truck, his bright red jacket unzipped and flying out behind him.

"Hi, Tom!" he said. "I wore my cowboy hat. It's like yours." He also wore cowboy boots.

Tom grinned down at the kid, thinking that he was a handsome child, with all that blond hair and those big blue eyes. If he had a son, Tom wouldn't mind if he resembled Mitchell.

"Can we leave now?" Mitchell asked, hopping on one foot and then the other.

Tom had planned to go in and talk to Beth, maybe cadge a cup of coffee, but she appeared in the doorway and waved. "Thanks, Tom," she said warmly. She was coiling her hair up off her neck as she spoke, pinning it in a twist. She was businesslike in a trim navy-blue suit and heels; this was a side of her he hadn't seen before.

"When will you be back?" she asked.

"I'd like to take Mitchell to the zoo," he said. "If that's okay. It means we won't be back until late."

"The zoo! Wow!" Mitchell said. "Can we go, Mom? Please?"

Beth smiled indulgently. "I guess that would be fine. If you really want to, Tom."

"Sure. It'll be fun."

"There'll be monkeys and every stuff. I heard about it from Ryan."

"That's right," Tom assured him.

Beth said, "Drive carefully and have a safe trip. 'Bye, honey. Behave yourself."

"I will, Mommy," Mitchell said as Tom opened the door of the pickup for him.

Mitchell climbed up, and Tom helped him fasten himself in. He was bouncing in his seat as Tom slid in under the steering wheel.

"Next stop, Austin," Tom said, when they were headed toward the interstate highway.

"Can we go to the zoo first?" Mitchell could have passed for a real cowboy in his miniature cowboy hat and boots, and even his foghorn voice seemed kind of appealing.

Tom shook his head. "Not until after lunch."

"Okay." Mitchell tugged at his turtleneck. "I wish Mom wouldn't have made me wear this shirt. The collar hurts. I wanted to wear a cowboy shirt to go with my boots and jeans and hat, but she said no."

"Moms do things like that," Tom said in a tone of commiseration.

"Boy, do they ever. Like my blue suit that she sewed for me. I hate that suit, but she makes me wear it for special occasions."

Tom recalled the velvet outfit that Mitchell had worn to the pancake breakfast. "I don't like to wear suits, either," he confided.

"You could tell her that. Maybe she won't make me wear it if your mother doesn't make you wear yours."

Tom tried not to laugh at this. Mitchell was totally serious. "I'll see what I can do for you," he said, thinking that there were a few other things that he could lobby for on Mitchell's behalf. Like maybe even a dog.

By this time, Mitchell was off on a different subject. "Have you seen Captain lately? Did you tell him I'm going to learn to ride him?"

This topic eventually led to discussions about what real cowboys actually did, how Tom had learned to train cutting horses when he was still in high school and how he'd spent his time in the marine corps.

"Did you really fight a war? Was it exciting?"

"Yes, I fought a war, but it was not fun at all."

Mitchell seemed to accept this, and they talked about how things could be fun but not exciting, which was how Mitchell regarded his kindergarten classes at day care. When they were through exploring that topic, they touched upon Jeremiah and his hamster, and the fact that Jeremiah had named the hamster Britney, which was a much better name than Ava. This reminded Mitchell of his new baby sister, which led to observations about life at his father's house. All of this gave Tom the impression that Mitchell was a relatively well-adjusted kid who was good company when he wasn't showing off to get his mother's attention.

"Hey, cowboy, how about telling me when the sign comes up for exit 234. That's the numbers two, three and four right next to each other."

"On a big green sign like that one?" Mitchell asked, point-ing to the one they were passing.

"That's right."

"Okay, Tom." He leaned forward in his seat, scanning the up-coming exit signs.

Tom relaxed and stopped wishing that Beth could have come with them. He wasn't worried anymore about what he would do to entertain Mitchell all day. He knew now that Mitchell was go-ing to entertain him.

ON HER WAY HOME from Kettersburg that afternoon, Beth stopped at the antiques shop where Chloe worked. As she slid out of the minivan, she noted the handwritten For Lease sign in the front window.

"I guess the sign makes the closing of the shop official?" she asked when she found Chloe arranging a collection of milk glass in a corner cabinet.

"We're out of here in two months," Chloe said as she closed the cabinet door. "Come with me. Before the holidays, we got in some things that might be perfect for the country club."

Beth followed her friend to the warehouse behind the shop, where Chloe showed her a row of elegant old bookcases that had recently been removed from a house scheduled for demolition.

"These will work beautifully for the library at the country club," Beth told her as she ran her fingers lightly over the sat-iny finish of the chestnut wood. "How long can you store them?"

"No problem," Chloe said, making a notation on the sales slip. "We'll have use of the warehouse as long as we need it."

Chloe led the way outside and back into the store through the rear entrance. They threaded their way through a thinned-out in-ventory of beds and dressing tables.

"Have you decided what to do about moving to Florida?" Beth asked her.

Chloe stopped beside a display of depression glass, her expression serious. "If I don't make a break now, I never will de-sign the kind of jewelry I really love."

"I felt the same way about starting my own design business," Beth told her.

"Remember how scared you were? How you worried that you wouldn't be able to make a living at it? That's how I feel now."

"My fears involved being on my own after five years of mar-riage."

"You're doing okay," Chloe said. "That contract for the coun-try club is a big deal. I'm so proud of you, Beth."

"Yes, but—" Beth, remembering how supportive Chloe had been when she was in a turmoil over the divorce, suddenly felt the urge to talk to her about Tom.

Chloe must have sensed Beth's inner conflict because she studied Beth's expression, her eyes going solemn and dark. "Hey," she said softly, "you *are* doing okay, aren't you?"

Beth heaved a giant sigh. "Professionally, yes. But person-ally, I'm not so sure."

"It's nothing to do with Mitchell, is it?"

"Oh, no. It's Tom Collyer." She winced, waiting for Chloe's gasp of amazement.

Beth wasn't disappointed. Chloe not only gasped, her jaw dropped. "Tom? *Collyer?*"

"The same."

Chloe appropriated Beth's arm and slid a dining chair out from under a table. "Sit," she said, indicating the chair. "I can hardly wait to hear."

"We've been seeing each other since the housewarming party at his house. We've—well, it's more than hanging out. It's ev-erything. Eating together, going places together, cooking Christ-mas dinner together, sleeping together. Don't look so shocked, Chloe. People *do* sleep together."

Chloe closed her mouth, opened it again. Closed it. "I remem-ber seeing the two of you at the Christmas pageant. I thought you were with Leanne and her family, had maybe splintered off from the group."

"No, it was a—a date. Go ahead and tell me what an idiot I am. Maybe that's what I need to hear."

Chloe took a deep breath and grinned. "You're not an idiot, Beth. The guy is gorgeous. Those gray eyes like smoke one day, silver the next. That abdomen—rock solid, I bet. What woman wouldn't want a shot at Tom Collyer?"

"I don't need a description of his appearance. I need to be told off and pulled back in line."

"No, Beth. You should have started dating right away after Richie left."

"I wasn't in the mood for it."

"Getting back into the singles life would have done wonders for your self-esteem."

"I have a son to consider."

"It worried me when you decided that the only man with whom you wanted a relationship was a preschooler." Chloe delivered this statement tartly, succinctly, making no secret about her disapproval.

"Don't be so quick to condemn. Most guys aren't nearly as interesting to me as Mitchell. Then Tom Collyer comes along, and all my standards go out the window. I fall hard and then find out he's no better than Richie. My ex-husband left me and his child for another woman. Tom walked out on his pregnant girlfriend. That doesn't say much about the character of either one. Why, oh why, do I keep finding guys with no integrity?"

Chloe drummed her fingers on the tabletop. "I'm not sure that's the case, Beth. Has Tom ever demonstrated that he's untrustworthy?"

"No, he's been above reproach from the get-go. He's seemed like someone I can count on in a pinch, and I can tell from the things he says that he really cares. Mitchell has grown to enjoy his visits—they're on the way to becoming friends. I considered Tom a good role model for my son. But he's still the same person who left Nikki Fentress to bear her child alone, and the whole town knew about it."

"He could have changed, Beth. Why not ask him about Nikki and give him a chance to explain?"

Beth shrugged unhappily. "I might learn too much."

"Which means?"

"You're going to say that I should have confronted Richie sooner about Starla and that I shouldn't make the same mistake again with Tom."

"It's hardly the same situation, but yes." Chloe patted her comfortingly on the hand.

"And if I don't like Tom's explanation, I should break it off now before Mitchell's heart gets broken."

"What about your heart, Beth?" Chloe watched her, eyes steady.

Beth only gazed back at her, unable to reply.

AFTER ARRIVING IN AMARILLO, Tom spoke to Beth once or twice from his motel, and for the most part, the conversations were unsatisfactory. She tended to be in a rush, uncommunicative and distracted. A few times, he managed to get a chuckle out of her, but it was always short-lived. He was growing resentful that she didn't respond to his attempts to draw her out.

The rodeo exhibition took place over a weekend, with shows on both Saturday and Sunday. On Sunday night, he was walking to the parking lot while silently congratulating himself on performing well, when he heard a vaguely familiar female voice behind him.

"Hey, Tom." The tone was seductive, which put him on alert.

He swiveled, squinted into the darkness, then realized that the person speaking to him was a woman who was sauntering along at the edge of a group. She had chin-length dark brown hair and a slightly chunky build, but she walked with the self-assurance of a woman who understood her own sexuality.

She wore a lightweight coat, thrown open to reveal a tight

sweater over her jeans. "You *are* Tom Collyer, aren't you?" she asked as she drew closer.

"Yes," he said. A name flashed into his head: *Dorothy. Dolores?* Something like that.

"We met at a rodeo in Laredo a long time ago. You competed in bronc and bull riding, and I was running the barrels. Dorinda Neville. Or at least that was my name then. I'm Dorinda Hardy now." She waited expectantly.

Tom recalled Laredo; he'd gone there when he was a teenager to compete in the annual rodeo. One of those years after all his events were over, he'd sneaked a few beers with Divver and Johnny and become violently sick to his stomach. A girl who had been tagging around after them all weekend had guided him to her parents' camper trailer at the edge of the parking area, where she'd provided soap and water so he could clean up. Then—oh, wow. He remembered it all now.

The girl was older than he was. Her parents had been off partying somewhere, and he was woozy from the beer, so she suggested that he sleep it off in her parents' double bed. When he woke up, she was beside him under the covers. Naked. And eager.

Dorinda.

"I—well, I do recall something about Laredo," he said.

"We ran into each other a few times after that," she reminded him.

"Dorinda," called one of the guys who had now moved ahead of them, "you going to Poco Loco with us?"

"Meet you there," she called back. She flashed a smile up at Tom, and for a moment, he remembered a girl with skin smooth as silk and dark hair that had swung in his eyes when she leaned over to kiss him.

"Want to go with us?" she asked. "We're going to knock back a few, then call it a night. I have to drive back to El Paso early in the morning—got to pick up my kids from my mother's house."

He fell into step beside her, thinking that the years hadn't been particularly kind to her. He noticed that she wore no wedding ring.

"So what you been doing all this time?" she asked, matching her shorter strides to his long, slow ones.

"Marine corps, Gulf War veteran, have a new venture going." He didn't want to get more specific than that.

Her car was an aging black Camaro coated with dust. She unlocked it and gestured for him to get in.

"Me, I've been married twice. Got a son from the first one, a daughter from the second. Picked the wrong person both times." Her eyes, illuminated as they were by other cars' headlights, reflected sadness.

"I'm sorry to hear that," Tom said.

"You ever been married?"

"No," he said.

"Seems I remember you had a girlfriend last time I saw you…it was a couple years after Laredo."

"Nothing ever came of it," he said. He'd left Farish because he hadn't wanted to defend himself or his actions, and he wouldn't do it now. The pain of what happened with Nikki—and Johnny, of course—had receded to a hard little core deep inside his soul. For a long time that part of him had been like an open wound. After a while it became an ache, then no more than a prickle of discomfort, like a burr under the skin. Now, he realized with a new and surprising awareness, it was merely a scar that he noticed once in a while when something happened to remind him, like Dorinda's remark.

He stared straight ahead at the taillights of the car in front of them. The truth was that the Nikki situation didn't matter to him anymore because of Beth. Because Beth was more important to him than Nikki had ever been. Because he loved Beth.

"Those relationships don't always work out," Dorinda was saying reflectively as they headed down a street lined with strip malls.

At first Tom thought she was referring to the one he had with

Beth, and he was ready to refute her statement. Then he realized
that she meant the kind of romance that develops between two
young people, like his with Nikki.

"I married young," Dorinda said wistfully. "The first time,
anyway. He was a bronc rider. I figured we had things in common. It turned out that he fell asleep after guzzling a six-pack
every night. We were divorced after a year. My second husband
died a couple of years ago. Serious illness."

"I'm sorry," Tom said, and he was. Dorinda had been a beautiful girl once, full of fire and spirit. Now she seemed discouraged and depressed.

"Them's the breaks," she said, rounding a corner into the
parking lot of the bar. She cut the engine and they got out of the
car. He slowed his step to accommodate hers, feeling he was out
of place walking with anyone but Beth.

Inside, they were hailed by her friends and invited to join
them. He and Dorinda crowded around a small table damp with
rings from the bottoms of beer bottles as everyone began to talk
about the day's events, but Tom found his mind wandering before five minutes had passed. He knew that back in Farish, Beth
would be tucking Mitchell into bed now. Afterward, she would
tidy up the kitchen before settling on the living room couch.
She'd watch TV for a while, maybe call her friend Chloe to share
a laugh or two. He hoped she might call him. Maybe she *had*
called him already.

Surreptitiously, he slid his cell phone from his coat pocket
and checked for messages. Only one, and it was from Divver.
He dropped the phone back into his pocket and drained his beer
before signaling for another.

A wheezy country-western band was playing, and couples
were circling the floor. "Let's dance," Dorinda suggested. Before a reasonable excuse came to mind, the band started to play
"Cotton-eyed Joe."

Dorinda brightened. "All right, Tom. No Texan worth his salt
would sit out 'Cotton-eyed Joe.'" A couple of the other mem-

bers of the group stood up, and before he knew what was happening, Dorinda had tugged him to his feet and he was being led toward the dance floor.

He forced a smile and took her in his arms. She was well padded around the ribs, and her lipstick was smeared too thick on her bottom lip. Life had not been kind to Dorinda Neville. Yet he couldn't help thinking about Beth and her hard breaks. Beth had managed to overcome a difficult childhood and an unwanted divorce without becoming cynical or discouraged.

Dorinda eased closer, her breasts pushing against his chest. She wasn't much of a dancer—had no sense of rhythm. She stepped on his foot really hard and apologized, and when he tried to hold her farther away from him, she stomped on his foot again.

He was praying for an end to the task of jockeying her around the dance floor when the band wound up the song and started to play another one, this one much slower. As he prepared to escort Dorinda back to the table, she pulled him closer and rested her temple against his cheek.

"Just one more," she whispered. "For old times' sake."

It wouldn't have been gentlemanly to turn down a lady, especially when she'd asked so desperately, so Tom gritted his teeth and tried to insert more space between them. The heavy scent of her perfume was cloying, and he hated the way she sang the words to the song with her lips beside his ear.

As the music drew to an end, he was itching to leave, but he realized with chagrin that he didn't have a way back to the motel.

Dorinda kept a tight hold of his hand as they walked back to the table.

"Dorinda, I really have to go."

"Oh?" she replied in dismay.

He began to perspire, thinking that he should have planned his escape earlier. "I'm afraid so. I'll get a taxi. It isn't necessary for you to cut your evening short."

"I'll drive you to your motel. Is it nearby?"

He cringed at her eagerness. "Well, I—"

"It doesn't matter. To tell the truth, I'd like to get out of here, too." She grabbed her purse and told the others that they were leaving. No one seemed too perturbed; they all turned back to their conversations, flirtations, drinking.

Great. This was all he needed—a woman who wouldn't give up when he was sending clear signals that he wasn't interested.

He flung enough money on the table to cover his drinks and tried again. "Honest, Dorinda, I don't want you to trouble yourself."

She aimed a too-big smile up at him. "No trouble. Let's boogie out of here."

They snaked their way in single file between the crowded tables. Outside, Tom stuffed his hands in his pockets and walked wordlessly beside Dorinda to her car. It was raining slightly, little stinging drops. She kept up an endless stream of chatter, which was totally uninteresting to him. One of the things he appreciated about being with Beth was that when they conversed, they engaged in a lot of give and take. That certainly wasn't the case here.

"Tell me which direction," Dorinda said as they waited in her car at the stop sign for a chance to nose into traffic.

"Hang a right," he said brusquely. He knew by this time that he should have insisted on a cab.

They rode for a mile or two, the noisy windshield wipers stuttering back and forth in front of them, and he caught her shooting little glances in his direction. Perhaps she was assessing his mood, or worse yet, maybe she was trying to muster the nerve to ask him something.

"I'm at the A-Plus Motel," he said. "It's a ways up the road."

She wet her lips, braked at a stoplight, drew a deep breath. "We don't have to go to your place. I have a room at the motel on the next corner. You could stay there if you like."

Damn. He hadn't invited this, didn't want it. Maybe this was standard operating procedure for her.

"I—" he began. He shook his head and started over. "Thanks,

Dorinda, but I'll have to pass. I appreciate the offer, though."
Sometimes, he knew, you had to tell little white lies in order to
propel yourself over the minor hurdles of life.

Her face crumpled. "Okay" was all she said.

"You can let me out here," he suggested, thinking this might
make it easier on both of them.

She slammed on the brakes and jerked the Camaro over to
the curb. A tractor-trailer rig behind them honked, then passed,
stirring up a whirlwind of soggy litter from the gutter.

Tom heaved a giant sigh and shook his head as if to clear it.
"I'm sorry," he said.

"No, you aren't. Guys never are," Dorinda said bitterly, refusing to meet his eyes.

He slid out of the car and shut the door. Once he was clear,
Dorinda rammed her foot down on the accelerator, and the Camaro shot away from the curb.

Tom pulled his collar up and hunkered down inside his coat
before striking off toward his room. Flickering neon reflected
in the puddles on the pavement, and somewhere he heard a si-
ren. It wasn't such a long way to his motel, and he could use the
exercise. As he walked, he checked his cell phone for messages,
but Beth still hadn't called.

Back in his room, he dialed her number. She didn't answer.
After he'd called her several times, he finally realized that she
wasn't going to pick up. He sat staring grimly at the phone in
his hand for a long time.

He'd been successful in convincing Beth to let down the bar-
riers. But it was clear that now he was going to have to work at
weakening her defenses.

Chapter Fourteen

Her deliberate distancing of herself from Tom didn't feel right to Beth, especially when it came to explaining to Mitchell.

His day-care center was in session again, and Beth had settled into her usual work routine, but she was unprepared for Mitchell's relentless questioning about Tom's whereabouts.

"When will Tom be back, Mommy?" Mitchell asked over and over again.

"I told you, later this week. He's gone to a rodeo."

"I wish he would have took me along," Mitchell said disconsolately.

"Had taken," Beth said absently. She was driving him to day care, her mind on work. She also reminded herself that she needed to phone Richie's parents and ask them if they still wanted her to visit next weekend.

"*Had taken* me with him," Mitchell said. "*Had taken* me to ride the pony."

"He said he would," Beth reminded him.

"He never comes over and lets me ride my scooter."

"He can't when he's in Amarillo."

"We had a good time at the zoo. He can make a face like a monkey." Mitchell made no secret of his admiration for this ability.

"That's nice," Beth said with a sigh.

"You *never* let me ride my scooter," Mitchell pointed out.

"I've had a lot of things going on at work."

"I hate work. Why do you have to do it?"

They'd been through this before. "So I can earn money to buy food and pay for our house."

"Oh. That's right. Why doesn't Tom have to work?"

"He does, honey, every day at Mr. Holcomb's ranch."

"Riding around on horses sounds more like fun," Mitchell observed.

Laughter bubbled up in Beth's throat. "Maybe Tom will show you more about his job when you have your first riding lesson."

"I hope so! I can't wait. When is it?"

"On your birthday, remember?"

"When's that?"

"In five more days."

Mitchell held up his fingers and folded them down one by one. "One, two, three, four, five," he recited.

"That's right." She shot him a cheerful glance. "Your birthday will be here before you know it."

"It seems like a long time," Mitchell said.

Not nearly as long as it seems since I saw Tom, Beth told herself. Since her revelatory conversation with Chloe about Tom's past, she had deliberately maintained her aloofness in preparation for the discussion she planned to have when he returned. She was dreading it, but she agreed with Chloe that Tom deserved a chance to explain before she decided whether to keep him in her life.

"Oh, neat, Ryan's got a hat just like mine!" Mitchell exclaimed as they stopped in front of Nancy's house.

Nancy, dressed for work, waved from the front door. "I have a surprise to show you," she called to Beth. "Wait just a minute. I'll come out to the car."

Beth got out to help Ryan into the back seat.

"Hey, cowboy," Mitchell said to Ryan.

"Hey, cowboy yourself," Ryan said back.

Nancy hurried down the path to the car.

"This is my Christmas present," she said, extending her hand to display her new engagement ring.

It was unexpected, though Nancy and Dennis had been dating for over a year. "Wow," Beth said. "Double wow. That's beautiful, Nancy."

"Thanks," said Nancy. "This makes it official."

Beth hugged Nancy and told her that she was happy for her. Which she was, but as she drove away, she realized that she was more depressed than ever.

TOM WAS IN AN EXPANSIVE MOOD when he arrived at Beth's house after stopping for a few minutes at his own place to freshen up. After returning from Amarillo, he'd called her from there, chatted with her briefly and learned that Mitchell wasn't home yet from day care. This meant that he and Beth would have a few quiet moments before Nancy dropped him off.

He couldn't wait to tell Beth how much he'd missed her. After the fiasco with Dorinda on Sunday night, the scene had gone from bad to worse. The next day, he'd found out that some of the equipment he wanted had been mistakenly sold to someone else, and he had ended up driving all over town to find replacements. On top of that, when he checked out of the motel, the inexperienced but officious desk clerk tried to overcharge him. All in all, he was glad to leave Amarillo behind.

He almost ran up the path to Beth's front door, hoping she would throw it open and envelop him in a big hug. Instead, she sidestepped him when he entered, and he realized immediately that something major was going on.

"Beth?" he said, following her into the living room. "Is everything okay?"

Before she could answer, a car door slammed outside. He glanced out the window and saw Nancy's small sedan in the driveway. Footsteps ran toward the house, and the front door burst open. Mitchell, attired in jacket and cap, entered and slammed the door shut behind him.

"Hi, Mom," he said. He ripped off his cap and rushed over to greet Tom.

"Hi, Tom," he said, clearly expecting a similar welcome from his idol. "Are you here to take me to ride Captain?"

Tom patted Mitchell awkwardly on the shoulder, trying not to show how disappointed he was that he and Beth weren't going to have time alone. "Not today, cowboy. On your birthday, remember?" His false heartiness didn't fool even him.

"Oh," Mitchell said. "That's pretty soon. Only four days."

"Right. I'm glad you're keeping count."

Mitchell grinned at him before handing a heavily crayoned picture to his mother. "I made this in school. Can we put it on the refrigerator? We were supposed to draw pictures of our Christmas presents, and I drew my scooter."

"Sure, honey. Let me help you with your jacket first."

"I'd better go," Tom said gruffly. "You're both busy."

"You're welcome to stay. I—well, I didn't expect Mitchell home so early."

Once divested of his jacket, Mitchell headed for the kitchen. "Can I have something to eat? I'm hungry."

"Wait a minute," Beth called. "I'll be right there." And to Tom she said, "I'll get you a beer."

Since Mitchell was out of sight, he pecked her on the cheek. "I missed you, Beth."

"I missed you, too," she said.

Her slight hesitation made him wonder—why wasn't she friendlier? She seemed wound up and radiated tension.

Mitchell appeared and skidded to a stop in the hall. "Is Tom going to stay for dinner?" he asked his mother.

Tom answered for her. "Not tonight," he said, and started for the door.

"It's okay if you stay," Beth said, but her reserved tone implied that maybe it would be better if he didn't.

"I've already made plans," he said. He was sure she'd assume that he was going to Leanne's.

She attempted a smile, and he left. He hated to do it, but there was no point in sticking around when they couldn't talk privately.

When he was almost to his pickup, Mitchell opened the door and yelled after him. "I'm glad you're home, Tom."

He knew he wasn't mistaking the forlorn undertone to those few words, and he turned and gave Mitchell a halfhearted wave.

As he was backing out of the driveway, he spotted Beth through the sidelight beside the door. She didn't wave, only let the curtain fall in front of the glass. *Some homecoming,* he thought. For a moment he considered turning around and barging back into the house, demanding to be told how he'd transgressed. But this wasn't the time to raise that topic, so he drove slowly home.

"Mommy, are you going to marry Tom?"

Beth almost dropped the plates she was carrying to the kitchen table. "Why would you ask that?"

Mitchell started to swing on the kitchen door. "Ryan's mom is getting married."

Beth still hadn't shaken the sense of sadness that had settled in after Nancy shared her good news. Not to be overjoyed at her friend's good fortune made her feel guilty. And yet, and yet… She *was* happy for Nancy. She was.

"Ryan's mom says they're going to go live in Kettersburg with his new dad. Ryan won't be at my day care after they move."

"You have lots of other friends there, and you and Ryan can play when he comes to visit his father in Farish."

"Ryan's going to have two dads, one he lives with and one he visits. You know, maybe you should marry Tom, Mommy."

"Just because Ryan's mom is getting married doesn't mean I should." She busied herself mixing spaghetti and sauce together.

"I don't think Tom likes us anymore," Mitchell observed. He stopped swinging on the door.

Keeping her back to Mitchell, she said, "Tom likes us just fine." She knew she'd managed to communicate to Tom that they had a problem, and she didn't feel comfortable about the way they'd left it hanging. She certainly didn't want to give Mitchell hints that anything was amiss.

Mitchell hitched himself up on the chair. "Tom looked funny when he left here today."

"Mitchell, get some napkins from the cabinet, please."

"What's for dinner?" He went to do her bidding, which would have encouraged her at any other time. Right now, though, she didn't care.

"Spaghetti and meatballs," she said, taking them to the table.

Mitchell's eyes lit up. "Oh, boy! Meatballs! That's exactly the kind of spaghetti I love!" His enthusiasm bubbled over as he climbed back onto his chair and eyed the food.

Beth felt a rush of love for her son. Even though she was tired and worried about her relationship with Tom, and even though the last thing she wanted to do at the moment was prepare dinner, this was what parenthood was all about. It wasn't all Kodak moments, bright and shining faces upturned in the sun. It was soothing painful earaches in the middle of the night, and struggling to keep a clean house when you'd rather take time for yourself, and being flat-out exhausted so that you couldn't get together with your friends as often as you liked.

But—and she didn't want to forget this—it was also being grateful that for your own particular kid, you were the one who endured those difficulties and inconveniences. And you persevered, no matter what, because you loved him.

She knelt beside Mitchell, who was clumsily spooning spaghetti out of the bowl and getting as much on the table as he was on the plate. "I love you, Mitchell," she whispered, hugging him so tightly that she felt his ribs beneath his shirt.

Mitchell, surprised, dropped a huge glob of spaghetti on the floor. "I love you, too, Mom," he said with a beatific smile, swiveling so that he could place his own cheek against hers.

Except for the spaghetti under the table, it might have qualified for a Kodak moment. She almost laughed, but instead, she kept hugging Mitchell for a long time, and then she went to get a paper towel to clean up the mess.

BETH WAS SURPRISED AND GLAD when Tom called later, and she carried the phone into her room, where she'd be able to talk to him more privately. Mitchell was in the living room, watching TV. She intended to broach the subject of Nikki over the phone; it might be easier to have the discussion if she and Tom weren't face-to-face.

"I was thinking," Tom said in that drawl of his, which always put her in mind of long lazy mornings in bed, of breakfast eaten in a leisurely fashion amid sheets tumbled after a night of lovemaking. "I'd like to cook dinner for you some night at my house."

That might be a good idea. At his place, she and Tom would be able to talk uninterrupted, and after a relaxed evening of good conversation and a few glasses of wine, asking him about his past wouldn't seem so confrontational.

She hesitated, and Tom said, "Well? How about it?"

Mitchell wandered in from the living room. "Is that Tom?" he asked, although he'd been instructed repeatedly not to interrupt her when she was talking on the phone.

"Yes," she said, waving him away.

"Can I talk to him?"

"Excuse me," she said to Tom, and to Mitchell, "You'll get your turn later."

"*Now,* Mommy. I want to ask him something."

Tom couldn't help but hear this, and as if to prove it, he said, "Beth?"

But she needed to deal with Mitchell, who had crossed his arms and stuck out his lower lip—a sure danger sign.

"I'll call you back," she said to Tom.

"Let's at least set a time for dinner," he said doggedly.

Mitchell stood there, immovable.

"Tomorrow's not good," she said, remembering her promise to stop by Zelma's house on her way home from Kettersburg. "I'll call you in a while and we'll decide on a night, okay?"

"Mom? Tom doesn't want to talk to me, does he?"

"Mitchell, hush."

"Beth, if you don't feel like coming for dinner—"

"Mom*my*," Mitchell said, almost wailing.

Beth knew she had to put an end to this. "Tom, I'll call you back. Would you prefer your cell or your home phone?"

"I don't want to talk to that dumb old Tom, anyway," Mitchell yelled, and he ran out of her room, slamming the door behind him.

"Oh, hell, don't bother calling either phone," Tom said, clearly put out by what was going on at her end.

"Tom?"

He had hung up.

This time Beth was really angry with Mitchell. She opened the door and marched straight to Mitchell's room, where he was standing in the middle of the floor, arms crossed, still pouting. He glared at her.

"You're going to bed, young man," she said firmly. "And no story tonight. When I ask you to do something, you're supposed to mind, and it's my job to make sure that you do. It's not good manners to keep talking to me when I'm on the phone. As for the yelling, it had better not happen again."

"I wanted to talk to Tom."

"I told you you'd have your turn later."

"Tom doesn't talk to me anymore," Mitchell said, his lower lip quivering. "I knew he didn't like us. I *said.*"

"Of course Tom likes you," she reassured him. "Didn't he take you to the zoo? Aren't you going to learn to ride Captain?"

"If he likes me, he wouldn't of hung up."

She wondered how to explain to a five-year-old that his own actions had been responsible for making Tom want to terminate the conversation.

She went to the dresser and found his pajamas in the drawer. "Put these on, please," she said wearily. "And brush your teeth."

But Mitchell was having none of it, and Beth sensed a tantrum coming on. She turned down his bedspread, hoping she could get him into bed before he erupted. Leanne, experienced at such things, had advised distracting Mitchell when he gave signs of being tired, stubborn and on the brink of losing his cool. Of course, Leanne hadn't suggested what to do if she, Beth, started to lose *her* cool.

"There you are," Beth said with forced cheeriness. "All ready for you to jump in between the covers."

"I don't want to go to bed."

"Mitchell—"

And then Mitchell lost control. He kicked the nightstand and threw himself on the floor.

"I hate Tom!" he cried. "I hate him, Mommy." His heels pounded the wood floor.

Beth decided not to deal with this irrational outburst; experience had taught her that paying attention to Mitchell's tantrums never made them any shorter or less disturbing. "Please don't say that. Tom doesn't deserve it. Put on the pj's, and I'll be back to tuck you in after a few minutes."

At one time she would have wasted words trying to reason with Mitchell when he was in this kind of mood, but she had learned a better approach. She left her son without a backward glance, ignoring the crying and kicking. Back in her own room, pretending to be deaf to the sounds in the other room, she washed her face, slipped into the T-shirt she wore for bed, and by the time she had done so, realized that the tantrum had ended. She breathed a sigh of relief and decided to give Mitchell a few minutes before going to tuck him in.

She was turning back her own bedcovers, when she heard terrible noises coming from the living room. They sounded like splintering glass, and pounding, and a couple of crashes that she would rather not identify.

She ran into the living room to find Mitchell standing amid a shambles of broken glass and ceramics. He stared angrily up at her, but at least he dropped the toy hammer with which he had wrought such mayhem.

"What have you done?" she cried.

Mitchell only burst into tears.

DURING THE SLEEPLESS NIGHT that followed Mitchell's destruction of much of her precious heart collection, Beth kept thinking about another thing Leanne had once told her: "Whenever you add or subtract a family member, it changes the dynamics. None of us relates to each other in quite the same way." At the time, Leanne had been reflecting on how life at the Novak house changed when Eddie was traveling or Maddy was babysitting Gretchen's kids for a whole weekend. But the observation could certainly apply to the situation with Tom, as well.

Beth had modified her family of two by including Tom, and it didn't matter that he wasn't really a member. By virtue of being part of her life, Tom had upset the equilibrium in her household. No wonder Mitchell was acting out. Being a sensitive kid, he had picked up on her uncertainty about Tom, on her sadness at the possibility of ending the relationship, and he was feeling angry. He was almost certainly upset with her for minimizing his contact with the man he had grown to idolize.

To make things even worse, Tom didn't call the next day or the next. Sick at heart, Beth gave up the idea of a warm, intimate dinner at Tom's house. He was probably out of the notion by this time.

Besides, she had enough to handle within her own four walls. By the next morning when he woke up, a chastened Mitchell had been contrite over the damage he'd done to her heart collection and even drew her a picture of a lopsided heart to atone for his bad behavior. Beth tacked it to the refrigerator next to the one he'd drawn of his scooter, but she also meted out a punishment: Mitchell was not to be allowed to go over to Jeremiah's to play over the weekend or during the week ahead. He was crushed at the prospect but accepted her pronouncement stoically. He clearly understood that he'd done wrong, and he *was* remorseful.

"Can—can Jeremiah come over here?" Mitchell asked, haltingly exploring the limits of his restriction.

"No, not until Friday of next week," Beth told him, circling the date on the calendar so he'd be able to keep track of how many days it was. She hated the way her son's face fell at the prospect of no playdates until then, but she was determined to stick to her guns. The damage to her beloved collection rankled, and it would be a long time before she got over it, even though she knew that, for her own good and Mitchell's, she needed to put the incident behind them and move on.

"I can still learn to ride Captain, can't I?"

Beth wasn't quite sure what to say to that, since Tom had not called back.

"Can't I, Mommy?"

"I'll talk to Tom about it soon," she promised.

But Tom didn't call.

A FEW DAYS LATER, Beth delivered two chairs to one of the model homes in the Hillsdale subdivision, which required that she pass the Holcomb Ranch. On her way back into town, she noticed Tom's pickup parked in front of the bunkhouse, signaling that he was there. Impulsively, she headed down the driveway, bumping over a series of ruts and rocks and past the windmill, on its spindly metal legs, turning slowly on her right. She pulled the minivan up next to Tom's truck and cut the engine. Divver's wife, Patty, waved as she drove by, probably heading to her job at the hospital where she worked as a pediatric nurse.

The temperature today was comfortable, not cold. A hawk wheeled overhead, and Beth heard voices on the other side of the barn where the corral was located. She slowly got out of the car and walked up the path to the bunkhouse. Near the equipment shed, Dallas perked up and trotted over, tail wagging. Beth indulged her in a companionable scrub behind the ears and continued into the bunkhouse. Finding no sign of Tom, she started for the barn.

There, the light from the open door was diffused by the bare branches of the trees outside. Horses in their stalls shuffled and whinnied at her approach. The familiar scent of fresh hay and horse made her feel less restless, less nervous about confronting Tom.

She found him in the feed room, checking off items on a list. His eyes lit up when she walked in.

"Beth," he said, coming to meet her.

"I—I needed to touch base with you," she said, her voice sounding high and uncertain. She swallowed and tried again. "I came to ask about Mitchell's riding lesson tomorrow. He keeps mentioning it."

She detected a momentary flicker of apprehension in Tom's eyes, but he was beaming down at her as if he never wanted to stop.

"I'll pick the two of you up tomorrow after lunch. Is that a good time?"

Beth nodded, not trusting herself to speak. She was overwhelmed with gratitude that Tom hadn't forgotten, that he was planning to honor his promise to Mitchell.

"What's the matter?" Tom asked, his voice full of concern.

"I wasn't sure if you'd be planning to—to—" Words failed her as she gazed up at his expression, at his eyes, at his mouth. His mouth, which was only inches away. Which she inexplicably found herself wanting to kiss in the worst way.

"Tomorrow's Mitchell's birthday. I haven't forgotten." He sounded incredulous, unbelieving that she might have doubted.

All she could do was stare at him mutely.

He took her hand and led her to a bale of hay. He sat and pulled her down beside him. "You thought I'd renege?"

"Not—not exactly," she stammered. And, hating herself for saying it, she blurted, "After the other night, when—when—well, you hung up. We haven't heard from you since."

Tom gazed off into the distance for a moment, then at her. "No," he said softly. "No, you haven't. I guess I have some explaining to do." He clasped her hands in his. "I needed time and space, Beth," he said gently. "It seemed kinder not to call or see you when I wasn't feeling positive about what was going on."

"I understand," she said heavily, and in that moment, she understood things from Tom's point of view. He must feel as if he'd been misplaced in her affections by her son. He didn't have any idea what else might be going through her mind.

Tom brushed a tendril of hair back from her forehead. "We haven't been apart very long, Beth, but I've been going through acute withdrawal. I'm not a poet, and I don't say things in a fancy way, but—" He lifted one shoulder and let it fall. "I want to make things right between us. I'm sorry I hung up. I should have called you back immediately, but, well, I've got a temper and sometimes it gets the better of me."

Now her tears really did spill over. She swiped at them with the back of her hand. "I didn't want to stop by here today, but I had to, for Mitchell's sake."

"I'm glad you came. Beth, I'm sure we can work everything out. About us, I mean." He pulled a bandana from his back pocket and dabbed at her cheek.

He stood and drew her up beside him, then planted himself squarely in front of her and wrapped his arms around her. It felt to Beth like a welcome, like stepping into a warm familiar place where when you go there, they have to take you in.

She found comfort in his strength, listening to her heart beating against his. His shirt smelled like sunshine and the outdoors. She closed her eyes, willing herself back to the time when everything had been so easy between them. Tom kissed her, gently at first and then more passionately, his beard rough against her cheek. He held her tightly. When, after a while, they relaxed their embrace, she was trembling and longing for more. Right here, in the barn on the hay with the horses nearby and Dallas outside, thumping her tail in the dust. She was shaken at the passion that drove her desire.

Even more of a revelation was her certainty that she'd never felt this way about anyone else. This new person that she had become was a stranger to her. And to everyone else, no doubt, including her son.

"I want to be with you tonight," Tom murmured in her ear. "It's been too long."

"After Mitchell goes to bed," she said in a rush. "Come over. I'll be waiting."

"How about asking Leanne if Mitchell can spend the night with Jeremiah? She probably wouldn't mind."

Quickly, Beth explained that Mitchell was on restriction. "I can't let him go to Jeremiah's house when I already told him he couldn't, but I want to be alone with you."

"We'll manage it. Phone me after Mitchell is asleep, and I'll sneak over in the dark of night. We'll have a secret tryst." He smiled mischievously.

"Tom," called Divver from the direction of the corral. "Hurry out here and give us a hand, will you?"

"Be right there," Tom shouted back.

"I'd better go," Beth said. "I'm supposed to pick Mitchell and Ryan up this afternoon."

"You have a lot of obligations," he said, "and mine are going to increase in the next few weeks as we rev up for the students' arrival. Don't worry, Beth. You're high on my list of priorities, and—well, if you're worried about Mitchell and me, don't be."

She merely stared at him, glad he was saying this but unsure how to react.

"Your son is part of you, Beth. I get along with him just fine. Like I said, we can work it out. Together."

"Together," she said, and it seemed a magical word, with the power to make everything right.

He kissed her forehead. "I'll be over tonight."

"Tom!"

It was Divver again, sounding impatient. "I'd better go," Tom said.

She held on to his hand until the last moment and stood watching as Tom headed out into the bright sunshine.

Not until she was halfway home did she realize that she'd forgotten all about mentioning Nikki. And in spite of all her doubts, the question didn't even seem relevant anymore.

From the *Farish Tribune:*
Here 'n'There in Farish
by Muffy Ledbetter

Amy Holcomb hosted a party at the skating rink in Kettersburg last week for her Sunday-school class at the First Church of Farish. Attending were Necie-Lizbeth Eubanks, Jennifer Morris, Alisyn Morris, Tara Clark, Emily Weiss, Margaret Wesloski, Jenny Ballinger, Rosie Cerratano and Sophie Pell. A good time was had by all.

As in every January, we have a whole bunch of people on our sick list this week: Teresa Boggs and Joe Gomez have colds, and Teresa's mother, Elsa, went to the hospital with pneumonia last week. Get well soon, Elsa. We miss your smiling face behind the counter at the hardware store. Doc Walter Lewis was down with the flu, but he's back on schedule now. If you missed an appointment because of a cancellation, call Miss Betty in his office and she'll set you up.

This week's column is short because I've got a whopper of a sore throat myself. Don't forget to call in your news to my cell phone, and leave a message if I don't answer. This week, until I feel better, I most likely will not be seeing anyone here 'n' there in Farish.

Chapter Fifteen

That night after Mitchell was asleep, Beth left her front door unlocked for Tom and waited for him in bed. She was dozing when she heard the latch click, and she came half-awake. His skin was still cold with the chill from outside when he slipped naked into bed beside her.

"Warm me up," he whispered as she turned toward him.

She felt her nipples tighten as his leg slid between hers. The hair on his chest tickled her cheek, his rough hands stroked her skin and he buried his face in her long, loose hair. It was so good to touch him like this, to feel him, to inhale him. His hands, creating the most wonderful friction, moved down to her buttocks to caress her with hunger and exquisite tenderness. She closed her eyes, feeling his breath blowing hot against her shoulder. She'd yearned to be with Tom like this every night, wanted to wake up to his smiling face every day, and longed with her whole being to make love with him whenever she wanted.

"Beth," he murmured. He wasn't cold now; she could feel the heat emanating from his body as she kissed him, his hardness pressing against her.

"Oh, my dear Tom," she said, opening to him on a gasp of pleasure, and quickly, surprisingly—just like that—he entered her, filled her, made her whole again. For their bodies to be joined seemed so natural, so right. In those moments, there was nothing in her world but Tom, the two of them one.

With a clarity that had previously escaped her, she knew that she and Tom were meant to be together, were supposed to be doing this. They had been created for each other, and this mutual passion of theirs could empower them to live fully and meaningfully. This was a profound revelation, whose significance only enhanced her experience.

Afterward, he held her for a long time, his breathing slowly returning to normal. She felt the tears swelling in her eyes, drawn from the well of deep emotion that had been tapped as they'd made love.

Tom noticed the dampness on her cheeks. "Are you okay?" he asked tenderly. "I didn't hurt you, did I?"

She shook her head. "They're happy tears," she said. "I love you so much, Tom. So much—" Her voice cracked, almost broke, but they were words that she had to say. Wanted to say. Needed to hear.

"I love you, too, honey."

"You're not just saying that because I did, I hope." She spoke with trepidation.

"No, Beth. I should have told you a long time ago."

"We only met before Christmas," she reminded him, feeling utterly content and fulfilled. Tom loved her. She loved him. It should be so simple, really.

He nuzzled her ear. "I fell in love with you at the pancake breakfast when I spotted you in that cute little elf suit."

Drowsy but amused, Beth put that statement away for future reference, but she smiled. She was so tired. "I'd better get to sleep. Tomorrow's going to be a busy day."

"Rest easy, honey," he said as he stroked her cheek. "I'll be gone when you wake up."

"Sorry," Beth murmured, but it was the way things had to be. Mitchell would come bouncing in first thing in the morning, and he didn't need to find Tom there with her.

TRUE TO HIS WORD, when she opened her eyes in the morning, the only evidence of Tom's presence the night before was his belt with the silver longhorn buckle, which he had evidently forgotten in his haste. Mitchell, who galloped noisily into her room at seven, wearing his cowboy boots and cowboy hat with his pajamas, recognized it immediately.

"Tom left this," Mitchell said, clearly mystified as he picked up the belt from the floor.

"Uh, well, it does resemble his, doesn't it." Beth was mortified, but she reassured herself that Mitchell wouldn't understand enough at his age to put one and one together and get two in her bed last night.

"It *is* Tom's, Mommy. I remember the longhorn on it."

"Mmm," Beth said. "You'd better give it to me and we'll return it to him today when we see him at the ranch."

Mitchell relinquished the belt without further comment. "Yippee! I can't wait to go horseback riding."

"Happy birthday, sweetheart. Happy six years old." She mussed Mitchell's hair even more than it already was and recalled the day she'd given birth to him. The long painful contractions and the controlled breathing had exhausted her, and at one point she was sure it was never going to end. Finally, with Richie at her side, the doctor had held Mitchell up and said, "It's a boy, Beth. Richard, you have a son," changing their lives forever for the better. Richie had been so relieved and happy that it was all over, and she had been overwhelmed with love when the nurse settled Mitchell in her arms. No moment before or since could compare with it for sheer joy. Even though things had gone terribly wrong later, she and Richie had done something right. They had made Mitchell.

Oblivious to her musings, Mitchell rattled on. "I hope Captain likes me. Will he?"

Beth had already started for the kitchen. There, she coiled Tom's belt and shoved it deep into her purse, which was hanging on the kitchen doorknob. "Of course he will." She poured cereal into a bowl and set it on the table.

"Ryan doesn't believe I'm going to ride a horse. He thinks I'm fibbing. You'll tell him, won't you, Mommy?"

"Right," she said. She scooped coffee into the coffeemaker and switched it on before taking a bagel out of the freezer for herself.

"Can I get dressed? And open my presents?"

She'd invited Ryan and Jeremiah over for tacos, ice cream and cake tonight; it was to be Mitchell's birthday party. She hoped Tom could come, too. "We should wait to open your presents when the boys and Tom are here. And you haven't finished your breakfast."

"I'm not hungry. I want to get ready to ride Captain." He slid down from his chair. "Can I wear my Shrek T-shirt? And my favorite jeans?"

That meant the pair with the tear in the knee, but Beth knew it wouldn't matter to Tom. "Sure," she said.

Mitchell went whooping down the hall, and Beth realized that she was in for a difficult morning of dealing with a rambunctious kid. Still, the afternoon would be fun, since she would be spending it with her favorite guys, Mitchell and Tom.

WITH MIXED FEELINGS, Tom watched Beth and Mitchell climb out of the minivan. On the one hand, he wished he could spend the afternoon alone with Beth. On the other, he warmed to the way Mitchell's eyes brightened at the sight of him.

Mitchell broke into a run. "Hi, Tom," he said. "Today's the day!"

Tom didn't know how it happened, but one minute Mitchell was running toward him, and the next his arms were outstretched toward the boy and he was swinging him high in the air. Mitchell laughed with glee before Tom returned him to the ground.

Dallas came bounding up, wagging her tail. She almost bowled Mitchell over, so they had to be introduced. Mitchell backed off when Dallas tried to lick his face, but after a few seconds of uncertainty, he threw his arms around her and embraced her wholeheartedly.

"I like this dog," Mitchell said as Dallas slurped at his cheek with her tongue. "Mommy, when can we get one?"

"Not yet," she said. She bent and scratched Dallas behind one ear, and the dog closed her eyes in bliss.

Mitchell refused to give up the idea. "Ryan's going to get a puppy, and his mom is going to stop being a teacher when she gets married. If you got married, you could quit your job, too."

Beth flushed and assiduously avoided Tom's eyes. She'd told him once that she'd never close her business. She'd worked too hard to give it up. He'd assumed that she meant that she'd want to keep working if she got married, but neither of them had steered the discussion in that direction. Now he was overwhelmingly curious about Beth's inclinations in the matter, and he wished he'd pressed the issue.

This wasn't the time, however. "Want to tour the Holcomb Ranch, Mitchell?"

"I sure do."

The three of them walked side by side toward the bunkhouse, where Tom held the door open for the two of them before following them in. He showed Mitchell the classroom as well as his office and Divver's. Mitchell's eyes widened with interest when Tom pointed out where the cowboys' bunks used to be.

"Maybe you and me and Jeremiah and his dad could camp out here in front of the fireplace some night like I used to when I was a kid," Tom suggested. "We could bring sleeping bags and make a pot of cowboy stew for dinner."

"You mean it?" Mitchell asked, eyes shining.

"I'll suggest it to Jeremiah's dad," Tom promised.

"What's cowboy stew?"

"We brown hamburger in a big pot, and then everyone adds a can of something, and we let it simmer over the fire."

"I'll bring a can of chocolate pudding," Mitchell said seriously. "That's my favorite canned thing."

"Maybe you'd better ask your mother what she thinks about that before you go shopping." He winked at Beth, who only smiled.

Dallas was waiting for them outside the front door, and Mitchell walked beside Tom with his hand on the dog's neck.

On the way to the barn, Tom got in a few important pointers about how the riding lesson would proceed. Beth followed behind, watching and listening.

In the dark recesses of the barn, Captain nosed at the door of his stall. The stocky little brown pony always perked up when kids appeared because he understood that he'd be getting some exercise.

Mitchell was wide-eyed as Tom saddled the pony and explained how the cinch held the saddle on.

"You've got to keep an eye on Captain," Tom told him. "Sometimes he'll inhale a lot of air, then blow it out later so the saddle will loosen."

"Pretty smart pony," Mitchell said.

Tom demonstrated how to mount Captain from the left side and how to hold the reins. He insisted that Mitchell wear a safety helmet, telling him that even though Captain was gentle enough for a beginner, it was best to stay safe.

"Like when I'm riding my scooter," Mitchell added, catching Beth's eye. His face was losing the contours of babyhood, developing planes and angles that she was sure hadn't been there a few months ago. To watch him changing into a man little by little, day by day, was bittersweet. Both of them, she and Mitchell, were changing.

She followed Tom, and Mitchell on the pony outside and braced herself against the fence, basking in the pleasant warmth of the midday sun.

"Mommy, I'm riding a horse! I really am!"

Beth put her hand over her eyes to shade them. Tom had allowed Captain, on a lead line, to pick up his pace a bit. "You look like a big boy up there on that pony," she said.

"I am, Mom. I'm six years old now, just like Jeremiah."

Tom grinned at Beth, and she smiled back. After last night, she felt comfortable with him again. The business about Nikki had receded to the back of her mind and seemed much less important. Tom had remembered Mitchell's riding lesson, and that had gone a long way to reassure her that he was responsible and considerate. She pushed away the voice of caution that continued to nibble at her consciousness. With Tom and Mitchell getting along so well, she had no interest at this moment in pursuing something that could destroy their relationship.

WHEN TOM WAS THROUGH with the lesson, he demonstrated how to remove the bridle and saddle, then how to rub the pony down before closing him in his stall. Mitchell hung on every word and ran to Beth after he'd fed Captain a carrot as a reward.

"I rode a horse, Mommy. Tom, can I have another lesson soon? Can I?" He grabbed Tom's hand as they walked back toward the parking area.

"Sure, cowboy. How about next Saturday?"

"Can I, Mom? Please?"

Tom addressed Beth. "Next week you and I could saddle up Ironsides and Daisy, the mare I told you about. Mitchell would do fine on a short ride up the trail."

"That sounds like fun."

"Really? We're gonna ride out like cowboys do?" Mitchell was bouncing up and down as they walked.

"That's right," Tom told him, and the statement sent Mitchell into a dither of excitement. He ran over to Dallas, hugged the dog, started whirling like a dervish in the path.

"Mitchell, slow down," Beth cautioned. He ignored her and tore off toward the bunkhouse, slapping his hand along the slats of the picket fence as he ran. Not to be outdone, Dallas started to chase him, barking all the while.

"Mitchell," Beth called. "Come here."

He heard her and looked back, but he kept running. Tom waited for Beth to inject more firmness into her next request. But despite her apparent discomfort with Mitchell's behavior, it was not forthcoming. After another minute or so of commotion, Divver stepped out of the bunkhouse. He spotted Mitchell and narrowed his eyes.

Tom decided to act. He cupped his hands to his mouth and called to the boy. "Mitchell, your mother said to stop that."

Mitchell, unaccustomed to the sternness of Tom's voice, halted. He turned toward Tom, his confusion clear. He stared for a moment, then switched his gaze to Beth.

This was a pivotal moment. If Beth showed signs of wavering, Mitchell would probably continue his annoying behavior.

Beth set her lips into a firm line. "Come over here, son, and thank Tom for the riding lesson. Shake hands with him the way I taught you." Her tone was kind and gentle, and Mitchell responded immediately by walking purposefully to Tom and extending his hand.

"Thanks, Tom. I really had a good time. I like Captain."

Tom gripped the small hand in his large one. "I'm pretty sure he likes you, too. I'll be over to your house in a while for tacos, okay?" Out of the corner of his eye, he spotted Divver dodging back into the bunkhouse.

Mitchell grinned. "You bet. I'm going to open my presents then. We'll have cake and ice cream afterward."

"Can't wait."

Beth took Mitchell's hand and smiled at Tom. "Is five-thirty okay?"

"Perfect."

He sneaked a kiss from her as Mitchell was climbing into the van. "Am I spending the night?" he whispered.

"I hope so." She rummaged in her purse and slid his coiled belt into his hand. "You forgot this."

"Oops," Tom said sheepishly. He flicked his eyes toward Mitchell, who wasn't paying attention. "Any fallout?"

Beth shook her head and got into the minivan. "Thanks, Tom."

"No problem," he said, because there wasn't. Mitchell had proved to be an attentive riding pupil, and Beth had stayed in the background throughout, as a parent should. Best of all, she hadn't interfered when he'd corrected Mitchell. She'd seemed to welcome it.

As he watched Beth drive away, he thought about how much

he'd enjoyed the afternoon. Once she was out of sight, he walked into the bunkhouse. Divver glanced up from his paperwork and treated Tom to a long grin.

"Things must be moving right along between you and Beth if you're stealing kisses."

"Yeah, well, she's great."

"And the kid?"

"Nice kid," Tom said.

"Tom, I heard him and saw him."

"Mitchell, well, he's got a few things to learn, but Beth's working on it."

"You brought him to heel quickly."

"He needs a firm hand sometimes."

Divver squinted up at him in the fast-fading light. "Is everything okay with you, Tom?"

"Sure," he said, though if Divver had asked him the same question a week ago, he probably would have poured out his concerns.

"Well," Divver said, getting up and shoving the papers into a folder. "Guess I'd better get back to the house and start cooking up some burgers for Amy and me. Patty's working tonight."

Tom hesitated at the door. "Divver, you've been married a long time."

"Fourteen years and counting."

"Is a monogamous relationship always like it is with Beth and me now? You grow apart, you pull back together, you go along for a while and everything's fine, and then the whole process starts over again?"

Divver clapped him on the back. "You've described it to a *T*, man. Patty and me—we're accustomed to times that aren't so easy. The key is that we love each other enough to ride out the difficulties."

Tom considered this. In the past, he'd allowed his experience with Nikki to define all women for him. Not until he met Beth did he learn that women had many facets—companion, sex partner, mother, playmate. During the long interim between Nikki and Beth, he'd never understood what women were all about or why he'd invite one into his life on a permanent basis. He'd contented himself with shallow, short-term relationships that went nowhere—but they weren't enough anymore.

He tucked his fingers in his belt loops and leaned against the door frame. "Thanks, Div. You've convinced me to ask Beth to marry me."

Divver stared, then broke into a wide smile. "I never thought the day would come when you'd settle down again with one woman. After Nikki, I mean."

"Me, neither." Tom rubbed his jaw, studied the faraway hills through the window, then focused on Divver's smiling face.

"Good luck. Any idea when you'll be popping the question?"

Tom replied in a jovial tone. "We're not even what you might call going steady yet."

"You'd better find out if she'd even entertain the notion. From what I've heard, her boy always comes first."

"You told me that."

"Well, good luck, Tom. Let me know how it goes."

After Divver stumped up the hill to his house, Tom set off toward home, feeling sure of himself and of Beth. As for Mitchell, the kid liked him. And he'd grown fond of the boy.

One thing, though. No way could he keep calling Mitchell by his given name. A kid didn't need a handicap like that to ruin his life. He should be called Mitch. Or something like Skip or Chip or Bud. Now, there was a fine, masculine name. Bud.

Tom began to run other possible nicknames through his head, but he had enough sense not to settle on any one in particular. He'd better consult Beth about it first.

BETH HAD MADE TACOS for the birthday boy and his friends, and after they'd driven them home and Mitchell had fallen asleep, Tom and Beth made love late into the night. As he had before, he left at the first light of dawn, rolling his pickup silently down the slope to the road and turning on the engine when he was well away from the house. Tom agreed with Beth that Mitchell didn't need to know he slept with her; this time, he made sure that he didn't leave his belt on Beth's bedroom floor.

He hadn't had a chance to talk to Beth about formalizing their relationship, whether by declaring that he wanted an exclusive arrangement, or by becoming engaged, or—well, whatever she wanted as long as they were together.

The discussion would have such importance that he wanted to initiate it when they couldn't be interrupted. On Sunday afternoon, he asked if he could stop by for a visit, but she'd already promised Mitchell they could go to the park. On Monday, she called to tell him that Mitchell had a cold and she was making him chicken noodle soup; she seemed distracted, but she told him she loved him.

"I love you, too," he said, the words sounding natural and right.

The next day Mitchell developed an earache and had to go to the doctor. He couldn't go to day care, so Beth had to take time off from work to stay home with him. Finally, on Thursday, Beth called to say that Mitchell was feeling much better and that on Friday night he was going to celebrate the end of his restriction by spending the night with Jeremiah.

"Does that mean I can stay over and not have to worry about waking Mitchell?" Tom asked hopefully.

Beth laughed. "It certainly does. Will you fix me one of your big breakfasts the next morning?"

"Yes, honey. I can't wait."

"Neither can I," she said.

On Friday night, when Tom stayed at her house, he and Beth returned to their pre-Mitchell degree of freedom. First, they went to Zachary's for burgers, and when they got back to her house, she lit a fire in the fireplace and popped a video into the VCR. Afterward, they lay on a blanket in front of the TV, feeding each other s'mores, which Beth hurriedly assembled from ingredients in her pantry. After making love, they nestled together before the glowing embers and fell asleep, waking intermittently to kiss and whisper endearments all through the night.

When Beth woke up, Tom was already cooking breakfast in anticipation of what he wanted to discuss.

Over the breakfast table, as Beth sat across from him, her hair still wet from her shower and so beautiful that his breath caught in his throat, he decided that it was now or never.

"Beth," he said, "we have to talk. I've been waiting for just the right time, and I'm not sure this is it, but I'm not willing to put it off any longer."

She stared at him, slowly lowering a bit of biscuit to her plate.

"I want us to—uh, well—the term used to be going steady." He felt suddenly abashed. "That sounds silly for two adults, but what it means is a commitment. Exclusivity. More later, if we mutually agree."

She gaped at him. "Like being engaged to be engaged?"

"You could say that," he said, gazing deep into her eyes and not sure that he understood the uncertainty reflected there. "I love you—you love me. For me, what we have together is meaningful and important. If it isn't serious with you, you should tell me."

"Oh, Tom. Of course I love you, but I have a lot to consider before making a commitment. Mitchell. My work. Everything."

"Yes," he said.

"There's something else, Tom," she said, avoiding his eyes.

A new and unidentifiable undertone made him wary. "What are you talking about?" he asked.

"Nikki," she said softly. "Nikki Fentress."

The last thing he had expected, when laying the groundwork to propose to the love of his life, was to hear the name of his former girlfriend. "I'm not sure how that factors into this," he said slowly.

"I can't stop thinking about it. About her predicament." Beth's expression was resolute, pained. Clearly, she didn't like talking about this any more than he liked hearing it.

He shifted uneasily, playing for time, trying to understand

what bearing Nikki had on their situation. "Maybe you should tell me what you've heard."

"She was pregnant. You enlisted in the military and left her to bear the child alone."

Through his growing anger, he couldn't help noticing that Beth was gripping her mug so tightly that her knuckles had turned white. She was tense, she was worried and he wanted to hold her in his arms and comfort her. But overriding those feelings was another more basic one—defensiveness. In the marines, he had learned that he didn't have to take anything from anybody. He had become as tough as he needed to be, a characteristic that had served him well. Because of his previous history, he couldn't help but interpret this as a hostile situation.

His answer shot back, uncensored and gruff. "Yeah, she was pregnant. I joined the marines. And yes, she bore the child alone. It's true." He felt his face flush and knew he couldn't do a thing about it. He wanted nothing more than to forget about Nikki. She was the past, and what he longed for now was a life and a future and some kids with Beth.

Who was studying him as if he were a specimen mounted on a slide. "You admit it. You left her when she was going to have a baby."

He pushed back his chair, unable to contain his anger now. "That's what they say. That's what you heard."

"Yes." The word was little more than a whisper.

He strode to the window overlooking the peaceful backyard, saw the Afghan pine that he'd bought her and that they'd planted together a few days after New Year's. His head jerked around when he spoke. "I stayed away for fifteen years. I wonder why I came back. These Farish folks never forget anything, do they?" He bit the words off sharply, not caring that Beth's face crumpled before his eyes.

"Good people live here, Tom," she said, stricken.

He shook his head. "This place was a gossip mill before I left, and it still is. I should have stayed in the service." He walked to the back door.

Beth stood. Her face had taken on an unusual pallor, and her eyes pleaded with him.

"Don't go," she said. "We should talk this out."

"Not now," he said, unsure whether he was more furious with her or with the suffocating mores of a small town. Well, maybe his anger was for the way everyone around here always knew everyone's business. But Beth had settled into Farish, Texas, and accepted the town's shortcomings. She lived by its moral values and defined her life by its parameters. That made her part of the problem.

Despite his love for her, he couldn't stand to be confined within these walls any longer. He wanted to break free for a while, saddle up Ironsides and embark on a long ride into the hills. Consider whether his love for her meant that he'd have to accept this town for what it was.

He slammed out of the house, Beth's pinched face so impressed on his consciousness that he'd have a hard time focusing on the other things. Still, he kept walking, climbed into his pickup truck and drove away. His gut churned. He knew he should have gone back to Beth and taken her in his arms, but at the moment he didn't care.

On his way out to the ranch, he passed landmarks familiar since he was a kid: the pond in the county park, the five-way stop where the highway diverged into a bypass, the historical marker where the first settlers in this county had built their cabins, the steel girder bridge over the slow-moving river. They reminded him of all the things he loved about Farish, and the realization that his roots were so deep here only plunged him into a deeper funk.

Even so, he kept seeing Beth's face and recalled the love shining from her eyes when she bent to talk to Mitchell or instruct him. Tom knew the same love encompassed him, and that was no small thing. He found it amazing, really, that Beth cared about him at all.

Damn, he was tired of being alone in a world of couples and families. All he really wanted was to be with Beth and Mitchell. The only thing that counted in life, when it came right down to it, was a good woman and the chance to create something worthwhile. He didn't want to waste his life searching for something he'd never find. He wanted to grasp this special happiness and make it his own before it was too late.

But because he couldn't bring himself to face Beth yet, because talking about Nikki was hard for him, he kept driving.

Chapter Sixteen

After Tom left, Beth cried.

She sank on her bed and sobbed uncontrollably. Why had she confronted Tom about Nikki? That episode in his life was over and done with, she knew that. Anything that she had hoped to gain by bringing it up was lost.

And yet she'd had to ask him. Had needed to find out why he'd left Nikki when she was pregnant with his child. Had hoped that his reaction would somehow reassure her. Perhaps he'd had good reasons for abandoning her. The last thing she'd expected was for him to fly off in a huff after criticizing the gossips here in Farish.

A honk sounded in the driveway, and she spotted Leanne's SUV. Mitchell was climbing out of it, pulling his overnight bag with him. She'd almost forgotten that he was due home so that they could head out of town for their overnight visit with Allen and Corinne.

"Hi, Mom," Mitchell said as he walked in. She bent over for a kiss, only to be confronted with a puzzled stare.

"Your eyes are all red," Mitchell said.

She pretended to ignore this statement. "Did you have a good time?"

"Uh-huh. Jeremiah's hamster rolled around in her exercise ball all night long. Me and Jeremiah fed her lettuce for breakfast."

"That must have been fun," she murmured as she trailed after Mitchell on the way to his room.

"Yeah, and I can't wait to see Grammy and Grampa today. I'm going to tell them about riding Captain."

"They'll enjoy hearing about your lesson. How about helping me pack your things for our trip?"

"What do I take?"

"Just put a few shirts and jeans in the duffel. Oh, and some underwear."

"I can do that." He stood watching her where she leaned against the door frame of his room. "Is something wrong, Mommy?"

"I—no. I've been very busy getting ready to go. Just—just— put your things in your duffel like I told you."

She went into her bedroom and began to rummage through her drawers. She missed Tom and wished he could be there to comfort her, but realized right away that it was a futile hope. An overwhelming sense of loss enveloped her as she tossed clothes into her overnight bag, and she debated whether to call Tom on his cell phone. When she reminded herself that her name would pop up on the call screen and he had the option of not answering, she decided against it.

At least she would have the visit with Allen and Corinne to distract her. Perhaps, like Tom earlier, she needed some time apart.

AFTER HIS RIDE IN THE HILLS, Tom simmered down to the point where he regretted having walked out on Beth that morning. He'd triggered at the thought of her listening to gossip about him, because that was precisely why he hadn't returned to Farish for years and years. He hadn't been able to stomach the idea that people were talking, Nikki was saying nothing to stop their rumors, and he'd been the bad guy.

That was only the public perception of him, however. The real story was something that only Divver knew. Even Patty, Divver's wife, hadn't been told the truth.

Now, Tom realized grimly, Beth should be informed about what really happened with Nikki. If Beth didn't believe him, they didn't have enough trust to proceed with a permanent relationship. This would be a test.

He drove over to Beth's house that evening, realizing that it was too early for Mitchell to be asleep. It didn't matter. After this morning, he knew that Beth would put Mitchell to bed as soon as it was practical and that she'd want to hear what he had to say.

He stood hat in hand on her doorstep and rang the bell repeatedly. He'd offer an abject apology, and if he was lucky, she'd accept it. He was counting on Mitchell to smooth over any awkward moments.

But no one came to the door. Even though it was almost dark, the only light inside was the small night-light that Beth kept in the foyer.

Then he recalled Beth and Mitchell were going to spend tonight with Richie's parents, and he cursed himself for being so forgetful.

For a moment he lingered uncertainly, considered leaving her a note and decided against it. He would come back when she was here, and he'd talk to her then. That would give him more time to frame his story in suitable words, to develop some eloquence in the telling of it.

She would understand when she heard what he had to say. He knew she would.

TOM'S TRUCK WAS PARKED OUTSIDE her house when Beth and Mitchell returned on Sunday afternoon from their visit to Stickneyville.

"Tom's here!" Mitchell exclaimed in delight as she pulled up, and at that moment Tom rounded the corner of the house with a wide smile on his face.

"Tom, I'm glad you came," Mitchell called, running to him immediately.

"Hello there, cowboy," he said, ruffling Mitchell's bangs, but his eyes remained on Beth as she got out of the minivan.

She advanced toward him, unsure of herself.

"Can I ride my scooter, Mom?"

"Sure, Mitchell. It's such a nice day that Tom and I can sit out here under the grape arbor and watch you."

Mitchell ran toward the garage, and Beth and Tom followed.

"I forgot you went to Mitchell's grandparents', and I stopped by last night. I wanted to apologize."

Beth kept her eyes on Mitchell's blond head. She didn't reply.

"I'm sorry, Beth. I shouldn't have left in such a hurry. I want to explain now, if you'll listen."

Beth unlocked the garage door with her key. Before she could lift it, Tom did, and Mitchell went immediately to his scooter.

"You don't have to help me," Mitchell objected when Beth picked up his helmet and handed it to him. "I can do everything, Mom."

"Be careful. Don't go too fast."

"She always says that," Mitchell told Tom. "That's because she's a mom."

"That's what moms are for," Tom agreed.

They watched while Mitchell headed up the driveway past the pickup and the minivan, his hair fluttering out from under his helmet, then Beth gestured toward the grape arbor.

"This will be a comfortable place to sit," she said.

Tom sat on the bench and stretched out his legs. "It's time to tell you about Nikki and me," he said.

"Go ahead." She clasped her hands around her knees and focused on Mitchell in the driveway. "I'm listening."

He blinked up at the sky, at the bare tree branches overhead, and began the story.

BACK WHEN NIKKI had been Tom's girlfriend, he'd been eager to become a rodeo star. At first his friends were as keen on rodeo life as he was, but before long, Divver fell in love with Patty, who hated everything about the rodeo and convinced him to quit, and Johnny sustained a leg injury that kept him out of competition for almost a year.

Even though Tom missed his buddies while traveling the circuit, he didn't mind going it alone. He made new friends, and he won enough bronc-riding and calf-roping contests to make a name for himself. He envisioned becoming a media star in the up-and-coming sport of rodeo, copping some lucrative endorsement contracts and making a decent living. Someday, he and Nikki would get married.

Nikki had been supportive of his career, but from the beginning, she was impatient with the time frame. "You expect me to wait a couple of years? While you travel around getting famous?" She wasn't happy, to say the least.

Tom had always dealt with Nikki's pouts by coddling her and making things as pleasant as he could. Nikki didn't have much of a home life. She lived with her father and her sister in a small run-down mobile home on the ranch where her father worked. One day when Nikki was twelve, her mother had ridden a bus out of town, taking all of her husband's money and nothing else, not even pictures of her two daughters. Her family never saw her again.

"We'll be married as soon as we can," Tom told Nikki whenever she got in one of her moods. He'd built a sizable bank account, and his savings would provide the down payment for a house.

"I hate living with my family," Nikki said.

"In less than a year, you'll be my wife," he promised. "You'll be the most beautiful bride Farish has ever seen."

"I'm going to have eight bridesmaids and a dress with a long train," Nikki told him. "Everyone in Farish will be there."

Tom went along with her fantasy. "When you walk down the aisle in that white dress, baby, I'll be the happiest man alive." He meant it, too.

Competing in rodeos required that he was almost always out of town on weekends, and although Nikki joined him sometimes, often he was too far away for her to make the trip. He justified his absences by saying that his rodeo winnings were important to both of them and to their future. When out of town, Tom was scrupulously faithful to Nikki. To take advantage of his growing prestige on the circuit by hooking up with any of the pretty girls who were available never occurred to him.

Nikki wasn't the type to sit home alone. Sometimes Divver and Patty invited her out with them to a roadhouse or a party, and occasionally Johnny, who didn't have a regular girlfriend, squired Nikki around town. Tom didn't mind. He was happy that Nikki was having fun.

Then, one night after he'd been traveling in Utah and Colorado for a month, when he and Nikki were parked at the local lovers' lane, she tearfully told him that she was pregnant. He was stunned. "But—but I always took precautions," he stammered in bewilderment. He'd never wanted to jeopardize their future by taking chances, and she knew it.

Even in his shock, he recognized something cagey about the glances she was giving him. Something calculated and shrewd— characteristics that he didn't associate with Nikki.

"Maybe I wanted to get pregnant," she said. "Maybe I'm tired of waiting to get married."

"Nikki, I—"

At that point, she threw her arms around his neck and started to cry. "Oh, please, Tom, let's just run away. Then we'll always be together."

The false note that he had detected earlier had become even more apparent with these histrionics. When he hesitated, in a turmoil about becoming a father, Nikki got hysterical and accused him of not loving her. Nothing could have been further from the truth, so, sick at heart, he calmed her the best he could, and by the time they drove up to her house, she wasn't crying anymore.

"Can you come over tomorrow?" she asked as he walked her to her door.

"I'll call you first thing."

"If we got married now, we could live in an apartment over my uncle's gas station," Nikki said. "It's vacant."

Tom knew the place, and it was a dump. "Let me sleep on this," he told her. "I'm still in shock."

"Want me to pack a suitcase? It's so romantic to elope."

She seemed so pathetically eager that he didn't want to ask what had happened to the goal of the big wedding and the white dress, so he only kissed her good-night and left. He hadn't felt like going home after Nikki's unsettling news. Feeling in need of male companionship, he drove to Dolan's, the roadhouse where he was sure he'd find Johnny and maybe Divver.

Divver wasn't around, Johnny said, because he and Patty were attending some family function. Johnny, with his arm around one girl and another hanging all over him, had been drinking heavily. Tom recoiled when he realized how drunk Johnny was, and he pried his friend away from the two women, thinking that he'd better pocket Johnny's car keys so that he couldn't drive home. As the two of them finished their beer, Tom talked Johnny into going outside to the parking lot for fresh air.

"Hey, bro, where's Nikki tonight?" Johnny asked while lighting a cigarette. The flame from the match flared, illuminating his handsome features.

Tom hesitated. "I dropped her off at her place a while ago," he said finally.

Johnny raised an eyebrow. "Nikki doesn't like to go home early." Everyone knew that she spent as little time there as possible.

"Yeah," Tom replied. He couldn't stop thinking about Nikki's news. He'd like to have kids someday, sure, but not now.

"Tom, is something going on with you two?"

He should have known better than to confide in Johnny. But at the time, he wanted to get it off his chest and he expected Johnny to console him.

"She's pregnant," he said quietly.

"She is?"

Tom nodded. "I was so careful."

Johnny seemed to turn this over in his mind; then, showing his agitation, he flicked his half-smoked cigarette onto the pavement. "You might have taken precautions, but not everyone did," he muttered in a voice so low that Tom almost didn't hear him.

Tom froze. Surely he'd mistaken what Johnny had said.

"No offense, Tom. Don't get mad. But you're not the only guy who, um, knows the pleasures of Nikki's charms. I've thought about telling you for a while, but I never had the nerve."

"What?" Tom said.

"Hell, man, she's been with me, she's been with guys she picked up somewhere, guys passing through town."

"Nikki wouldn't do that." A rage began to build inside Tom.

"Well, if that's true, how would I know about that little tear-shaped mole way down low?"

Johnny smirked, and that did it. Tom was well acquainted with that mole, and it was located where no one would find it unless…

His rage blossomed into a fury, exploded in his brain. For the first time since they became friends back in first grade, he hit Johnny. Punched him smack in the jaw and knocked him cold.

Leaving others to tend to Johnny, crazed by what his friend had said, Tom jumped into his truck and tore back to the mobile home where Nikki lived, pounded on the door until she appeared and unlocked it. He wrenched the door open, scaring her. He didn't hurt her. He would never hurt a woman, and he loved Nikki more than anyone. But he yelled and accused and told Nikki what Johnny had said. She confessed tearfully, and when he informed her that the engagement was off, she became angry, too. She drew herself up and taunted him.

"Oh, you're hot stuff, Tom Collyer, aren't you. Well, it's not yours, do you hear me? It's not yours! My baby is Johnny's. You weren't man enough to get me pregnant, but Johnny was."

As much as he didn't want a baby right now, as disgusted as he was by her cheating, he still loved her and couldn't believe that she had willfully destroyed their relationship. But he read the truth in her eyes; and worse, her scorn for him and her pity.

He rushed out the door and embarked on a week-long drunk in the old homestead cabin at the Holcomb Ranch. Divver brought him food and water and kept his presence a secret.

Divver volunteered to act as intermediary between him and

Johnny, but Tom wouldn't allow it. Making peace with Johnny was his last concern. He was grappling with how he was going to get over Nikki and panicking over what he would do with the rest of his life now that his dreams were shattered.

He awakened one morning and realized that as long as he stayed in Farish he'd be seeing Nikki around town, growing larger with Johnny's baby. He considered, when he was finally stone-cold sober, that he might want to marry her anyway and raise the child as his own. Her infidelity, however, was something he couldn't stomach, and he knew that in his heart he would never trust Nikki again.

That night, he left Farish, and the next morning, he enlisted. He didn't go home before he was shipped off to boot camp, didn't come back for Johnny's funeral. The sad conclusion of the story was told to him by Divver: When she'd learned that Tom had left, Nikki had confronted Johnny at Dolan's, where he and Divver were hanging out, informed him she was carrying his child and begged him to marry her, saying that she'd loved him all along. Johnny had laughed in her face. Then, while Divver was trying to calm Nikki, Johnny had stolen somebody's new Corvette from the parking lot and roared away without fastening his seat belt. Shortly afterward, he'd crashed into a bridge abutment while traveling ninety miles an hour. He was killed instantly.

Nikki, bitter and embarrassed because Johnny hadn't wanted her, had done nothing to refute popular opinion that her baby was Tom's and that he'd left her after finding out that she was pregnant. Divver had begged to spread the true story after Johnny died, but Tom wouldn't let him.

In the end, it seemed more honorable to let Nikki say what she would. If what Divver subsequently heard around Farish was true, the father of little Angelica could have been any one of half a dozen guys, as Johnny had said.

It didn't matter. By that time, Tom had embarked on a satisfying military career, and when, after years of absence, he finally came back to Farish, it was only for a few days now and then to visit Leanne and her growing family.

Nikki raised her daughter alone until she married and moved away, which happened years before Tom's return to his hometown. For a long time, Tom had thought about her every day, and he'd gone on loving her in spite of what she'd done.

But now, that was over. He'd finally moved on with his life. He'd found Beth, and his future was with her.

"SO NOW I'VE TOLD YOU what really happened," Tom said earnestly, taking Beth's hand. "Yes, I walked out on the woman I loved, but I didn't abandon my child. Nikki wasn't the aggrieved party in that situation—I was. But I chose the high road. I decided to do the gallant thing, even though it ruined my reputation around here."

Beth stared at him. "I can't believe you let people go on thinking it was your baby."

Tom shrugged. "I was far away from home. I didn't care what Nikki said, and I'm not sure she passed along a whole lot of information. Because we'd been together for years, people surmised her baby was mine. They talked. I hated them for it, but what if her child wasn't Johnny's, either? Should I have exposed Nikki to her friends and family for what she really was? It didn't seem like the right thing to do to a girl who'd already had a miserable life and was faced with raising a baby on her own."

Beth turned his hand over, studied the lines on his palm, then closed her eyes briefly and made herself concentrate on all the things he'd said.

"Last summer, I quit the marines to come back to Farish because when I heard what Divver planned to do with the kids in the ATTAIN program, I wanted to be part of it. I found that as I grew older, as I had even more ties here with Leanne's kids, I couldn't go on letting people in Farish think I was no good. Working with at-risk teenagers seemed like a good way to regain my reputation."

"You should tell people the true story, Tom." Beth concentrated on sitting quietly, her backbone straight, her expression as neutral as she could make it.

He blew out a long breath. "There's a young girl named Angelica out there somewhere. Nikki is her mother, and I don't want Angelica to find out anything bad about her mom. I hope they're both happy in their family situation. I heard that Nikki had a couple more kids after she got married, and maybe she managed to create the kind of family she always wanted. I don't want to hurt Nikki, ever."

"You sound as if you suspect Angelica might be your child after all," Beth said, suddenly worried.

He rushed to set her straight. "I knew Angelica wasn't mine. I hadn't even been in town when Nikki got pregnant. Consulting a calendar made me sure of that, and I always took precautions. Eventually, paternity tests proved I wasn't the father. I insisted on finding out for sure because I gladly would have contributed financial support to any child of mine." He paused, his eyes searching hers. "You believe me, don't you, Beth?" He seemed to be holding his breath as he waited for her reply.

She answered slowly, considering every word. "I never did believe you were the type of guy who could abandon someone who was going to bear your child."

"I love you, Beth. Only you. I should have told you about Nikki and me a long time ago, but I kept putting it off. I figured that you'd probably heard the rumors and that all those things that happened back then didn't matter. It was such a long time ago."

"True. Oh, Tom, I'm glad you told me." Relief flooded through her as she realized that at last she was free of all doubt.

"So am I." He stared off into the distance for a moment, then seemed to pull himself back from whatever he was thinking. "I guess I've talked too much. Is there anything you want to say? Anything else I need to clear up?"

Beth shook her head mutely.

He slid a hand up and around the back of her neck, leaning toward her so that their foreheads touched. "Whew," he said. "I can't tell you how glad I am that you know the truth. How about if you leave the door unlocked for me tonight and we finish our discussion then?" He smiled down at her.

208 Breakfast with Santa

"I'll be waiting," she said.

He stood, and she rose with him. He kept his arm around her as they walked toward his pickup. When they reached the truck, he hugged her. "We're okay? You're okay?"

She closed her eyes and rested her forehead against his chest. "Yes," she murmured. This was her man. He was a decent man. That was all that mattered at the moment.

Mitchell zipped past them on his scooter. "Tom! Are you going home?"

Tom let his arms drop. "Yep, that's right. Your mom's going to fix your supper, and you both have things to do."

Mitchell pulled up beside them. "I'm not ready to quit riding yet."

"You can have about ten more minutes," Beth said. "Then we'll go inside."

"Okay, Mommy. 'Bye Tom." He started to get back on the scooter.

"Wait a minute," Beth said hastily, restraining him. "Tom's going to back out of the driveway, and you'd better stay right here with me until it's safe."

"He can watch out for me—right, Tom?"

"You'd better stay with your mother like she says."

"It'll take a while to get back into the swing of things here," Beth told Tom with a meaningful flick of her gaze toward Mitchell. "Allen and Corinne have different rules at their house." Spending time with them, as she had on several other visits, she'd noticed how lax they were about certain rules. In fact, she had grown to understand how Richie could have turned out to be so irresponsible; his parents hadn't held him to any standards, and if Beth would allow it, they'd let Mitchell do anything he wanted when he was with them.

"You'll handle it," Tom told Beth.

Beth and Mitchell both waved as Tom turned onto the road, and after his pickup was out of sight, Beth went into the garage to sort a pile of carpet samples that she'd stored there. Only a

few more minutes remained until it would be too dark to let
Mitchell continue to play outside, and she figured she might as
well put the time to good use.

As she tossed some pieces of carpet onto a pile to put in her
minivan and another to send back to the manufacturer, she kept
running Tom's story through her mind. She could well imagine
the scene with Nikki when she'd told Tom she was pregnant; it
could have been Beth and Richie. That was where any resemblance to her story ended, however. She couldn't condone
Nikki's attempt to force a man to marry her by getting pregnant
by his best friend. This was deceit of the worst kind. Now that
Beth knew the way it really was, she didn't identify with Nikki
at all. All her sympathies were squarely with Tom.

She gathered up the carpet samples. They'd better go inside
so she could start supper.

Because of the way the minivan blocked her vision, she
hadn't realized that Mitchell was riding his scooter in loops at
the end of the driveway and that some of them overlapped the
road. As soon as she realized that he was in forbidden territory,
she called to him sharply.

"Mitchell! Let's put the scooter away."

He looked back at her, all smiles. "Just another minute, Mom."

She was all too familiar with that tone. It was the way he
spoke when he knew he could coax and charm her into giving
in. He was heading back toward the street.

"Mitchell—" she began, intending to tell him that he was to
put the scooter in the garage right this minute. And then her heart
stopped.

Barreling around the curve in the road was a red coupe. And
her uttering Mitchell's name had caused her son to turn his head
so that he didn't see the car bearing down on him.

Before she even heard the terrifying squeal of the car's brakes,
Beth dropped the pieces of carpet and began to run. If she could
get there fast enough, she'd be able to pull Mitchell out of
harm's way.

But she couldn't. Forever engraved on her brain would be Mitchell's expression of shock and fear when he saw the car, the ashen face of the driver as she swerved to avoid the inevitable, and the horrible *thud* of Mitchell's body before it flew through the air.

Chapter Seventeen

Mitchell's small frame was dwarfed by the big hospital bed, and he was so pale. He was hooked up to a variety of machines in the intensive care unit and had an IV needle in his arm. Beth felt as if she were living a nightmare, but at least she wasn't alone. Tom had arrived at the emergency room almost immediately; Patty Holcomb, who worked in the hospital's pediatric unit, had called him as soon as she'd heard from a friend in the ER that Mitchell had been admitted. Chloe hurried over and Leanne stopped by.

Don Weiss, a local doctor whom Beth knew from church, had been grave. "Beth, I'm afraid that Mitchell has a brain concussion. We've done X rays and a CT scan. The good news is that he doesn't have a skull fracture, only a contusion of the scalp that required sutures. He's not out of danger, of course. We'll be watching him so that if he develops a brain hemorrhage, we can deal with it promptly. Brain damage is also a concern."

"Brain damage," Beth repeated, devastated.

"We're hoping for the best. He also has two broken ribs. We have a good team taking care of him, and we're doing our best. Of course, if necessary, we can always move your son to Austin for medical care, but right now we're confident that we can deal with his problems."

Though his words didn't provide her with any certainty, Beth had taken heart from his reassuring manner. Dr. Weiss was a highly respected physician in the community, and she trusted him.

Now she sat amid the machines and the tubes that were supposed to save her son's life and tried not to panic. She'd knelt beside Mitchell seconds after the car hit him, and by that time the shaken driver had already been dialing 911 to ask for help. An ambulance had arrived within minutes, and the crew, two of whom were acquaintances, had been professional and kind. She'd ridden beside Mitchell all the way to the hospital while the medical techs worked to keep him alive. He hadn't regained consciousness, and she was terrified that he never would.

She couldn't seem to take her eyes off his face. Mitchell was as beautiful as a sleeping angel, and if not for the large bandage on his head and the fact that they'd had to shave off some of his hair, he might have been merely sleeping. If only he'd give her some sign that he knew she was there—if he'd just open his eyes! But maybe that was asking too much. She prayed that he'd go on breathing, that none of the monitors would start beeping to signal something terribly wrong, though at the moment, nothing was right. Mitchell was just a little boy. He wasn't supposed to be lying here all waxy pale and silent. He should be laughing and running around and making too much noise. And now she didn't know if he would ever be able to do those things again.

"Beth." Someone touched her shoulder, but she was so numb she almost didn't feel it. She looked up blankly, expecting Mitchell's doctor.

It was Patty Holcomb, who couldn't have been more kind and caring during this ordeal.

"Why don't you go out for a while and get something to eat, Beth. Tom's brought you a sandwich from the cafeteria."

"I couldn't," Beth whispered, stricken at the thought of leaving her son alone in this frightening environment. What if he woke up and she wasn't there? What if he needed something?

Patty smiled reassuringly. "Go on. I'll stay right here with Mitchell, and his nurses are nearby. You have to keep your strength up."

For whatever ordeal is to come. Beth silently finished the sentence for Patty.

"Come on." Patty slid an arm around her and helped her to her feet. For the first time, Beth was aware of her bloodstained clothes.

She cast a worried glance back at Mitchell. "You'll find me if—"

"Yes. Tom is in the private waiting area near the elevator. You can be alone there."

Beth made herself move her feet toward the small room at the end of the hall. She went directly into Tom's arms to be comforted by his stalwart presence.

"Oh, Tom, I'm so scared." She sighed, and he smoothed her hair and said that everything would be all right. Beth wasn't sure that it would be, but it was good to have someone to tell her so.

He produced a canvas bag that Chloe had dropped off, and it contained a change of clothes for Beth. She went into the nearby rest room and put them on, sure that she'd never wear the bloodstained slacks and shirt again. Then Tom tried to convince her to eat, and she managed to force down half a chicken sandwich. After she'd finished eating and drinking a cup of hot tea, Allen and Corinne, grim expressions on their faces, had arrived, and Beth was able to describe Mitchell's condition without breaking down.

After Richie's parents excused themselves to get coffee, Tom took Beth aside. "I want to be with you," he said. "Right there with you and Mitchell."

"They don't allow anyone but his immediate family in the ICU," she told him doubtfully.

"Don't be so sure." A determined expression settled over his features.

Shortly after she returned to Mitchell, whose condition hadn't changed, Tom slipped into the room.

"I pulled a few strings," he said, and she smiled gratefully up at him as he brought a chair closer to the bed.

She thought Mitchell's eyelids flickered when he heard Tom's voice, but even though she called to him and tried to get him to repeat the movement, she wasn't successful.

"He's got to be all right. He's got to!"

"He will be," Tom said, and when she glanced at him, she saw that even he was shaken by Mitchell's appearance.

Her eyes filled with tears, but she knew she had to remain strong. She held Mitchell's hand in one of hers and Tom's in the other, and they sat like that for a long time, until a nurse arrived and asked Tom to leave.

"Your son has another visitor," she said with a meaningful lift of her brows, and through the glass window that allowed a view of the hallway, she saw Richie.

Tom squeezed her hand and left, walking slowly past her ex-husband and making no secret of his curiosity. As soon as Tom had passed, Richie brushed past the nurse.

Beth merely nodded at Richie, whose eyes were rimmed by dark circles; he appeared as upset as she was. She had no doubt that seeing their son in this condition affected him deeply.

"Has he awakened at all?" Richie asked. Like her, he didn't seem able to stop gazing at Mitchell's face.

"No," she said.

"Has the doctor shown up since Mitchell's been in the ICU?"

Beth shook her head. "He's going to stop by later."

Richie sank onto the chair beside her, the one that Tom had so recently vacated. She wondered if Richie had brought Starla, and then she realized that it didn't matter. The most important thing at the moment was for Mitchell to get well.

BETH MOVED INTO THE HOSPITAL, and she rarely left Mitchell's side. At night, she slept on a reclining chair near his bed, waking every time someone turned on a light or wheeled a cart past the room. During the day, she attended conferences with Mitchell's doctors and fielded inquiries from friends, all of them concerned, all of them asking if there was anything they could do to help. Chloe brought her fresh clothes every day and carried the ones she'd worn home to wash for her. Allen and Corinne commuted from Stickneyville and made themselves available to run errands for Beth. As for Richie, he was beside himself with worry.

Beth felt like a zombie, and even though everyone urged her to go home once in a while, she refused. Sometimes she took a break from her constant vigil, but she always ended up wandering the hospital corridors aimlessly, fretting about Mitchell.

One day, when she couldn't cope anymore, she stopped by the hospital chapel to pray. There she found Richie on his knees behind one of the pews. Beth hesitated before joining him and adding her prayers to his. When Richie stood, she did, too. In that moment, with all her resentment over the divorce stripped away, when she could relate to Richie as the father of her son rather than the husband who had betrayed her trust, she dismissed all the things she might have said. In light of the horrible tragedy that they were both facing now, nothing mattered except that Mitchell recover.

So she only gazed up at Richie with tears in her eyes, and he gathered her into his arms. The gesture was one of solace between two human beings sharing a common interest in one little boy who needed both of them now more than ever. Their embrace didn't last long, but it ensured that no bitterness would be allowed to interfere as they did their best to recover, along with their son, from the disaster that had taken over their lives.

They broke apart self-consciously, but Beth realized that she and Richie had rounded a corner in their relationship. She could let go of the sadness and anger that had accompanied her divorce and replace it with understanding. By forgiving Richie and even Starla, she was creating an atmosphere in which they could, perhaps, work together as an extended family for the good of all.

"I—I'd better get back to Mitchell," Beth said.

"Me, too," Richie replied.

They left the chapel together, riding the elevator silently upstairs. As they made their way to Mitchell's room, Patty Holcomb came flying around the corner.

"Beth, Richie, hurry!"

Beth's heart almost stopped. "Mitchell—is he—?"

Patty appropriated Beth's arm to hurry her along. "I stopped in to check how he was doing and he opened his eyes. I called his nurses and came to find you."

By this time, they'd rushed into Mitchell's room. His eyes were closed, and at first, Beth was sure it was a cruel hoax, that Patty had been wrong, that nothing had changed. But when she curved her hand around Mitchell's, his eyes fluttered open.

"Mommy, I want to go home," he said. The words were no more than a whisper, but there was no mistaking them.

And in that moment, Beth's fractured world came back together again. She bent low to brush Mitchell's forehead with a kiss, her joyful tears falling on his cheeks. "As soon as we can, sweetheart. As soon as we can."

Behind her, Richie made a strangled sound, and when she turned, she realized that he was crying, too. He gripped Mitchell's other hand in his, and Beth knew that their prayers had been answered. Their son was back.

THE NEXT FEW DAYS proved to be difficult, and Mitchell wasn't always in the best of moods. His ribs hurt, and he kept pulling at the bandage on his head. Still, he developed a hearty appetite, didn't require an IV anymore and began to agitate to leave the hospital.

"When am I going to be able to ride Captain again?" he pestered.

"Soon, cowboy," Tom told him.

He visited every morning and every night, even though he was deeply involved at the ranch now that the ATTAIN kids had arrived. Beth couldn't have managed without Tom. He made Mitchell laugh, he sat in on her conferences with Mitchell's doctors. He even got along with Richie. When Beth discovered Tom and her ex engaged in a deep conversation about NCAA basketball, she realized that the two men had conquered whatever animosity they initially might have felt for each other.

On the night before Mitchell was scheduled to go home, when Richie, Allen and Corinne were eating dinner with him, Tom stole Beth away from the hospital and drove her to Zach-

ary's, where he ordered steaks with all the trimmings. Beth dug
into hers with gusto, also polishing off a huge salad with Gor-
gonzola dressing and scarfing down half a loaf of Zachary's special cheese bread.

Richie had told them earlier that he was planning to spend
the last night of Mitchell's hospitalization in his room, so Beth
allowed Tom to take her home. There he propelled her straight
into the bedroom, where he sat her on the bed and slipped off
her shoes for her.

"Let me pamper you. You've been through hell and I want you
to relax completely for a change." He started to massage her feet.

"Tom, I—"

"Humor me."

She started to laugh, not sure if he was removing her clothes
more for her benefit or his, but she let him ease her out of her blouse
and slacks, then her bra and her panties. He led her into the bathroom, where he adjusted the shower to a fine spray. He stepped in
beside her, and then she was standing warm, wet and naked in his
arms, with the water running off their bodies and nothing between
them. She'd thought once or twice that she'd be smelling like a hospital until Mitchell was released, but as Tom soaped her all over,
the scent of lavender and vanilla from the soap began to replace
the antiseptic odor that she'd grown to dislike so much. After he
rinsed her off, he soaped himself, and then he kissed her lingeringly.

"Relax," he murmured in her ear. "This is going to be a night
of pleasure for both of us."

"No loudspeakers squawking all night long? No carts with
squeaky wheels trundling through the halls?"

"No bright lights in your face in the middle of the night, and
no one asking if you want anything when all you need is a good
night's sleep."

"It sounds lovely" was her heartfelt reply.

He dried her with a fluffy towel, swept her into his arms and
deposited her on the bed. Then he slid beneath the covers and
cradled her close. She fell asleep with Tom's body curved pro-

tectively around hers, and felt, for perhaps the first time in her life, completely and utterly cherished.

OF COURSE HE WOKE HER the next morning with breakfast in bed. As an additional surprise, he wore a Santa Claus cap.

She started to giggle as soon as he appeared. "What's the cap about?" she asked. "It's not Christmas anymore. In fact, it's closer to Valentine's Day."

He set the tray down beside her and sat on the edge of the bed. "I wanted to put us both in mind of that wonderful December morning when I first fell in love."

"I didn't love you. You came across as a jerk."

"Keep in mind that I wasn't in a good mood at the time. I wanted to wring Leanne's neck for getting me into that situation."

"I didn't much care for the elf outfits she made the helpers wear, either."

"I like you better with no clothes at all. Like now." He caressed her bare shoulder.

She pulled the sheet up. "I'd better eat in a hurry and get back to the hospital. I can hardly wait to bring Mitchell home."

"Hospital checkout isn't until eleven o'clock. I asked. So you have plenty of time to eat a few pancakes."

"You shouldn't have," she protested as he settled the tray on her lap, but they were blueberry, her favorite.

"This morning, I wanted to remind you of the day we met," Tom said. "It was the beginning of us, Beth."

She sensed an uncommon seriousness in his words. "Aren't you going to eat?" she asked.

"I already have."

"What's that behind your back?" She leaned slightly sideways to see what he was concealing.

Tom's lips clamped together in an unsuccessful effort to suppress a smile. "It's a gift."

"Why? It's not Christmas or my birthday." She nonchalantly stabbed another piece of pancake with her fork.

"Maybe you can think of another special occasion, although it hasn't exactly happened yet."

"What in the world are you hiding, Tom?"

"Nothing ever again," he said with a rueful laugh. He produced a clumsily wrapped package and handed it to her.

"May I open it?"

"You sure can."

She tore off the sloppily tied ribbon, which looked suspiciously as if it had been used before. The paper ripped away easily, as well, considering that it was only taped in one place. A white box presented itself, and she lifted the lid.

Inside was something made of ceramic. Two somethings, actually, and she pulled them free of tissue paper to hold them up for inspection.

"Heart bookends!" she exclaimed. "They're so pretty." Each bookend was a bright red half heart resting on a wooden base.

"I found those in the hospital gift shop and bought them to replace some of the hearts in your collection that got broken. When I consulted with Mitchell, he agreed that you'd like these."

"Tom, that's very sweet of you," she said, smiling at him.

He took the bookends from her and held them so that they touched. "Together, the two halves make a whole heart." He moved them slightly away from each other. "Apart, each half can stand independently. This is my idea of how a good marriage should work. When together, beautiful and strong. When apart, able to stand alone."

Beth picked up a book from the nightstand and placed it between the bookends. "Also, quite capable of supporting something else when working toward the same goal," she said, thinking of children, or running a home, or pursuing a dream. She had an idea where this was going, and she didn't want to rush the moment. She wanted to savor it as long as possible.

Tom replaced the hearts carefully in their box and the book on the nightstand before tipping her face toward his. "There's one more heart I want you to have, Beth. Mine. Will you marry me?"

She was mindful of the gravity of Tom's request and the earnestness with which he spoke, but the Santa cap was so incongruous. Not that his appearance rendered this marriage proposal in any way unwelcome to her ears.

"Of course I'll marry you," she said demurely.

"You've made up your mind just like that?"

"You didn't expect an argument, did you? And when are you going to kiss me?"

He began to smile and quickly enveloped her in his embrace. Her head settled into its customary position in the hollow of his shoulder, and when she tilted her head back for his kiss, she saw that the Santa cap had slipped down over one eye. She reached up and adjusted it.

"My darling Beth," Tom said unsteadily. "I love you so much."

"I love you, too. And Mitchell thinks you're wonderful."

"You know what he asked me yesterday? If I already had kids. He said that if I didn't, could I please be his other dad? What could I do? I told him yes."

"Tom, I—"

He stopped her from talking by placing a gentle finger over her lips. "I intend to be the best stepfather ever," he said. "I'm going to take Mitchell to ball games and shoot basketballs with him in the driveway, and I'll make sure he's a good rider, and teach him how to lasso—"

"You'll be what he wanted for Christmas," Beth said, her eyes sparkling. "A live-in daddy."

"When he asked for a father at Breakfast with Santa, I told him I couldn't bring him one. I guess I didn't say that I couldn't *be* one."

They laughed over that, and then they kissed. Somehow, afterward, the Santa hat ended up on the floor along with all of Tom's clothes. That was okay, because they didn't have to pick up Mitchell for another two hours—plenty of time to seal their intentions with more than a kiss.

As THEY DROVE TO THE HOSPITAL LATER, Tom glanced over at Beth. She had fastened her hair back with a barrette. Wispy tendrils covered her small pink ears, and she wore little makeup. In Tom's eyes, she was the most beautiful she'd ever been in her life, but maybe that was because of their new commitment and direction.

He cleared his throat. He wanted to talk to her about something that he considered important.

"About Mitchell," he began as she raised her eyebrows questioningly. "If I'm going to be his live-in daddy, I can't call him Mitchell. A kid deserves a nickname."

"I've never cared for nicknames," Beth began doubtfully, but he shook his head.

"Mitchell might prefer one."

"The three of us could discuss it," Beth said.

"You wouldn't mind?"

She squeezed his hand. "No, I've learned a lot from my husband-to-be about bringing up boys," she said. "And I have a feeling that I'm going to learn a lot more."

He smiled at that and pulled into the hospital parking lot. After he'd slotted the pickup into an empty space, they took time for a quick kiss before entering the building.

"The elevator's full," Beth said as she spotted people piling into it at the other end of the lobby. "Let's use the stairs."

Then, holding hands and running up the steps like two carefree kids with the best secret in the world, they hurried to tell Mitchell their wonderful news.

Epilogue

Four months later

Mitchell—who wanted to be called Mac now—sang at the top of his lungs while Beth put the finishing touches on her makcup for her wedding.

> *"Here comes the bride*
> *All dressed in white,*
> *There goes the groom*
> *As he hides out of sight!"*

"I hope not," Chloe said as she handed Beth a pot of eyeshadow. "Dab this frosty stuff under your eyebrows," she suggested. "It'll give you that dewy bridal glow."

"Do I need 'dewy bridal glow'?" Beth asked.

"Go for it."

"Is everyone here yet?" The wedding was being held in Beth's backyard on one of the most beautiful days of spring. Beth and Tom would exchange their vows under the grape arbor, and guests had been arriving for the past half hour.

Chloe peeked out the window. "Eddie is bringing more folding chairs from Leanne's SUV."

Mitchell picked up Beth's eyebrow pencil and experimentally poked the tip with a finger.

"Stop that, son," Beth said. "You'll make a mess."

Mitchell dropped the pencil and clasped his hands behind his back. He and Tom had convinced Beth that it wasn't a good idea for him to wear the blue velvet suit that she'd made him for the pancake breakfast, and it was true that he'd almost outgrown it. Beth had nixed the sweatshirt-and-favorite-jeans alternative Mitchell had suggested, and they had compromised on a rented ringbearer's outfit similar to the suit Tom was wearing. This morning Mitchell had proclaimed happily that the rented clothes didn't itch. He and Tom had exchanged an exuberant high five over this, which Beth didn't understand at all.

"Five minutes," Leanne said, popping her head in the door. Her eldest daughter, Madelon, was going to play "The Wedding March" on a piano that Beth had rented for the occasion.

"What's Tom doing?" Beth asked. She studied her reflection in the mirror, liking the way the pale-peach-colored gown showed off her figure. It had cap sleeves and a scoop neckline, and the bodice tapered to a bell-shaped skirt.

"Eddie took him out behind the garage to bolster Tom's resolve with a talk. Not that Tom needs it, Beth. I've never seen anyone more eager to be married in my life." Leanne hurried away to the kitchen to supply plenty of jalapeño cheese puffs for the reception.

Chloe judiciously twitched her own ice-blue gown into place over her hips. "I'm glad you chose a dress I can wear again," she said as she turned to study the back.

"Maybe it will come in handy for one of those society balls in Palm Beach," Beth told her. "I'll bet your cousin's godmother will make sure you're invited."

"Fat chance," scoffed Chloe. "Anyway, when I get to Florida, it won't be the social season. Summer is boring there, from what I can tell."

"Not if you meet someone," Beth pointed out.

"Never going to happen," Chloe said.

"That's what I said, Chlo, and I'm a bride!"

"And a gorgeous one."

Maddy played the first bars of "The Wedding March," and Chloe handed Mac the pillow with the ring tied to it. "You go first, then me, then your mom," she told him.

Beth had decided not to be escorted down the aisle, since there wasn't really anyone to do it except Eddie, who had offered but certainly had his hands full keeping tabs on his five children while Leanne was supervising food preparation.

With Mac leading the way, the three of them filed through the foyer to the kitchen, where cookie sheets filled with jalapeño cheese puffs and miniature quiches and other goodies covered every surface. Chloe, in front of Beth, looked elegant, her hair all one color for a change.

When Beth glanced out the window over the sink, she saw Tom waiting for her under the arbor, beside the pastor. "Mitchell," she said to her son, "do you know what you're supposed to do?"

"Mac," he corrected, sounding surprisingly grown-up. "I'm Mac now. All I have to do is hold up the pillow so Mr. Holcomb can untie the ring and give it to Tom, right?" He and Tom and Divver had worked out an elaborate system of signals beforehand.

"That's right, sweetheart." She leaned down. "How about a good-luck kiss?"

Mac smooched her on the cheek. "You sure are pretty, Mom." He beamed at her.

"Thanks, Mac. All right," said Beth. "I'm ready."

Mac opened the back door and began to walk ceremoniously toward the arbor. Chloe was smiling brightly as she followed. And then Beth, her eyes never wavering from Tom's, walked—or maybe floated—past her assembled guests. Patty Holcomb was sitting beside Chloe's sister, Naomi, and her three daughters. Gretchen and Julie, with their husbands, occupied the second row. Even Richie had driven all the way from Oklahoma, and with him was Starla, holding their baby in her lap. Allen and Corinne were there, too, and, in fact, Corinne had baked the wedding cake.

When Beth joined Tom under the arbor, he bent and kissed her cheek, then drew her close as the pastor began the ceremony.

Everything proceeded almost flawlessly, except that Divver dropped Beth's wedding band, which disappeared under Jeremiah's seat in the first row. While Jeremiah was retrieving it, everyone had a chance to admire the bride's dress and to remark upon how handsome Tom was. After the minister finally pronounced them husband and wife, the newly married couple kissed for so long that the bride's son could be heard uttering an impatient sigh. This had the effect of putting an immediate end to the embrace, and Beth was blushing as she and Tom turned to face their friends and neighbors.

"Now can we have some cake?" Mitchell was heard to whisper to Tom, who only laughed and ruffled his hair.

The top layer of the wedding cake was adorned with three figures—Beth, Tom and Mac—instead of the customary two. At first Mac had lobbied to include a model of a dog, but Tom had objected, claiming that since they didn't have the dog yet, it wouldn't be right.

While Beth and Tom were cutting the cake, Mac opined that since Dallas had recently given birth and they were going to adopt one of the pups, it would *too* have been fair to include a dog figure. Beth shushed him, and then she and Tom fed each other their ceremonial slices, after which Mac told his friend Jeremiah in a very loud voice that when the puppy came to live with them, it was going to be named Blackie.

"Wait a minute," Tom said, picking up on this. "Those puppies are all the same color as Dallas. They're yellow. Blackie isn't a good name for a yellow dog."

"We could name the dog Goldie."

"Topaz?" Beth said. "Would you go for Topaz?"

"That's kind of a neat name," Mitchell agreed.

It was a long time before Tom managed to get Beth to himself in a corner of the backyard. "How does it feel to be Mrs. Collyer?" he asked her playfully.

"Wonderful," she sighed, fitting into the curve of his arm.

They watched Mac playing with Jeremiah, Ryan and some of his other friends. The boys were engaged in a rousing game of hide-and-seek in the shrubbery at the side of the house, thankfully staying well away from the other guests.

"It was a nice touch," Tom said. "Having a figure of Mac on top of our cake to symbolize that we're now a family."

"At least I talked him out of the dog," Beth said with a grin.

"It's funny how insistent he was about that," replied Tom.

Beth turned to Tom and slid her arms around his neck while gazing deep into his eyes. "Actually, there could have been another figure on top of the cake, but I wasn't ready to announce it yet."

Tom cocked his head in puzzlement. "What do you mean?"

"That there are going to be four of us before long. You, me, Mac…and the new baby."

"A baby?"

She nodded solemnly. "I wasn't sure until this week, but it's true."

"A baby! Oh, Beth, that's wonderful, honey." And then he crushed her to him for a kiss that held all his love and hopes for them as a couple. No, as a family. Because that was what they were now, and would be forever.

"I love you, Beth. And I love our baby already."

She didn't reply. She didn't have to. Beth rested her head against Tom's broad chest and considered how lucky she was that she would be having breakfast with this particular Santa for the rest of her life.

From the *Farish Tribune* the following December:
Here 'n' There in Farish
by Muffy Ledbetter

Nothing makes me happier than to report a new little Farish resident. Mr. and Mrs. Thomas Collyer and their son, Mac McCormick, announce the birth of a daughter and sister, Noelle Elizabeth, at the Bigbee County Hospital on Christmas Day. Yes! That's right, on December 25! Noelle must be a really special Christmas package to arrive on that day of the year in a season that already means so much to Tom and Beth. The new parents met at Breakfast with Santa last year.

Mac is thrilled with his new sister. He wanted to name her Blackie but finally agreed that Noelle was a prettier name. Beth says that she'll soon be back to work at her Bluebonnet Interiors, so y'all call her if you need any draperies or bedspreads or things like that. She's turned her bungalow out on the highway into a decorating studio, since the Collyers have moved into Tom's newly renovated house to have more room for their growing family. As for the daddy, he's proud as punch and continues to do good work in the ATTAIN program at the Holcomb Ranch.

In my other news, Chloe Timberlake, who left Farish a few months ago to start a new life in Florida, hasn't exactly disappeared from our radar screen. You remember Chloe, who makes that beautiful jewelry from sea glass (I admit to buying a few pieces myself.) Well, you'll never believe what the former Farishite says about her new life. It seems that she met The One down there in the Sunshine State, and I'll be telling you more about that soon.

Remember, if you have any news to share about our friends and neighbors, give me a call on my cell phone, the number of which you'll find at the end of this column.

Till next time, I'll be seeing you here 'n' there in Farish. Happy New Year, everybody!

It's time for some BLOND JUSTICE! This is Kara Lennox's third book in her trilogy about three women who were duped by the same con man. Sonya Patterson's mother has been busy preparing her daughter's wedding—and has no idea the groom-to-be ran off with Sonya's money. Will the blondes finally get their sweet revenge on the evil Marvin? And how long can Sonya pretend that she's going through with the wedding—when she'd rather be married to her long-time bodyguard, John-Michael McPhee? We know you're going to love this funny, fast-paced story!

Airplane seats were way too small, and too crowded together. Sonya Patterson had never thought much about this before, since she'd always flown first class in the past. But this was a last-minute ticket on a no-first-class kind of plane.

She'd also never flown on a commercial airline with her bodyguard, which might explain her current claustrophobia. John-Michael McPhee was a broad-shouldered, well-muscled man, and Sonya was squashed between him and a hyperactive seven-year-old whose mother was fast asleep in the row behind them.

She could smell the leather of McPhee's bomber jacket. He'd had that jacket for years, and every time Sonya saw him in it, her stupid heart gave a little leap. She hated herself for letting him affect her that way. Didn't most women get over their teen-age crushes by the time they were pushing thirty?

"I didn't know you were a nervous flier," McPhee said, brushing his index finger over her left hand. Sonya realized she was clutching her armrests as if the plane were about to crash.

What would he think, she wondered, if she blurted out that it wasn't flying that made her nervous, it was being so close to him? Her mother would not approve of Sonya's messy feelings where McPhee was concerned.

Her mother. Sonya's heart ached at the thought of her vibrant mother lying in a hospital bed hooked up to machines. Muffy

Lockridge Patterson was one of those women who never stopped running all day, every day, at full throttle with a to-do list a mile long. Over the years, Sonya had often encouraged her mother to slow down, relax and cut back on the rich foods. But Muffy seldom took advice from anyone.

Sonya consciously loosened her grip on the armrests when McPhee nudged her again.

"She'll be okay," he said softly. "She was in stable condition when I left."

A comfortable silence passed before McPhee asked, "Are you going to tell me what you were doing in New Orleans with your 'sorority sister'?"

So, he hadn't bought her cover story. But she'd had to come up with something quickly when McPhee had tracked her down hundreds of miles away from where she was supposed to be. She'd already been caught in a bald-faced lie—for weeks she'd been telling her mother she was at a spa in Dallas, working out her pre-wedding jitters.

"I was just having a little fun," she tried again.

"A little fun that got you in trouble with the FBI?"

This is the first book in an exciting new miniseries from Jacqueline Diamond, DOWNHOME DOCTORS. The town of Downhome, Tennessee, has trouble keeping doctors at its small clinic. Advertising an available position at the town's clinic brings more than one candidate for the job, but the townspeople get more than they bargained for when Dr. Jenni Vine is hired, despite Police Chief Ethan Forrest's reservations about her—at least in the beginning!

"Nobody knows better than I do how badly this town needs a doctor," Police Chief Ethan Forrest told the crowd crammed into the Downhome, Tennessee, city council chambers. "But please, not Jenni Vine."

He hadn't meant to couch his objection so bluntly, he mused as he registered the startled reaction of his audience. Six months ago, he'd been so alarmed by the abrupt departure of the town's two resident doctors, a married couple, that he'd probably have said yes to anyone with an M.D. after his or her name.

Worried about his five-year-old son, Nick, who was diabetic, Ethan had suggested that the town advertise for physicians to fill the vacated positions. He'd also recommended that they hire a long-needed obstetrician.

Applications hadn't exactly poured in. Only two had arrived from qualified family doctors, both of whom had toured Downhome recently by invitation. One was clearly superior, and as a member of the three-person search committee, Ethan felt it his duty to say so.

"Dr. Gregory is more experienced and, in my opinion, more stable. He's married with three kids, and I believe he's motivated to stick around for the long term." Although less than ideal in one respect, the Louisville physician took his duties seriously and, Ethan had no doubt, would fit into the community.

"Of course he's motivated!" declared Olivia Rockwell, who

stood beside Ethan just below the city council's dais. The tall African-American woman, who was the school principal, chaired the committee. "You told us yourself he's a recovering alcoholic."

"He volunteered the information, along with the fact that he's been sober for a couple of years," Ethan replied. "His references are excellent and he expressed interest in expanding our public health efforts. I think he'd be perfect to oversee the outreach program I've been advocating."

"So would Jenni—I mean Dr. Vine," said the third committee member, Karen Lowell, director of the Tulip Tree Nursing Home. "She's energetic and enthusiastic. Everybody likes her."

"She certainly has an outgoing personality," he responded. On her visit, the California blonde had dazzled people with her expensive clothes and her good humor after being drenched in a thunderstorm, which she seemed to regard as a freak of nature. It probably didn't rain on her parade very often out there in the land of perpetual sunshine, Ethan supposed. "But once the novelty wears off, she'll head for greener pastures and we'll need another doctor."

"So you aren't convinced she'll stay? Is that the extent of your objections?" Olivia asked. "This isn't typical of you, Chief. I'll bet you've got something else up that tailored sleeve of yours."

Ethan was about to pass off her comment as a joke, when he noticed some of the townsfolk leaning forward in their seats with anticipation. Despite being a quiet place best known for dairy farmers and a factory that made imitation antiques, Downhome had an appetite for gossip.

Although Ethan had hoped to avoid going into detail, the audience awaited his explanation. Was he being unfair? True, he'd taken a mild dislike to Dr. Vine's surfer-girl demeanor, but he could get over that. What troubled him was the reason she'd wanted to leave L.A. in the first place.

"You all know I conducted background checks on the candidates," he began. "Credit records, convictions, that sort of thing."

"And found no criminal activities, right?" Karen tucked a curly strand of reddish-brown hair behind one ear.

"That's correct. But I also double-checked with the medical directors at their hospitals." He had a bomb to drop now, so he'd better get it over with.

This is the final book of Dianne Castell's
FORTY & FABULOUS trilogy about three women living in
Whistlers Bend, Montana, who are dealing (or not dealing!)
with turning forty. Dixie Carmichael has just had her fortieth
birthday, and gotten the best birthday present of all—a second
chance at life—after the ultimate medical scare.
One thing she's sure of—now's the time to start living life
the way she's always wanted it to be!

Dixie Carmichael twisted her fingers into the white sheet as she lay perfectly still on the OR table and tried to remember to breathe. Fear settled in her belly like sour milk. *She was scared!* Bone-numbing, jelly-legged, full-blown-migraine petrified. It wasn't every day her left breast got turned into a giant pincushion.

She closed her eyes, not wanting to look at the ultrasound machine or think about the biopsy needle or anything else in the overly bright sterile room that would determine if the lump was really bad news.

She clenched her teeth so they wouldn't chatter, then prayed for herself and all women who ever went, or would go, through this. The horror of waiting to find out the diagnosis was more terrifying than her divorce and wrapping her Camaro around a tree rolled into one.

God, let me out of this and I'll change. I swear it. No more pity parties over getting dumped by Danny for that Victoria's Secret model, no more comfort junk food, no more telling everyone how to live their lives and not really living her own, and if that meant leaving Whistlers Bend, she'd suck it up and do it and quit making excuses.

"We're taking out the fluid now," the surgeon said. "It's clear."

Dixie's eyes shot wide open. She swallowed, then finally managed to ask, "Meaning?"

The surgeon stayed focused on what she was doing, but the news was good. Dixie could tell—she'd picked up being able to read people from waiting tables at the Purple Sage restaurant for three years and dealing with happy, way-less-than-happy and everything-in-between customers. *Oh, how she wished she were at the Purple Sage now.*

The surgeon continued. "Meaning the lump in your breast is a cyst. I'll send the fluid we drew off to the pathologist to be certain, but there's no indication the lump was anything more than a nuisance."

Nuisance! A nuisance was a telemarketer, a traffic ticket, gaining five pounds! But the important thing was, she'd escaped. She said another prayer for the women who wouldn't escape. Then she got dressed and left the hospital, resisting the urge to turn handsprings all the way to her car. Or maybe she did them, she wasn't sure.

She could go home. In one hour she'd be back in Whistlers Bend. Her life still belonged to her, and not doctors and hospitals and pills and procedures. She fired up her Camaro and sat for a moment, appreciating the familiar idle of her favorite car while staring out at the flat landscape of Billings, Montana. This was one of the definitive moments when life smacked her upside the head and said, *Dixie, old girl, get your ass in gear.*

You've wanted action, adventure, hair-raising experiences as long as you can remember. Now's the time to make them happen!

Welcome back to Laramie, Texas, and a whole new crop of McCabes! In this story, prankster Riley McCabe is presented with three abandoned children one week before Christmas. Thinking it's a joke played on him by Amanda Witherspoon, he comes to realize the kids really do need his help. Watch out for Cathy Gillen Thacker's next book, *A Texas Wedding Vow,* in April 2006.

Amanda Witherspoon had heard Riley McCabe was returning to Laramie, Texas, to join the Laramie Community Hospital staff, but she hadn't actually *seen* the handsome family physician until Friday afternoon when he stormed into the staff lounge in the pediatrics wing.

Nearly fourteen years had passed, but his impact on her was the same. Just one look into his amber eyes made her pulse race, and her emotions skyrocket. He had been six foot when he left for college, now he was even taller. Back then he had worn his sun-streaked light brown hair any which way. Now the thick wavy strands were cut in a sophisticated fashion, parted neatly on the left and brushed casually to the side. He looked solid and fit, mouth-wateringly sexy, and every inch the kind of grown man who knew exactly who he was and what he wanted out of life. The kind not to be messed with. Amanda thought the sound of holiday music playing on the hospital sound system and the Christmas tree in the corner only added to the fantasy-come-true quality of the situation.

Had she not known better, Amanda would have figured Riley McCabe's return to her life would have been the Christmas present to beat all Christmas presents, meant to liven up her increasingly dull and dissatisfying life. But wildly exciting things like that never happened to Amanda.

"Notice I'm not laughing," Riley McCabe growled as he

passed close enough for her to inhale the fragrance of soap and brisk, wintry cologne clinging to his skin.

"Notice," Amanda returned dryly, wondering what the famously mischievous prankster was up to now, "neither am I."

Riley marched toward her, jaw thrust out pugnaciously, thick straight brows raised in mute admonition. "I would have figured we were beyond all this."

Amanda had hoped that would be the case, too. After all, she was a registered nurse, he a doctor. But given the fact that the Riley McCabe she recalled had been as full of mischief as the Texas sky was big, that had been a dangerous supposition to make. "Beyond all what?" she repeated around the sudden dryness of her throat. As he neared her, all the air left her lungs in one big whoosh.

"The practical jokes! But you just couldn't resist, could you?"

Amanda put down the sandwich she had yet to take a bite of and took a long sip of her diet soda. "I have no idea what you're talking about," she said coolly. Unless this was the beginning of yet another ploy to get her attention?

"Don't you?" he challenged, causing another shimmer of awareness to sift through her.

Deciding that sitting while he stood over her gave him too much of a physical advantage, she pushed back her chair and rose slowly to her feet. She was keenly aware that he now had a good six inches on her, every one of them as bold and masculine as the set of his lips. "I didn't think you were due to start working here until January," she remarked, a great deal more casually than she felt.

He stood in front of her, arms crossed against his chest, legs braced apart, every inch of him taut and ready for action. "I'm not."

"So?" She ignored the intensity in the long-lashed amber eyes that threatened to throw her off balance. "How could I possibly play a prank on you if I didn't think you were going to be here?"

"Because," he enunciated, "you knew I was going to start setting up my office in the annex today."

Amanda sucked in a breath. "I most certainly did not!" she insisted. Although she might have had she realized he intended to pick up right where they had left off, all those years ago. Matching wits and wills. The one thing she had never wanted to cede to the reckless instigator was victory of any kind.

Riley leaned closer, not stopping until they were practically close enough to kiss. "Listen to me, Amanda, and listen good. Playing innocent is not going to work with me. And neither," he warned, even more forcefully, "is your latest gag."

Amanda regarded him in a devil-may-care way designed to get under his skin as surely as he was already getting under hers. "I repeat," she spoke as if to the village idiot, "I have no idea what you are talking about, Dr. McCabe. Now, do you mind? I only have a forty-five-minute break and I'd like to eat my lunch."

He flashed her an incendiary smile that left her feeling more aware of him than ever. "I'll gladly leave you alone just as soon as you collect them."

Amanda blinked, more confused than ever. "Collect who?" she asked incredulously.

Riley walked back to the door. Swung it open wide. On the other side was the surprise of Amanda's life.

Home For The Holidays!

While there are many variations of this recipe, here is Tina Leonard's favorite!

GOURMET REINDEER POOP

Mix 1/2 cup butter, 2 cups granulated sugar, 1/2 cup milk and 2 tsp cocoa together in a large saucepan.

Bring to a boil, stirring constantly; boil for 1 minute.

Remove from heat and stir in 1/2 cup peanut butter, 3 cups oatmeal (not instant) and 1/2 cup chopped nuts (optional).

Drop by teaspoon full (larger or smaller as desired) onto wax paper and let harden.

They will set in about 30-60 minutes.

These will keep for several days without refrigerating, up to 2 weeks refrigerated and 2-3 months frozen.

Pack into resealable sandwich bags and attach the following note to each bag.

I woke up with such a scare when I heard Santa call…
"Now dash away, dash away, dash away all!"
I ran to the lawn and in the snowy white drifts,
those nasty reindeer had left "little gifts."
I got an old shovel and started to scoop,
neat little piles of "Reindeer Poop!"
But to throw them away seemed such a waste,
so I saved them, thinking you might like a taste!
As I finished my task, which took quite a while,
Old Santa passed by and he sheepishly smiled.
And I heard him exclaim as he was in the sky…
"Well, they're not potty trained, but at least they can fly!"

Home For The Holidays!

Eat, drink and be merry with Kristin Hardy's Ultimate Hot-Buttered Rum Mix

Treats make the holiday bright

One of my favorite holiday treats is hot-buttered rum. Not just any old hot-buttered rum, though. This is the ultimate, as revered by J. J. Cooper in *Under the Mistletoe* (Special Edition, December 2005). You'll be seeing J.J. again, so keep an eye out for him.

Hot Buttered Rum Mix

1 lb butter	dash salt
1 lb white sugar	1 qt light cream
1 lb brown sugar	1 tsp vanilla

add:

Hot Buttered Rum

1 tbsp Hot-Buttered Rum Mix
1 shot dark rum (Myers is good)
Hot water

Cream butter, sugar and salt until emulsified. You want it light and fluffy, as if making a cake, so don't rush. Combine cream and vanilla. Add about a half cup at a time and let blend in thoroughly before adding more. It should have the consistency of buttercream at the end. Makes about four cups.

To make hot-buttered rum, add the hot-buttered rum mix and a shot of dark rum (I like Myers) to a mug. Fill the rest of the way with hot water. Delicious.

Note:

This recipe makes enough to share. I put it in glass jars with a pretty label on the front with directions and a ribbon around the lid. It's an instant holiday gift, and one that almost everyone will love. For more recipes, go to www.kristinhardy.com.